The North Side of Happiness

Sharon (Lucy) Robson

The North Side of Happiness
Copyright © 2023 by Sharon (Lucy) Robson

All rights reserved. No part of this publication may be reproduced, distributed, or transmitted in any form or by any means, including photocopying, recording, or other electronic or mechanical methods, without the prior written permission of the author, except in the case of brief quotations embodied in critical reviews and certain other non-commercial uses permitted by copyright law.

tellwell

Tellwell Talent
www.tellwell.ca

ISBN
978-1-77941-204-1 (Paperback)
978-1-77941-205-8 (eBook)

For Michael

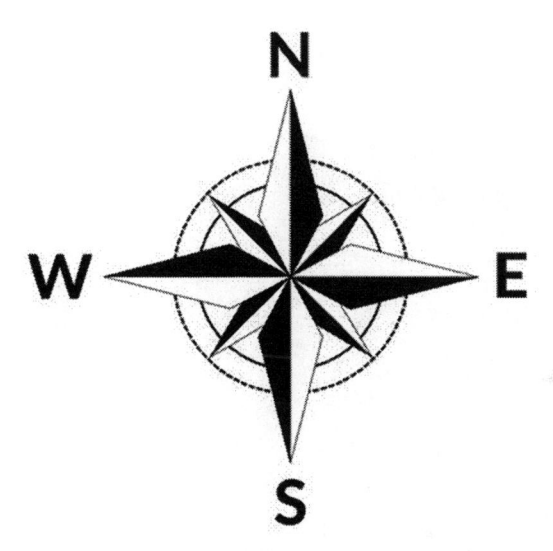

"For last year's words belong to last year's language
And next year's words await another voice.
And to make an end is to make a beginning."
T.S. Eliot

Prologue

A story can start from the simplest of moments: a glass of iced tea placed fondly into a friend's hand; a throw blanket wrapped around a shoulder waiting for the bonfire to grow bigger, warmer; or perhaps a sit on a swing in a late-night park, side by side, innocently twisting the chains, feet scuffing the earth. But my story had none of that innocence, that casual spontaneity ... my life story was carefully planned and had a gentle nervousness to it. A mother's slow steady voice, but with one fluttering hand clenching the other one still.

My mother decided that the evening of my 18th birthday would be the date. The time to tell me the disturbing circumstances of my birth. The way I came reluctantly into this world, like a beached right whale or a premature baby goat.

"Sweetie, come sit with us. I need to talk to you ... about your dad. It's time you know the facts." Mom's voice cracked over the word "facts."

I knew instantly that something weird was happening. There was a totally different vibe in the air. As I slumped down into a lawn chair, I was sure I didn't want to hear what she was going to say.

All my friends had left after a sunny pool party in the backyard, the best chocolate cake Mom had ever made, and a fun toast with a small glass of real wine. During the toast, Mom asked everyone to say a compliment about me or a fond or funny memory, which was kind of lame and embarrassing. Even though it was awkward at first, my friends got into it and tried to outdo each other. It ended up being really fun. After the party they all went off to a beach bonfire on The North Shore and I wanted to go with them and continue our celebration. Mom insisted I stay home.

"Aunt Shimi and Uncle Eddie have driven from Halifax to see you, so I'd like you to spend some time with them," she explained.

Begrudgingly, I agreed.

All afternoon I had worn Uncle Eddie's gift; a tacky Dollar Store tiara on my head, adorned with a huge sparkly 18 on top. I was surprised that it never fell off. Uncle Eddie is a bit of an enigma to me, the strong, silent type with his intense far-off stare, but he is my only uncle and perhaps the gentlest man I have ever met. For my fourth birthday he gave me a King Cavalier Spaniel puppy, who he said he had temporarily named Wilma. I said I loved that name and sweet Wilma was my best friend for the next thirteen years. Whenever I had video chats with Uncle Eddie, I always had Wilma on my lap. That seemed to make the sad lines around his eyes crinkle with happiness.

Last year, when Wilma became too old and ill to have a good life, Uncle Eddie called the vet and she came to our house. Dr. Andrea talked to me for a long time and I kept thinking, "Why doesn't she simply give Wilma the needle and get it over with?" Eventually I discovered why. Uncle Eddie roared into our driveway in his rickety old olive-green Jeep. As soon as Mom saw him, she gave a huge sigh of relief. Wilma was curled up on her little bed next to the fireplace. He sat down on the floor next to me, held my hand and put his other hand on Wilma's little head. I held Wilma's paw. He kept gently repeating, "Such a sweet girl," as our little Wilma was put to sleep. That's my Uncle Eddie.

Every good or bad event I have shared with Uncle Eddie. He's about the only man in my life, but with a guy like him, I figure who needs a whole bunch of brothers or uncles, or even a father for that matter.

After she arrived this morning, Aunt Shimi walked up to me and handed me the most beautiful card addressed To the Best Niece in the World, with a note inside saying she had transferred twenty-five thousand dollars into my bank account. "To add to your university fund," she said.

Mom said, "Absolutely not, Shimi!"

But Aunt Shimi had said, "I'm helping with university. And we're not arguing about it."

Aunt Shimi has been another constant in my life, although she is not quite as affectionate as Uncle Eddie or Aunt Bellabell. She is somewhat reserved in her attention to me, but I see her studying me when she thinks I'm not looking. She listens intently. One thing I love about her ... she's the kind of adult who when she asks, "How are you doing?" it sounds like she really wants to know. Nothing is casual with Aunt Shimi. One gets the feeling her words and actions are deliberate, calculated, but whenever she gives me hugs, there are often tiny tears in the corner of her eyes. I love that about her.

My mom and Aunt Shimi are best friends, and they have a weird little ritual. When most people visit each other, don't they typically bring a bottle of wine, or flowers? Whenever Aunt Shimi comes, she brings Mom a package of cheese. She finds different types of cheese from local producers at the Halifax market, or really exotic stuff from foreign countries. As Aunt Shimi hands Mom the cheese, they always say the same thing at the same time, "Thank Goddess for cheese," and then they laugh. They sit down at the kitchen table and make a lunch of cheese and crackers, with little bottles of spicy jam ... and they talk and talk and talk.

Of course, my wonderful Auntie BellaBell, in all her glory, was here at my party. With her great flowing red and green caftans and colourful tattered head scarves. She has curly grey hair now that she wears in braids and dreads, and she always wears large beaded earrings or thick silver hoops. She is a rainbow of colour and a library of laughter. There is no one quite like Auntie BellaBell. She's eighty-four now, but you'd think she is about seventy. Her joie de vivre is hard to match. She brought me a really cool backpack in the Pride colours. She said, "So when you travel, it's so strangers know they can talk to you about anything."

Unfortunately, Aunt Gloria couldn't make the party, but sent a pair of concert tickets. She used to work in the music business and still has good connections. So, thanks to Aunt Gloria, I'm off to see the Tokyo Police Club in Halifax next month. Can't wait.

I've been accepted into the University of Toronto's Biology program. I'm quite interested in getting into Audiology in the future, but I have decided to take a year off, so I have enrolled in an eight-month international volunteer program in Cambodia that runs an orphanage for deaf children. Aunt Shimi said she'll visit; Mom said she'd try; Aunt BellaBell said, "No way, my feet swell up too much already, without flying in a tin can for 20 hours. And why would I want to sit close enough to someone so they could count my chin hairs?"

Aunt Shimi replied, "But what if she was really cute?"

Aunt BellaBell said, "If she was cute, I'd hand her my tweezers." And of course, she roared with laughter. Then she looked at me tenderly and added, "I'm going to miss you big time, Baby, but video chats will have to do, my dear."

I had invited five of my best friends to my party. We're all going off in different directions this fall, to colleges and universities, so we are really excited, but kind of freaked out at the same time. When my friends arrived, Mom had them put their cell phones in a basket by the door. My girlfriends, Coreen, Sue, Donna, and Poppy, and of course Jake, who is almost a girl, had all groaned, but obliged when Mom said, "Come on, have a screen free afternoon, for a change."

She was right. The party was fun. However, near the end, she did allow the phones to come out to take a few photos of all my friends and some selfies. All of us laughing. A day I will always remember. The day when I still felt innocent and sure of myself ... the unfettered time before I knew the truth.

As Mom began her nervous story, the only guests left were my Aunt Shimi, Aunt BellaBell, and of course, Uncle Eddie. The two women sat quietly, nodding their heads and looking down at the glass of wine in their hands. Aunt Shimi played with a thread on the left leg of her jeans, while Aunt BellaBell kept softly sighing. Uncle Eddie was bent over, with his elbows on his legs, clenching a big mug of black coffee between his knees and simply staring straight ahead, like he was memorizing the many colours of the perfect summer sunset.

I hadn't seen much of them all afternoon, as they had cloistered in the kitchen, pretending to help Mom with stuff, always stopping their conversation whenever I walked into the room. Now I know why. Uncle Eddie eagerly manned the barbecue all afternoon, to keep his nervous hands busy … we had more than enough veggie burgers, kebobs, scallops, and shrimp to send everyone home with a doggie bag. But thinking back, I realize my mom and my two aunts had been preparing this "talk" together, behind closed doors.

As I listened to their story, with some sentences coming out rather jumbled, and incomplete, I still knew it was all rehearsed. Most words were carefully chosen. Important details were stressed. Perhaps some were left out, I don't know. But I was given a carefully planned story, like it took all their resolve to tell this once, and they didn't want to go back and have to do it again. There was no room for error.

I had long asked about my deceased father, as there were few photos of him in the family photo albums, but plenty of empty spaces where photos had been taken out. I didn't look at all like my mother, but several relatives on my dad's side of the family had said I was the spitting image of him. A man I had never met, and people seldom spoke of, yet it gave me some weird sense of comfort that I looked like him. I wanted to know more about my father, yet now listening to the urgency of my mother's words, I felt both intrigued and afraid, like the time in grade seven when I had tried smoking a cigarette with Sakda Kinds.

Gradually the story came tumbling out of Mom. Whenever she paused or didn't seem able to continue, my two aunts would help her, adding a bit more to the incredible story. I sat silently. Their words flowed over me with a lassitude I had never felt before. The story was muddled at first and appeared as an abstract painting that begs to have some kind of focus, some kind of logic to the dashes and swirls of colour. But soon the story became real, with a reality I could never have imagined.

Everyone has a creation story. Although I had always bombarded my mother with questions about my birth, I never thought mine would be this complicated and troubling. And I can no longer take that information back, unknow what I now know.

I now empathize with my mother and realize there is no perfect time for this type of story ... no perfect age ... no perfect circumstance ... as there is never a perfect time to hear things you don't want to hear.

I
(before)

She always had a far-off look about her. A deep gaze from her grey eyes that seemed beyond present tense, beyond the foreground. Some thought it was a snobbishness, that she was simply turning up her nose to the common people who orbited her life; some felt it may be a shyness, that kept her truth tucked deep within her. For years locals gossiped she was self-medicated, some sort of pot-smoking, artist type, who created ridiculous types of cheese from her yard of fancy goats. But a few, the few who really knew Shimi Montray, knew she was none of these things. She simply lived in the past as much as she did the present. They knew that every single day she desperately tried to not have the texture of her life defined by one vile night. They knew she owned a fear that was totally rational, yet a fear that surpassed all understanding and brokenness. They knew that Shimi acted the way she did to protect herself and four other people she desperately loved. They also knew Shimi worried that if people knew what happened that year ... that they may learn the deeper truth, a truth that she could not bear.

Shimi, who was born Shirley Ann Montray, became Shimi at a very early age. Her parents, Gus and Mabel loved to dance to Elvis Presley music after dinner in the middle of the living room, and four-year-old Shirley loved to be included. She would shake her little bottom back and forth and twist around, while her dad laughed, "That's it, Shirley, do the shimmy-shimmy shake." And so, she became Shimmy, which she felt was much more fitting, than the serious name of Shirley Ann. And as she grew and became a teen, Shimmy became Shimi. She was a delightful child, full of life and curiosity, and despite a dark moodiness that set upon her as a teen, her parents were certain their Shimi had a brilliant future ahead of her.

Shimi was in her third year at Dalhousie University in Halifax, living in a rowdy apartment with three moderately-focused nursing students when she first learned that life can change in a heartbeat, or more accurately, by a simple knock upon a late-night door.

Fatima, who was always the last one up, ushered Aunt BellaBell into the apartment, down the hall and knocked on Shimi's bedroom door, "Shimi honey, you awake? Your auntie is here."

When Shimi opened her bedroom door and looked at the face of her aunt, she knew. She simply knew. Her parents were dead.

Aunt BellaBell sat on the edge of Shimi's bed, held her strong arm around her niece's shaking shoulders and explained how her parents' car had gone off the icy road and down a steep embankment, flipping several times, crushed beyond recognition. Despite seatbelts and airbags, the police had reassured Belladane Johnston that her best friends had most certainly died instantly.

The two women, Belladane, a tall, robust black woman in her early forties and Shimi, a petite, auburn-haired 20-year-old, with a smash of freckles across practically every part of her body, slid off the bed and sat on the floor, their backs against the bed. Then surprisingly, Shimi curled herself into a ball and quickly slid under the bed.

Aunt Belladane knew that being under the bed was Shimi's safe place. A place where she, as a child, had always felt secure. Although it was rather peculiar to see Shimi now as a young woman under the bed, the aunt simply held onto Shimi's ankle and gently rubbed it. Within a few minutes she said, "Shimi honey. Please stay here with me. Come sit with me."

Shimi remained under the bed weeping silent tears, then finally sobbed, "I know it's stupid. I just need a few minutes. A few minutes."

"It's not stupid but I'd love you to sit out here with me. My head's too big … well it's mostly my big gorgeous head of hair, of course … who am I kidding? … ALL of me is too big to get under the bed with you."

Belladane could hear Shimi give the slightest chuckle. She continued to gently stroke her niece's ankle, until Shimi finally crawled out. The two women grieved together for several hours, while Shimi's three caring roommates kept silent vigil outside her bedroom door, sitting on the floor, their backs against the wall, knees drawn to their chests.

There was a patience to Shimi's tears that her Aunt Belladane had not seen in other aspects of her life. Shimi had always been an impatient child, prone to wanting to do things well before her time. Perhaps because Shimi was an only child; perhaps because she was intelligent beyond her years; or maybe because her parents would encourage her with what some would describe as wild abandonment, she accomplished whatever she set out to accomplish. Yet, often that sense of accomplishment was mixed with disappointment that the goal, such as riding her bike without the training wheels at the age of four, wasn't as great as she thought it would be.

Instead of revelling in these significant childhood accomplishments Shimi would wonder, "Is that all there is? What was all the fuss about?" And then, she'd aim for the next big milestone. Even as a child, there was a dissatisfaction about her life, a longing for something greater, more profound, that provoked her every thought like a pesky, unwanted fly. She wondered at times, if perhaps her entire life would be anticlimactic.

So, just like many of her milestones that happened far too early, Shimi lost her parents well before her time. She had always realized they would die someday, leave her all to herself, maybe when she was sixty and they were in a retirement facility somewhere, where they would eat rice pudding and Jell-O for dessert, and have a difficult time remembering what they had for breakfast, even though it was the same every day.

Luckily, she had her Aunt BellaBell.

Belladane Johnston had lived next door to her parents' farm as long as Shimi could remember. She was a solid woman, standing almost six feet tall, with a mass of braids and dreads coiled on top of her head, which made her look even taller. She was originally from Jamaica, but immigrated to Nova Scotia with her parents in her teens. As an adult, she jumped on the ferry to visit Prince Edward Island one summer weekend, fell in love with the white sand dune beaches and red rolling dirt roads and decided to stay. She worked hard, made all the right contacts, and quickly became part of the province's growing arts community.

Six-year-old Shimi loved to sit on Aunt Belladane's kitchen stool and watch her create one of her fabulous paintings. Landscapes were good sellers, especially during the summer tourist season. Paintings of white lighthouses and red rocky shores with sea grass dunes rolling in the distance kept her humble life afloat, but it was the abstract portraits that both Shimi and Belladane really loved. Belladane used vibrant reds and purples to show sorrow and joy lines on a person's face. She especially loved painting the quiet, unassuming, some might say "unattractive" people one meets on the street every day…the ones with a hairy mole on their chin, or a nose too large to be forgotten. Painting was salve for Belladane's lonely soul. It always felt like a colourful, therapeutic rubdown.

Shimi's parents and Belladane were instant friends despite their obvious differences. Gus Montray was a successful, button-down accountant by day, amateur ballroom dancer by night. His wife, Mabel Caper, a petite, quiet-spoken woman, from a wealthy Maritime family, was a talented web designer who loved to cook Thai food and bake the most finicky pastries. Belladane was, for the lack of a better term, a starving Bohemian artist, whose uninhibited, boisterous laughter could spin a weather vane in the opposite direction. She wore bright, colourful scarves wrapped around her head, long flowing cotton trousers, wild batik tunics of linen and second-hand silks, and often loved to roam around barefoot, with her toenails painted turquoise, a colour that reminded her of her Caribbean Island home: the little turquoise houses, and the sparkling turquoise waters that swirled upon the shore. She would point to her toes and say, "Reminds me of my sparkling Jamaica." And then she would release her hearty laugh.

The kindred friendship of these three adults blossomed immediately upon Belladane's purchase of the old farm house across the road, and soon Shimi was told to call this wonderful, exotic woman, Aunt Belladane. Shimi much preferred Auntie BellaBell and being an only child herself, Belladane was delighted to finally be an auntie, and to such a talented and precocious child was an added bonus. These four extraordinary people soon became a family.

But now, Shimi's parents were dead. Just like that. She would never see them or hear their voices, never laugh together over some funny experience shared during their Sunday phone chats or some silly thing shown on the evening news. Life was suddenly totally different.

Although Shimi loved her university classes, after the death of her parents, all she wanted to do was pack up her things and go home. She knew she would miss the intricate ponderings of her human psychology courses. She was thrilled in learning things such as the different chemical and molecular makeup of human tears. It was a fun pleasure to study that joyful tears were molecularly different from sad or angry tears. And typically, only sad tears leave puffy eyes, whereas tears from cutting onions or tearfully laughing with friends do not. Shimi knew sitting on that bedroom floor, crying alongside Aunt Belladane, that her eyes tomorrow would be puffy, and perhaps for many days to come.

Despite the joy of learning, Shimi no longer felt the joy of being away from home. She wanted to be back in her old single Ikea bed in the upstairs corner of the farmhouse, with the quilt of pink tulips handmade by her Grandmother Cia tucked around her neck. She wanted to lie in that bed where she could stare at her posters of the solar system, the periodic table, and a vintage Beatles poster, handed down from her dad. Perched on her headboard was a tattered and torn cloth monkey from her childhood. He held a tiny white plastic banana in his left hand. She had sucked all the yellow paint off that banana years ago, chewing on it endlessly when terrified of the monsters in her closet. All these things at home gave her comfort. All these things were the life she shared with her parents and now she needed that familiarity. That sense of home.

After the funeral, Belladane tried to convince Shimi to go back to university and her friends, but there was no argument strong enough to convince the young woman to return to her previously planned life. Shimi cancelled her courses, packed up her stuff, leaving her Coldplay and The Strokes posters on the apartment wall and told her aunt she could either help her or not, but she was coming home.

She automatically assumed the life of her parents, taking over their hobby farm, with their chickens and four mischievous goats. To fill in the days and make a bit of money (although her parents' life insurance policy would have kept her comfortable for life) Shimi learned how to make cheese from the goats' milk and as time passed, she added to her herd and her production. It became a full-time job.

Six months after her parents' death, she closed the door on her teenage-themed bedroom and moved downstairs into her parents' master suite filled with dark mahogany furniture and heavy tapestry drapes. At first, it felt strange to sleep in her parents' large king bed and use the night stands that her parents had filled with magazines, old book marks, and leaking pens clipped to crossword puzzle books. Standing in the walk-in closet was the most difficult, as every garment held a memory, reminding Shimi of either her parents' daily routines or special occasions.

Belladane helped her empty the closet. They carefully took each garment from the hangers, and without thinking held them to their face, taking in the scent of Gus's aftershave or Mabel's perfume. All the items were folded into boxes and donated to the local thrift shop. Shimi kept a couple of her father's Shetland wool sweaters he had bought during a trip to Scotland, even though they practically fell to her knees, and some of her mom's slip-on felt clogs. She also kept her dad's grey plaid housecoat and her mother's blue floral silk kimono she had purchased on their honeymoon trip to Japan. She placed them on hangers and hung them side by side on the wall, pinning the sleeves out with tacks like they were two humans holding hands. Belladane found their presence slightly creepy, especially in the evening, when their shadows were long across the ceiling of the room, but the garments gave the bereaved daughter comfort so the loyal aunt remained silent.

Their lives fell into a comfortable rhythm. Shimi went across the road to Belladane's kitchen every evening for dinner. Belladane was an excellent cook, preparing popular Cajun meals, like gumbo with spicy red beans and rice, and her own one pot delights from whatever was in season in her prolific garden. Shimi had no interest in cooking. And as the years passed, she simply left fifty dollars every week in her aunt's antique cookie jar shaped like a fish to buy groceries for the following week. It wasn't really an arrangement they discussed; it simply evolved through time, love, and the necessity for company and comfort food.

Time did not pass slowly. The years sped along through the humid summer nights, the dark snow-covered fields, and the twisty goat-shaped weather vane that swirled relentlessly in the Maritime winds. There was a predictable pattern of seasons and special occasions. The two women celebrated birthdays, Christmas, and all the special holidays together. They became a force to be reckoned with, a mother-daughter-type duo of artistic talent and cheesemaking excellence.

The one drawback of their unique lifestyle was that despite their beauty and interesting personalities, neither found her soulmate. Belladane spent many years looking for a female partner. She used dating sites, Women Seeking Women, and had a few exciting flings over the years, but never was able to find a woman who wanted to share her solitary lifestyle in the country, in a drafty, old house filled with paint brushes, piles of The Economist magazines, and well-worn furniture.

Belladane had encouraged Shimi to go out with friends to Halifax on the weekends, go clubbing, find a nice guy, settle down. "Or just get out and have some fun," Belladane would often say. "You don't want to be old before your time." Belladane tried to instil in Shimi that every minute life starts over again. One never loses the opportunity to begin anew.

Shimi appreciated her aunt's art of not-so-gentle persuasion. She tried the dating scene for a few years, as she knew it would have also made her parents happy to know she was comfortably settled with a strong life partner. She experienced several relationships with young men, but she never stayed with any of them longer than a few months, eventually finding fault in the smallest of traits. She would walk away pondering why she sabotaged her chances at love. Why did she prefer her single life instead? Why couldn't she allow herself to be romantically happy?

After a few years of these sporadic relationships, Shimi began to turn down the invitation of friends to go out together or try a new dating site. She simply stayed at home. Often, her weekly trip to the Charlottetown Farmers Market became her only outing.

Belladane worried about Shimi's reclusive nature, but tried not to question or analyze too much, hoping in time her niece would find her own way to happiness. She also knew she was not the perfect role model for her Shimi. Sometimes Belladane, herself, felt like she was simply sleepwalking through her days … painting the same paintings, cooking the same meals, having the same conversations with herself until they became rote in her head.

The years passed succinctly and predictably, but then one day serendipity happened. Belladane splashed a container of paint across her chest. To save the expensive paint, Belladane pressed a canvas to her chest, knowing she would use it as her background colour. The effect was appealing with the ripples and streaks. So, the explorations began. She moved into abstract art and began painting with her bare breasts. She would brush wide swaths of paint across her bare chest and hold the canvas up to her body and paint great circles and daps with her generous breasts. Sometimes she would lay the canvas on the table, lean over it, and simply move to the rhythm of the music she chose for her mood that moment. Her nipples made great accent points to the abstracts, and she never tired of the process, gladly leaving the years of precise, predictable landscapes behind.

"I find the whole experience quite titillating," she would say with her raucous laugh.

She also found it hilarious that people from all over the world were intrigued with her breast art and ordered paintings from her online website, spending hundreds of dollars on paintings that looked like a child had made them with big, clumsy fists. Belladane would include her business card with each order, which had a photo of her bare breasts, covered in vibrant paint. She thought this gave the painting an authenticity that couldn't be denied, and since the photo was headless, Belladane also believed she kept her modesty intact.

Meanwhile, Shimi graduated from the initial hobby farm she inherited from her parents to a lucrative working farm. Within two years, she had added to her herd of goats and learned to make goat's cheese and began milking them twice a day. After a few years, she became bored with the simple process of making feta cheese and began to explore different types of cheese, like gouda and chevin. But soon this too became stale, and she looked for her next big change.

One day while watching Belladane dance to wild music while she cooked their dinner, Shimi pondered the relationship between sound and food. Does music enhance the flavour of food, or simply the mood one is in while creating or eating it? This was the question that sparked a unique approach to her caseiculture.

Shimi began to divide the batches of cheese into separate soundproof rooms. With their accurate temperatures and humidity, she cured the cheese while playing different music on a continual loop. In one cheese room she would play soft piano music; in another she might play heavy metal; and in the third room, perhaps traditional folk love songs. After the cheese cured, she would sample each, to determine whether the sound vibrations had made any difference on the taste of the cheese. She was certain it did.

Many of her fellow vendors at the market thought she was crazy selling Piano cheese, Heavy Metal cheese, or Love Song cheese. What a ridiculous gimmick, most quietly gossiped behind her back. Some secretly thought it was genius. *Everyone likes a new thing.* A few folks laughed in her face. Regardless, people came from miles around to taste Shimi's unusual but delicious cheese and soon she had a lucrative business far beyond her expectations.

And so, the years passed. Belladane painted her wild breast paintings and every three to six months Shimi would choose three new types of music to play to her cheese. She tried everything from Loreena McKennitt harp music, to ACDC. Then she branched out to other forms of music, such as the sound of the surf, whale songs, and train whistles. She was certain the different sounds created subtle differences in the cheese and was thrilled when the discerning turophiles tasting her free samples could differentiate between Heavy Metal cheese and Gregorian Monks chanting cheese. She was certain it simply wasn't a lucky guess.

The decades passed and the two women enjoyed each other's company, with the added bonus of Shimi's eight rambunctious goats, six productive hens, and a mutt she had picked up at the SPCA two years earlier. She had fallen in love with the young pup, described as an Aussie Shepherd-Golden Retriever mix. He wasn't a handsome dog, but he was a good listener, cocking his head from side to side when she spoke to him through the metal cage. He had an intense, sincere face she couldn't forget, so she drove back two days later and adopted him. He looked at her like he had been waiting. With the sparkle in his eyes, she was sure he was saying, "What took you so long?" Shimi named him Darcy, after an elderly neighbour she had adored as a child. This new Darcy became Shimi's constant loyal shadow and instant irritant to Belladane's old tabby cat, Meadow, who had arrived on Belladane's doorstep one quiet Sunday morning.

Shimi and Belladane busied themselves, each with their own unique art forms. They didn't require any other company. Or so they thought.

Then Eddie Savenko arrived in the lengthening shadows of a hot June day.

II
(provided)

THE BUTTONS ON her coat were made of bone. Her great grandmother, Pearl, had made the buttons from the antlers of a deer shot by her husband during the Great Depression. These six round discs had been passed down for generations. Shimi felt that it was both her privilege and obligation to continue to wear the buttons which were the only thing she had left of her great grandmother's family. Every few years when she bought a new winter coat at the local thrift shop, she always bought one with front buttons the same size, so that they could be easily replaced by the antique ones. She liked the smoothness of the bone, the yellowing along the edges, stains from all the women before her, who pushed, with their long work-worn fingers, these buttons through the holes in their own wool coats. Shimi loved the fact that they were handmade and would never wear out, unlike the memories of her parents which were slowly fading with each passing year.

As Shimi walked down the lane towards the century-old barn, she fingered the buttons on her coat and wondered what the women before her, especially her mother, would think of her and her life. Would they be pleased with her quiet, simple lifestyle? Or would they sense her loneliness and encourage her, like Belladane, to "get out there, while you're young." She pondered this often. She also pondered how much of her life was dictated by choice or simply fate. She knew with fate there is a final choice, to accept that fate or not ... or to change the direction of that fate. The sudden death of her parents had created the pathway to this current life ... or was it purely her choice? Choices? Had she made the right choices in her life after the tragic death of her parents? Over twenty years had passed, and still she was contemplating these two questions.

She loved the silence and stillness of the night. Sometimes she worked long after midnight, listening to CBC radio and making her cheeses. She felt blessed with the simple life of making cheese for others to enjoy, carrying on her mother's dream, but at the same time part of her resented it. Her life seemed like a revolving potter's wheel of predictability and routine. What would her life have been like if her parents had lived? What if she had finished her degree and had a career she loved in an energetic city? A lively circle of friends? And maybe her own family? Would that have been a better choice?

The distant train whistle was a welcome break from her thoughts. She loved hearing it late at night, always half past midnight. She understood the Proust phenomenon well and knew she experienced it also for sounds. Shimi lived with it daily, for the train whistle often stirred feelings of melancholy and loss, but it also churned up loving childhood memories. How her dad would help her count all the train cars whenever they were stopped at a crossing. Their largest train was one hundred and thirty-nine cars. How her mom had taken her on the train when she was seven from Moncton to Montreal, to have a "girls only holiday" and visit Gramma Cia. They had looked out the window at the massive rolling hills covered in trees, and were always excited when they spotted a river below them or a deer standing by the tracks, its ears twitching as the train rumbled past. They had eaten hard boiled eggs, salty crackers and drank Tang. Shimi had found the trip ever so exciting.

Now the late-night train whistle held an intimacy and a nostalgia, like it was there for only her to hear. And she loved that.

She checked on her eight goats in the side yard. They were hunkered down for the night, under the canopy roof that sloped out from the barn. She kept them outside during the summer, but in the cold months she moved them into the barn at night. She had two Nigerian dwarfs, four Oberhasli, and two Nubian. They were milked twice a day and were good producers. But the eight girls, Wilma, Betty, BamBam, Pebbles, Lucy, Ethel, Mary and Rhoda, were more like rambunctious pets, often escaping the yard and eating Belladane's prize azaleas. Shimi's buck, Ernie, a gorgeous Sable, was her pride and joy, and had a healthy abundance of romantic charm. The kids, born in early spring, were typically sold to people who wanted a pet goat for their hobby farm. Shimi loved taking evening drives on the back roads and spying on some of her past kids that were growing like wild weeds and living a playful life in barnyards equipped with old tires and teeter-totter boards.

When she entered the barn, she flipped on the light switch at the edge of the door, illuminating a large room of glass cabinets. Each was filled with rounds of cheese piled upon each other like a brick wall. Shimi called this space her "Ready Room." Once the cheese was cured and labelled, it was stored here, ready to be piled into the red cooler boxes in the corner and taken to the local market each Saturday.

Behind the Ready Room was the kitchen. It was her gleaming state of the art stainless steel sanctuary. Two long counter tops ran the length of the room. A commercial gas stove sat at one end, and a large refrigerator filled with bottles of lemon juice and pails of goat milk sat at the other. There were shelves with jugs of vinegar, salt, spices and steel utensils. Huge rolls of muslin, white waxy paper, and her labels hung from the ceiling. There were 12 large hooks above a sloped counter where the cheese could drip dry, allowing the droplets to run into a stainless-steel sink at the end. The only adornment was a huge poster entitled France's Favourite Cheeses and a large sunny window that looked out to the goat yard.

Along the other side of the Ready Room were three white metal doors. Behind each door, was a small six-by-eight-foot room, with shelves from floor to ceiling, filled with cheese being cured and aged to perfection and the music that flavoured their growth. She opened the door that held the sign, Whale Music. The room was chilly, about 10 degrees Celsius and the beguiling call of the whales made her shiver. The whale music played on a perpetual loop, piped in from a speaker on the wall. She didn't really understand how it worked, but her techie friend, Julie, set up the musical system for her and for each new batch of cheese. She wondered if making her cheese this way was totally crazy, yet she couldn't stop. There was something comforting about playing music to the cheese. The cheese that sustained her livelihood. And this particular whale music made her feel close to the right whales that passed through The Northumberland Strait each year and were sadly dwindling in numbers. She hoped that the people who bought the whale music cheese would also gain more empathy for the plight of these whales. She thought perhaps she should write a small statement about the whales and attach it to each piece of cheese. Maybe she should donate part of her profits to a whale organization? She would work on that idea soon.

Everything looked neat, tidy, and professional. A CBC journalist named Leon Birkshire had purchased some of her cheese two weeks prior at the market and returned the following week to request an interview. He was keen to explore her unusual cheesemaking philosophy. Reluctantly, she said yes. She didn't want to open herself to analysis and perhaps ridicule, but Belladane had convinced her, saying, "What the hell. Who cares? Whatever he writes, it will only increase sales."

Shimi was confident the journalist would be impressed with her cheesemaking business. How could he not? Shimi turned off the lights, and as she was about to lock the barn door, a soft cough came from behind her. She knew that cough instantly.

"Hey Eddie." Shimi turned the key, pocketed it and then turned to face Eddie.

"Hello Shimi." A man in his early fifties, with curly brown hair greying around the edges and loose baggy clothes, stepped out from the shadows. He had a long, handsome face, with a short, tidy beard.

There was a slight stoop to his walk and a tiredness about his eyes, typical of an older man.

"Making your rounds, are you?" Shimi asked.

"Just getting some air," Eddie replied.

Shimi knew that was far from the truth. She knew that every evening Eddie walked around the six properties that lined Gooding Road, checking in on things, doing his own unique type of neighbourhood watch. Everyone knew old Edna Lorhan often absentmindedly left her keys in her door, and Eddie, upon finding them, would lock her door and quietly slip them under her pot of geraniums. Shimi knew Eddie fed Mabel, the Barrymore's neglected barn cat, giving her a huge handful of kitty kibble from his pocket. Mabel sat on the picket fence and waited for him and the tiny morsels of Meow Mix that kept her comfortable during the night. Shimi also knew Eddie took the elderly folks' garbage cans to the road, when they were forgotten, and then dragged them back the next day. She knew that Eddie picked apples off the ground in the Stinson's darkened orchard and fed them to the Gordon's skinny mule. Shimi knew the many things that Eddie did at night as he walked by the darkened houses ... at night when everyone else in the neighbourhood was fast asleep.

Shimi knew all these things as she had secretly followed him one night, when Eddie first began his nightly walks. What she didn't know was that Eddie knew she was following him, but pretended he didn't. He liked that she was suspicious of a stranger who was a new friend to Belladane, and realized Shimi wanted to make sure he was worthy of her aunt's friendship.

Shimi was happy she had followed him that summer night and saw the kindness that he spread throughout his walk. The silence that he breathed in. The night air that appeared to fill him with calm and peace. She knew he avoided the business of daylight; the people, the conversations he would rather not have to fake; the noise; the blinding sunshine; the questioning eyes that followed him with pity or concern. Eddie was their very own night watchman. Shimi was happy fate had brought him here, and he had made the choice to stay.

One hot June day earlier this year, Eddie had simply appeared in Belladane's side field. He had a heavy, brown backpack, with a sleeping bag on top, and a large hole in his left shoe. He took his shoes off at the edge of the stream, rolled up his trousers to his knees and simply stood in the cool shallow water for the longest time. Belladane watched him from her kitchen window, fascinated, frozen in place. A stranger. The curiosity of it all.

Finally, she got back to her day: her drying paint brushes; her loaf of bread rising on the kitchen counter; and collecting her sheets from the clothesline. Yet she couldn't get him out of her mind. She was pleased when she saw him standing by her stream again, a few days later. And so it began, Eddie would appear at the stream several times a week, take a long drink, then fill up his water bottle, which Belladane was sure was not healthy, have a quick wash and then disappear.

The next time she saw Eddie at the stream, she quickly walked down the field, through the knee-high meadow grass, swatting the flies as she went. She was eager to meet this stranger.

"Hi there," Belladane said, as she came up behind the man.

"Hey," he replied. As he turned, the shadow of the trees and the sparkle of light off the water, created a jigsaw puzzle pattern across his tired face.

"How's it going," Belladane asked.

"Fine. Lovely day," Eddie remarked.

"My name is Belladane. I live in that house right there." She pointed to her house beyond the trees.

"I'm Edward Savenko. Sorry, about trespassing. I'll be on my way," he said, as he began to pick up his backpack.

"No worries, my friend. Stay as long as you want. I've seen you down here at the river before," Belladane said.

"Yes, it's a mighty lovely spot," Edward said.

"Do you live around here?" Belladane asked, even though she knew it was obviously a stupid question.

"No. I'm just passing through," he said, hoisting the large pack up onto his back.

There was something about the man Belladane liked. He smelled like fir trees and wet grass. She didn't get much information out of him during that first encounter, but she found out enough to know she trusted this stranger and wanted to help him.

"Listen, I have an old twenty-foot Winnebago trailer in the barn. It hasn't been used for years, probably smells like moth balls, but it's weathertight, and you're welcome to use it. My neighbour, with his tractor, could pull it down here by the stream, if you'd like."

Edward looked rather embarrassed and nervous. "Oh, thank you, but that's a lot of trouble, and I don't know how long I will be in these parts." Then he hesitated and added, "But it is pretty countryside ..."

"Look, it's no trouble. I will have my neighbour pull it down here tomorrow morning, and you can take a look at it, and stay as long or short as you like. You're welcome to stay in it in the barn, but it would be much nicer to be outside in this glorious weather. What do you say? And down here you'd have lots of privacy," Belladane added.

Edward looked at the ground and stuck his hands into his jean pockets. As quickly as falling in love with a three-legged dog on a string, Belladane felt an instant tenderness for this man.

Edward said gently, "You're very kind. I'd be much obliged. You won't even know I'm here. And we can work out some kind of a deal. I pay my way."

"Don't worry about that. I'm happy to meet you and happy the old trailer will get some use. Be forewarned, it probably will be a bit musty. See you tomorrow morning." Belladane wanted to stay and ask him a hundred questions, but she knew she might frighten him off, so she made herself turn towards the house.

"My friends call me Eddie," the man said, as she began to walk away.

Belladane turned to face him, but kept backing up as she talked. With a radiant smile, she said, "Then Eddie it is."

At dinner that evening, she told Shimi about the stranger she had invited to stay in her trailer.

"You did what?" Shimi said, stopping her chewing to stare at her aunt. "You don't even know this guy. He could have escaped from prison. He could be an axe murderer!"

"Well, I guess you'd better hide your axe, as I have invited him to stay and I'm not reneging on the invitation. I think he's a good guy, who just needs a break in life," Belladane said. "Let's give him a chance."

Shimi stood up and walked to the window to look down to the river, thinking she might see this man standing there. Meadow, Belladane's sleek black cat, who was sleeping on the sunny windowsill, woke up, yawned, stretched, and jumped down with a huff.

"My goodness Belladane, sometimes I don't know what to do with you. One of these days your big, fat heart may get you into trouble. And if he's American, like you think, well then, he won't need an axe. He probably has a gun," Shimi said with a worried sigh.

Belladane simply grinned and shrugged.

It was a couple of days before Shimi met Eddie. From behind her living room curtain, she had seen him on the road straightening out Belladane's crooked mailbox post. He was carefully adding another brace to keep the box level, so she thought it was a perfect place and time to pretend she coincidentally bumped into him. She walked casually down the lane.

"Hi Eddie, I'm Shimi," she said, extending her hand.

"Hi Shimi, I'm Eddie," he said with a laugh, as he dropped the hammer on the ground and wiped his hand on the side of his jeans. When he shook her hand, he placed his left hand over their clasped hands for a quick moment, which she thought was a rather curious and intimate thing to do. Her dad had always said you could tell a lot about a person by their handshake.

Immediately, Shimi noticed that Eddie was missing the last two fingers on his left hand. Although she wanted to ask how he lost them, she didn't. And despite being very curious, she and Belladane never did ask. They simply thought, over time, Eddie would explain his hand injury. And as time passed and he didn't mention his missing fingers, they assumed the story was too horrific to be told.

They spoke briefly that morning by the mailbox, but Shimi, like Belladane, got a good feeling about the man and walked back to her house knowing she would no longer be hiding her axe.

Eddie was indeed honest, for he instantly proved he liked to pay his way. And so, a symbiotic relationship began between the two women and this stranger. Belladane would go out to the garden and discover it had already been hoed and weeded. She would come home from shopping and her grass had been cut, or her outside windows were washed, without a streak, and she could never get them streak free. The fence behind the barn that had been falling down for years was suddenly upright and secure. In the fall, the leaves would be raked, the apples picked, the eavestrough cleaned out. All the routine or seasonal jobs were done without barely seeing this mysterious man doing them.

Belladane often bragged to Shimi over dinner, telling her a list of chores that Eddie had done. She would exclaim, "That man is as handy as a pocket on a tee shirt."

Within a couple of weeks of his arrival, Eddie had branched out to Shimi's property. Shimi would find a damaged board on the barn swapped out for a new one, a rotten fence post replaced, or a hole in the gazebo screen mended. Eddie seemed to know what needed doing, and without drama or questions he would get it done. In return, Shimi kept him well stocked with fresh cheese, some gourmet potato chips and Anne of Green Gables chocolates she liked to buy for herself. All the necessities in life, she liked to think. She discovered giving him things directly made him uncomfortable, so she started leaving them in a basket on the back porch at night. She would put Eddie's name on them, and hoped the local marauding raccoons could read. The goodies would be gone the next morning, and often he wrote a simple "thanks" on the note. She liked this sweet communiqué. It was clandestine and playful.

Belladane also loved having Eddie included in her flock. She shared with him all the veggies, apples, or grapes that grew on her property. During the day while Eddie slept, she would quietly leave them or a freshly baked loaf of molasses bread on the steps of the trailer. Her gifts often included freshly squeezed lemonade or some apple pie. As the weather cooled, she dropped off blankets, hats, and a man's warm pea jacket that had been hanging in the attic for years. She knew he used the outdoors as his toilet and the stream as his bathtub, but she knew the colder weather would make that lifestyle impossible. Plus, the trailer had no electricity running to it, which also posed a problem. She couldn't imagine him spending the winter in the trailer, and she most certainly didn't want the man to leave.

It was early October when Belladane insisted the trailer be taken back into the old barn on her property, where there was better shelter from the wind, and access to water and electricity. Eddie didn't argue too much.

And so, Eddie became a constant in the lives of Shimi and Belladane. He was their very own Boo Radley; he was always there, but not there. Seen, but not seen. He spoke as little as possible, but over the months, they learned he was an ex- veteran from the Afghanistan war, with excellent skills in marksmanship, could swim forever under the water holding his breath for extraordinary amounts of time, and had worked several years as an under-water welder. For being homeless and malnourished, he was incredibly fit. He had fought valiantly for his American homeland, and now he was homeless. After months roaming aimlessly around the northern states, he unintentionally wandered into Canada through the back roads of New Brunswick and began hiking throughout

Nova Scotia. He decided one day to jump on the ferry to see Prince Edward Island and started wandering the roads throughout Queens County. He soon discovered he never wanted to wander back to his American home.

"I'm an illegal alien, Belladane. Does that not trouble you?" he asked her one day.

"Nah! It took my family a few years to fill out the paperwork when we got here. And anyway, I judge a person by their character, not their immigration status." Belladane gave Eddie the biggest smile. "I will help you however you need, if you want to apply for citizenship. It won't be easy. I've heard the paperwork is a nightmare. Maybe I could sponsor you or something. Just don't ask me to marry you. I'm not into monogamy." Belladane punched his shoulder, and laughed at her joke.

"Thanks, Belladane. You're the best," Eddie said.

"No, just the best you've got," Belladane laughed. "And anyway, I'm sure Canada has bigger things to worry about than Edward Savenko."

Perhaps Canada didn't worry about Edward Savenko, but he did. His PTSD moments could happen without warning, and during those times, Eddie would simply stare straight ahead like he was reliving a devastation beyond words. Then he would quickly walk away. Shimi and Belladane never pressed him for more information. They respected his privacy and his emotional wounds, wounds they knew they could never truly understand.

Now Shimi saw Eddie almost every night as she made her last rounds at the barn. She was not surprised to hear his gentle cough behind her. She liked the fact that he was cognizant not to walk up to her quietly and scare her in the dark.

"Good night, Eddie," Shimi said as she walked back to her house. "Have a good one."

"Good night," Eddie murmured. Then he stuffed his hands into his pants pockets and turned back into the darkness he so preferred.

For Eddie Savenko the light quickened everything, made everything more extreme, more glaringly frightful. All the torments of his mind happened in the blaring sunlight of the Afghan desert ... the bullets, the blood, the explosions ... they came back with the flashing of images ... a helmet flying through the air, a bent head over a fallen friend, a hand over a gushing wound, and the screams ... always the screams. They came back to Eddie through the slam of a door, the beeping of a transport truck backing up, or a delighted scream of a child in a sunny playground. The memories were an asphyxiating box of fear that could be delivered at any moment.

The comfort of the night. The nights ... the nights were his. No haunting memories. The night welcomed him like a new landscape, a landscape that was cinematic and pretty. At night as he sat quietly by the stream, or leaned against a rail fence, he felt he could hear the grass growing and the heartbeat of the moon. He would watch for long periods of time the tree tides, as the plants moved microscopically slowly to follow the light of the moon. These night sights and sounds were miraculous and serene, and always comforted by the lonesome whistle of the distant train.

June 2022
Dear Elsa,

    I know I've been avoiding your calls, and you want me to call, or at least text, but I wanted to take the time to think about what I wanted to say to you. I know you think I have given up and run away, and maybe I have, but it's what I need to do right now. I'm sorry I have deserted you, made you worry and probably really pissed you off. I was always the strong one, and now you are the strong one, and I feel weak. But just know I'm working on things and starting to feel some better.

    I am presently in Canada, in Prince Edward Island to be exact. Remember, Anne of Green Gables ... all those books you read as a kid? Well, everything here is Anne of Green Gables; you can even buy a straw hat just like Anne's with funny red braids attached. I will get you one, before I leave. Ha!

    I am staying on a farm, helping out an artist. Belladane is a funny, kind Jamaican woman in her sixties and a very good cook! Shimi lives across the road and is also becoming a friend. She makes gourmet cheese, which is cured while she plays music to it. Weird, right? But they both have adopted me, and for now, that's okay. They also give me my privacy, and don't ask too many questions. So, it's all good.

    I don't know when I'll be back. I've got a lot of thinking to do, and a lot of decisions to make. But I will write to you every so often, so you don't worry too much. And as my dad would say, "We live until we die." And if Tanzania is calling you, go on that safari trip we had planned on taking together. Don't wait for me. Live your life, Elsa. Follow your bliss.

    I love you very much ... don't forget that. But I just can't be who you want me to be, right now.

IloveyaandImissya!
Eddie

III
(once)

WHEN SHIMI SAT down at table the next night to have dinner with Belladane, her aunt was eager to hear all about the interview with the journalist. It was a big deal for Shimi to be interviewed by the CBC. Belladane knew Shimi and her family had been lifelong fans and financial contributors to the Canadian Broadcasting Corporation. It was a dream come true to be featured as one of their local interest stories.

"So, how did it go?" Belladane questioned while piling a heap of seafood paella onto Shimi's plate.

"Good, I think. Well at least he didn't laugh at me," Shimi replied. "It will be interesting to see how he sets it all up. What slant he takes."

"What are some of the things he asked you?"

"Oh, he asked about the goats, the process, how I got started, how I got the idea of playing music to my cheese, just stuff like that. He took some pictures of my girls, the cheese room, the barn, and me holding some cheese. I'm not sure why, since it's only going to be on the radio. He wanted to know how I decide which music to play, and whether I have ever held an open house, kind of a taste-testing party."

"You give very generous samples every week," Belladane said. "What was Birkshire like?"

"He was nice. Friendly. Probably about my age, maybe a tad older, mid-forties. Well built. Smart dresser. He wore this really nice leather jacket with a black turtleneck underneath and nice jeans. He recorded everything of course, and he said it would be on the radio probably next week. He said he'd let me know when it would be aired. I think it went well. I hope it turns out well, and he doesn't make me look ridiculous." Shimi shovelled some paella into her mouth. It was delicious, as usual.

Belladane sat up straight like a meerkat. "Oh, stop with that! You're always worried about what people think of you. Who cares? And anyway, you haven't done one bad thing in your entire life. So, what if your cheesemaking is a tad eccentric; people love eccentric."

"I haven't done one bad thing in my life? If you only knew?" Shimi said, with a mischievous smile.

"Okay, try me. I bet your bad thing is you took a chocolate bar as a kid, and then went right back to the store and put it back, right? Am I right?" Belladane intently leaned across the table.

"Okay, I can't believe I'm going to tell you this. It's wicked, but kind of hilarious now. Do you remember when I was a teen, I used to babysit for the Wilsons? Remember the family with three bratty kids who used to live on Woodley Road? Well, Margaret Wilson was a real piece of work. She'd pay me a buck an hour and leave me all the kids to bathe, the dishes to do, the laundry to fold, and then … then even sometimes she'd ask me to do some vacuuming. All for a buck an hour. I know the poor woman was exhausted, but really? All of my friends would babysit one kid and they would watch cartoons together, eat popcorn and drink pop. I was watching three kids, and cleaning an entire house."

"Pure child abuse! So, what did you do?" Belladane inquired.

"Well, this one time I had put the kids to bed and was vacuuming her bedroom, and I couldn't help myself… I decided to nose around in the drawer of the bedside table. It was a friggin' hot night, and I was so pissed having to vacuum. There was a pile of condoms inside the drawer. So, I took them out, got a pin from her sewing basket, and I put a pin prick in each of the condoms, then I threw them back in the drawer."

Belladane practically spit the paella from her mouth. "What the hell, Shimi? No way! That is some crazy shit!" Belladane laughed hysterically, then added, "She ended up with two more kids you know."

"I know, I know. Don't make me feel any worse than I already do. I told you, I'm far from perfect." Shimi laughed and took a big gulp of wine. "I can't believe I told you that. I promised myself I would take that to my grave."

"I bet that was one prick Margaret never expected to find in her prophylactics," Belladane snorted.

"Oh you!" Shimi laughed.

"Ah, don't worry about it. Those kids got better the more of them there were. The first three were kind of clueless, if I remember correctly. The last two were more with it. Margaret Wilson used to brag about the marks and accomplishments of her two youngest. You did her a favour."

"I don't think I'd go that far, but I'm glad the last two were little geniuses. I stopped babysitting when she was pregnant a couple of months later. I couldn't look at her pregnant belly without my face turning red. I just couldn't. Mom always kept asking me why I quit. Then I got a job scooping ice cream at the Dairy Bar, so she finally quit asking."

"Ah, your mom was probably suspicious. Mabel was pretty psychic, she was. Or maybe she was worried Mr. Wilson had come onto you. He was a hottie, if I remember correctly," Belladane laughed.

"You're right, Mom used to often know what I was up to, even before I did. Maybe it's that sixth sense mothers have." Shimi shrugged and took another spoonful of paella. Then she continued, "I guess Mr. Wilson was hot, but at fourteen I didn't really register that. I remember he was very nice to me. Now my dad ... there was a good guy. As you probably know, he was one of the kindest men you could ever meet. Remember for years he would play Santa to all his friend's children? He'd drive around on Christmas morning and hand out their gifts. And remember how he'd put coins in expired parking meters, or those years he planted that huge garden just to supply the food bank. And all those years he volunteered for the Rotary Club."

"One of my fondest memories of your dad was the time he got wind that some folks in need, or maybe it was the food bank organizers, I can't remember which ... whoever ... they were coming to a potato field in the fall to pick up the potatoes that got missed by the harvester. They were allowed to pick them for free. Your dad didn't think there were enough potatoes left behind so he went out and bought a hundred pounds of potatoes and the night before they arrived, he scattered them in the field. Can you imagine? The farmer thought he was crazy, but your dad swore him to secrecy. He just wanted to make sure they had lots to pick up. What an amazing man he was." Belladane finished her story with a soft sigh.

Shimi nodded silently and stared at her glass of wine.

"You know, you take after both of your parents, Shimi. You're both intuitive and kind, despite sabotaging condoms all those years ago." Belladane gave Shimi a playful wink. She leaned over and picked up Meadow who was twirling around her ankles. The cat relaxed in her arms, began to purr loudly and rub her head under Belladane's chin.

"Ah, thanks. Well, what about you, Bella, my dear? Tit for tat! What did you do that you're ashamed of or are you the perfect one?" Shimi inquired playfully.

Belladane hesitated for a brief moment. "Ha! No! Far from it! Where should I begin? There are so many." Belladane tilted back in her chair and then smiled. "Well, as a teenager, I used to give decaffeinated coffee to the customers who were rude to me when I worked in a coffee shop."

"Oh, such a nasty girl," Shimi scraped her plate clean and then poured herself another glass of wine. "And? Dig a little deeper, my dear."

"Well, this is really bad. I mean really bad. I used to get bullied a lot, being one of the few black kids in my school. I always wanted to stay in the library at lunchtime and simply hide and read books, but the old librarian, Mrs. Carmichael, used to shoo me outside and say, 'go make friends.' She never took my plight seriously. So, one day I found a whole bunch of tiny frogs on our lawn. They were about an inch long. Just babies, I guess. Within a matter of minutes, I must have picked up around fifteen frogs. The next day I brought them to school in my lunch pail, and when Mrs. Carmichael wasn't looking, I took random books from the shelves and put a tiny frog inside, closed it tight, then put it back on the shelf."

"What the hell?" Shimi banged her wine glass down on the table. Meadow startled, jumped from Belladane's arms and fled into the living room. Shimi continued, "Belladane, oh my nerves! You didn't! Those poor frogs!"

"Yup, I did, unfortunately. Even now, all these years later, I can't look a frog in the face without feeling guilty. I squished all of those innocent baby frogs to death in those books. It took about three or four days before one of them was discovered. Then another book was discovered with a flattened frog in it. They had to remove every book from the shelves and go through them all, one by one. The books were ruined, of course, and the principal, well I had never heard her so upset. I was in grade five, in Ms. Turner's class and I sat at my desk while she raged over the loudspeaker. I can simply remember her saying the word 'sick' over and over again. And I thought, yes, I guess I am a really sick kid."

"Come on, you made that story up, just to make me feel better about my evil condom story, didn't you? Didn't you?" Shimi questioned earnestly.

Belladane smiled, raising her wine glass in the air as if in a toast. She said, "Well you will never know for sure, will you, my little condom-pricker?"

IV
(because)

Several weeks went by before Shimi got word that her interview would be on the radio. It was a Saturday afternoon program called Changing it Up. Shimi made a big pot of green tea with local honey; Belladane made some blueberry scones; and they all rallied around Shimi's kitchen radio, eager to hear what Leon Birkshire thought of Shimi's musical cheese endeavours. Even Eddie got up early to have a listen.

Shimi was old school and still preferred her parent's kitchen radio to her computer, even though the reception was crap. She constantly had to keep touching the dial, while at the same time sit in a particular spot at the kitchen table, so the damn thing wouldn't go fuzzy.

"Why does every God-awful country music station come in perfectly, but I can never get the CBC clearly?" Shimi groaned.

"Sit down and stop fussing. You're making me nervous," Belladane said, while carefully peeling bits of blue paint off her fingernails.

Eddie poured the tea, and they all sat around the table. Then the interview came on, and they fell silent.

"Welcome to Change it Up, a weekly endeavour to bring you interesting folks doing wonderful things in our community. I'm Leon Birkshire and this week we're talking about one of my favourite things: cheese. I recently had the pleasure of meeting one of our extraordinary farming entrepreneurs, Shimi Montray, from the village of Gooding. Many of you may know of her and her famous goat cheese that she sells at Charlottetown's Farmers Market every Saturday. She is a fascinating woman with an even more fascinating attitude towards cheesemaking.

Hello Shimi, thanks for allowing me to visit your wonderful establishment. What made you get into the cheese business?"

"Well, I took over my parents' hobby farm when they passed away, years ago, and after a while decided to make it into a lucrative business. I already had a couple of goats, so I learned how to make cheese, and it just kind of blossomed from there."

"So, the goats provide the milk for your cheese?"

"Yes, I have 8 goats I milk twice a day, and whatever they give me I turn into cheese."

"Ah, but your cheese isn't any ordinary goat cheese now, is it? Tell me about that."

"Well, I made what you call ordinary goat cheese for several years, and then I got thinking about the molecular makeup of cheese, the enzymes, and all the factors that go into a good round of cheese. I was fascinated for instance that our very own tears have different molecular makeup, depending upon the mood we are in, or the reason for our tears. So, cutting-up-onion tears don't leave you with puffy eyes, whereas sad tears do. This got me thinking about how other molecules change under different circumstances."

"Interesting! I didn't know they were chemically different. How did you incorporate this idea into your cheese?"

"I knew music enhanced food in various ways. I mean we all can relate to eating a meal, while listening to our favourite music ... the meal tastes great. If you eat while listening to grating, irritating music you hate, you likely won't enjoy the meal as much or maybe you will not notice the taste of the food at all. Something is happening in your brain on a molecular level. Or maybe, just maybe ... perhaps ... something is happening to the taste of the food as well? That was my question. So, I thought, what if the sound vibrations of the music are also changing the molecular makeup of the food. Wouldn't that be cool to test out?"

"So, what exactly do you do?"

"Well, I make my cheese the same way I always have, except now I play a certain type of music to that batch while I am making it, and while it cures and ages. The music runs on a continual loop for about three to six months in the soundproof sealed, curing room."

"Wow, that's a really long earworm."

"Yes, I suppose, but I haven't had any complaints from the cheese so far."

"So, what types of music do you play in your cheese rooms?"

"Well, I choose different music for every new batch. I've tried Rock and Roll; Classical, especially Beethoven; soft love songs like The Carpenters; and then louder, heavier stuff, like Heavy Metal, ACDC, stuff like that. I kind of feel sorry for that batch!"

"And what did you determine? Does it really taste differently?"

"I have some loyal customers, and I often do taste testing at the market, and many feel they can tell the difference between the cheeses. For people with discerning taste buds, you can tell the difference. Yes."

"Wow, that's incredible. Can we give it a try?"

"Sure. I have here four pieces of cheese ready for you. Give it a try. Cleanse your palate with this soda water between each. Take your time."

"Okay folks, thanks for listening to me chew there for a few minutes, but I have now tried all the cheeses, and I do think they taste slightly different. But I also think, but I'm not positive, that number one tastes exactly like number three. Sorry!"

"Wow! I can see why you're also the food critic. I tried to trick you. But you're right, number one and three were the same cheese. Well done!"

"And what was the music played to these three cheeses? Or should I be able to discern that as well? Should Heavy Metal taste louder and angrier than, let's say, The Carpenter's cheese?"

"That would be the next level of taste, but I'm not sure we are quite there yet. I'm still working on that."

"So, what types of music are your cheeses listening to right now?"

"I have three on the go, and have moved from what we think of as traditional music, to musical sounds of nature as well. Right now, I have Whale Songs on the go, which are rather beautiful I must admit. Another room features Gregorian Monks chanting which is also very melodic and moving; and in room three I have the 90's group, ABBA, playing. So, we will see what those taste like in another month or so."

"So, Shimi, there must be all kinds of folks who think playing music to food is a totally ridiculous idea, just a gimmick, let's say. What do you have to say to them?"

"Of course, and they have every right to their opinion. But science is learning more and more about sound vibrations, and how they affect our bodies on a cellular level. Many of these principles have been used for thousands of years, when you think of ancient religions that chant, or use bells, or the Buddhists who use gongs or the singing bowls. So, it makes sense to me that if the resonating sound is changing the molecular structure in our own body's cells, then it quite possibly is also changing the molecular structure of other forms of matter, like cheese, and that in turn could change the flavour."

"Alright, that does make sense, and for those of you who want to give this theory a try, Shimi Montray's Music Cheese can be found at the farmers market every Saturday. Good Luck Shimi, and make a special batch for me someday, okay. I am a big Garth Brook's fan!"

"Thanks so much! Who knows? Maybe some Garth Brook's cheese will be in the future."

When the interview was over, Shimi clicked off the radio, exhaled a long deep breath and looked at her friends, saying, "Just for the record, there will be no Garth Brooks cheese in the future!"

"That was great, Honey! You did great!" Belladane exclaimed.

"Yes, you did really well, Shimi. You explained it all really well. Made sense to me, and I have no clue about cheese," Eddie said.

Belladane nudged Eddie's arm and said, "Eddie, maybe you should go on Saturday as she will need to take a lot more cheese with her this week. I think, Shimi, you're going to be overrun with customers after that great interview."

Shimi dropped her head into her hands, and said with a playful sigh, "Oh dear, what have I done?"

When Friday evening rolled around, Shimi began filling her coolers with cheese, ready for the early drive to the market. Eddie volunteered to come with her, and Shimi was grateful for the help. The next morning, Eddie lifted eight coolers full of cheese into Shimi's truck, and helped her unload them at her stall. Then he disappeared, afraid Shimi would ask him to help her sell. Having to talk to all those customers was not in Eddie's skill set, and definitely not his idea of a good time. It made him sweat just thinking about it.

People were practically lined up waiting for Shimi's special goat cheese.

One old lady said, "Well I've never heard of anything so crazy in all my years, but I like the taste so I'll buy just a tiny bit. On a fixed pension you know." At which point Shimi smiled, gave her an extra-large slice, and secretly charged her half price. The old woman scuttled away with a scowl.

One young woman with brightly dyed blue hair said, "It's cruel to steal the milk away from the mother goats. What about her kids? Why don't you milk yourself?"

Shimi pointed to her small chest and said, "Maybe in my next lifetime."

A young millennial couple sampled everything, were sure they could taste the difference, and then bought two pounds of all three types, exclaiming, "We consider ourselves turophiles and this will go wonderfully with our Kopi Luwak coffee."

Shimi rolled her eyes as they walked away with their bag of cheese and fresh artichokes slung over the husband's shoulder.

Leon Birkshire dropped by and asked how the sales were going. Shimi was pleased to see him and thanked him graciously for the lovely segment on his show. She wrapped up some cheese and insisted he take it home, as a gift. He continued to hang around wanting to chat, while Shimi was busy selling to others. She noticed this and said several times, "Thanks Leon, have a good day" hoping he would leave, but he continued to stand close by and wait for a break between customers to start up more small talk.

Midafternoon, Leon finally left with a wave of his hand. Shimi was relieved as she realized she was feeling a bit self-conscious around him. He was a good-looking man.

Shimi also noticed two young men standing near the food court for a very long time, and every time she glanced their way, they were looking at her. She would smile and hope they were simply waiting to come over to her booth, but they continued to lean up against the wall and simply take in their surroundings. Perhaps they were waiting for someone who was shopping and didn't have anything better to do, Shimi thought. Yet they seemed quite fascinated with her and her cheese, which left Shimi once again feeling self-conscious and uncomfortable. She tried to shake it off, knowing being gawked at is often an occupational hazard for many women.

The day passed quickly, and just like clockwork Eddie reappeared at closing time to help Shimi tear apart her display, put the coolers in the truck, and head back home. None of that took long.

Shimi Montray's Music Cheese had sold out!

V
(consequently)

SHIMI WORKED TIRELESSLY over the fall. The orders were continuing to come in and she knew if she was going to have enough cheese in stock for the Christmas season, she would need to keep her goats in excellent milking condition.

She was averaging 14 gallons of milk a day, which could make about 11 pounds of cheese. It was a good amount for her small herd, but Shimi worried that she wouldn't be able to keep up with the demand. She wondered if she should find a supplier, so she could buy more milk, but she didn't want to do that. She loved that her cheese was made from her own goats. Farm fresh, from field to table.

"Don't sweat it," Belladane said at dinner one night. "You produce what you produce. If there is a growing demand, then put your prices up. The higher demand, the higher the price. Simple Economics 101."

"I'm not sure I want to put my prices up. I want to keep my cheese affordable for people," Shimi said.

"There's your dad talking," Belladane said, giving Shimi's arm a gentle pat.

"Thanks ... but all the pressure: the milking, caring for the goats, making the cheese, the curing, the market ... it is beginning to get a bit overwhelming."

"You do work really hard, Shimi. You certainly do."

"This isn't really what I had in mind when I started this. It was fun at the start, but now it's a huge drain and so much work. I'm out in the cheese room sometimes in the middle of the night."

"Well, you shouldn't be out there alone at night. Treat it like a 9 to 5 job, and then call it a day," Belladane advised.

"Right! How many small business owners can do that?" Shimi argued. "Sometimes I think I should simply get a real 9 to 5 job, stop breeding my goats, and have an easier life."

At forty-three, Shimi knew she was missing out on her own life. There were other things she wanted to do: travel to Asia, learn French and Spanish, read some good books, take yoga and maybe some pottery classes. Belladane was always on her to pick up a paint brush, but she never did. She always complained she had no time.

"I'm not sure I want to continue in the cheese business. I've been doing this for twenty years now. I want something exciting to happen in my life, know what I mean?" Shimi sighed.

"Oh, come on! You're good at it. Maybe you just need a break," Belladane offered. "And you've really carved out a name for yourself. Shimi, the witchy cheese woman." Belladane laughed. She rolled her spaghetti in her spoon and then added, "Maybe you need to hire an assistant, then you'll have more time to get some excitement in your life."

"I don't think my business is lucrative enough to pay a helper, but the irony is, sometimes I feel it's too big for just me. I guess that's the plight of many small business owners." She poured more hot sauce on her bowl of pasta. "And you're right, I do kind of like the little bit of notoriety and all my regular customers. They are always so sweet and I like getting to know them. But maybe I should quit."

"You don't cut off part of your foot when your shoe is too tight," Belladane scowled. "Why be so extreme? Just take a break or slow down. Do only what you can do. And why not ask Eddie for some help."

"Eddie is already helping with the milking a few days a week, but he's not consistent. Maybe I need to ask him if he can milk every other day, make it a set schedule. But I hate to bug him. I know he mainly sleeps during the day. Where has he been lately anyway? I haven't seen him for a couple of days."

"Yes, but you know just because you haven't seen him, doesn't mean he hasn't seen you. But you're right. I'd better check in on him," Belladane replied, then helped herself to another piece of garlic bread.

After Shimi finished the dishes, she walked down Belladane's dark lane with her loyal Darcy by her side. She hugged her wool coat around her, then lifted up her high collar and decided to do up her coat, pressing the heirloom bone buttons through their buttonholes. The November wind was coming in off the bay. She stopped at the barn and said good night to her goats. She touched each of their faces gently in the dim barn light. They were huddled together on the fresh straw she had laid out for them today. Pebbles licked at the back of her hand. Wilma tugged on her sleeve. She left the bottom half of the Dutch door open, so they had access to the barn yard even at night. She found this routine meant less cleaning inside the barn.

"How could I ever sell them?" she thought. "They are such beautiful, sweet souls!"

At the same time, Belladane wrapped a tea towel around a loaf of her warm, fresh bread and filled a thermos with hot cocoa. She bundled herself up against the November night, commanded Meadow to stay in the house, took her flashlight and headed out to the distant barn, where the trailer and Eddie was housed. The wind was growing stronger and the boards rattled on the side of the barn. Oh, how she wished Eddie would simply live in the upstairs of her farm house. She never used the rooms up there, and it seemed ridiculous for him to be out here living like a hermit, when her house was warm and half of it was empty.

Inside the barn she turned on the light switch and walked towards the trailer. Eddie had built a windbreak wall of old square bales along the north side of the trailer, which Belladane thought was quite clever and resourceful. She hoped that was keeping the trailer a little warmer.

"Eddie? Eddie, are you in there?" Belladane called when she reached the dark trailer.

There was no answer.

She tugged on the trailer door and peered into the darkness. Then she switched on the interior light. Eddie was nowhere in sight, but the place was a disaster. There were empty beer bottles everywhere, two empty wine bottles on the floor, and a 24-ounce bottle of vodka half empty on the small table. A chipped coffee cup sat beside it.

Belladane pulled back the curtain to the small bedroom area, and Eddie was lying face down on the bed. His arms and legs were splayed out, like he was a dead body floating on a pool of water. She rolled him over, started slapping his face, and calling out, "Eddie, Eddie, wake up. Are you okay? Eddie! What the hell is going on?"

Finally, she was able to revive the man and got him sitting up. He took a glass of water from her hand, reluctantly. As he drank, half of it spilled down his shirt.

"Eddie, you said you don't drink much. What happened? What's going on?"

It took a while for Eddie to talk, but he finally said, "It's too much. It's just too much."

"What's too much, Eddie? Talk to me," Belladane looked earnestly into her friend's eyes, sat down on the bed beside him and held his arm. "Talk to me!"

"Why am I here and they're not? It's just not right. What's the point?" Eddie held his head in his hands. His eyes were glassy, and his scraggly hair fell about his unkept beard. He looked and smelled like he had just walked out of the bush. "Why did I come back and they didn't?"

"The point is you're here now. Maybe you're here for a reason. Yes, you came back from that God-awful war when many of your friends didn't. And I know I don't understand how hard that is …

but you've been given a second chance. So, you don't throw that away. You need to woman-up and put one foot in front of the other and get on with it. Your friends would slap you silly if they knew you threw it away. A chance for a better life. You don't need to feel guilty about that ... that is simply how it goes sometimes."

Eddie leaned his elbows on his legs and put his head in his hands. "Every day is such a struggle. I am a ghost of myself. And I can't seem to get it together."

Belladane encouraged Eddie to move into the kitchen and sit at the tiny table. They talked while she heated up a can of mushroom soup, found some of Shimi's cheese in his bar fridge, and cut generous slices of the cheese and the warm bread. She wiped out the chipped coffee mug and poured the steaming cocoa into it. She put the food in front of him.

"Eat!" she said.

He ate ravenously.

"I don't want to be your mother, Eddie, but I'm damn proud to be your friend. And sometimes we simply need a friend to get us back on track. Now you need to pour all your strength into your overalls and get back into the game of life," Belladane said with a huff, then she turned to tidy the dishes so Eddie wouldn't see the tears forming in her eyes.

The two friends talked long into the night. Belladane had never heard Eddie string so many words together in a row. She felt honoured to be allowed inside his heart and share some of the secrets of his past. To be a trusted confidante.

It was almost three in the morning before she wandered back to her own house. Eddie had finally asked for her help. And they had made a plan.

October 2022
Dear Elsa,

    Things are okay with me. I've been struggling a lot with my PTSD lately, and as you know, I have been drinking too much. Have my days and nights mixed up, which doesn't help, as I just try to avoid people during the day. But I'm working on it.

    I kind of hit rock bottom, so I have joined some AA meetings. I hitch a ride with Belladane when she drives to her art classes twice a week. Also joined some online meetings. It's going okay so far. She also wants me to go to Veterans Affairs to see about PTSD counselling or support groups, but that kind of scares me, as they will figure out that I'm an illegal alien here. I'm certainly not ready to be shipped back to the States, but I promised Belladane I would do this, so I will try to talk to them and see what happens. Fingers crossed.

    I also have started working regular hours for Shimi, milking her goats each evening. She has too much on her plate with her cheese business and even though I didn't think I was the farmer type, I must admit I really like the goats. They are very cool animals. Curious and sweet.

    Belladane insisted I have dinner with them more often. Her quote was, "I want your skinny ass at my table at least three times a week. No more canned soup and beans." She also said, I was to shower upstairs and be at the table by 6pm. I feel like a delinquent kid around her sometimes, but I know she means well. She has become a great friend. She puts me in charge of the dishes those nights. And I must admit there is nothing more comforting after a great meal than your hands in hot, soapy water washing dishes. And there usually is a pile of them! Ha!

    Hope you and California are well, my dear. It's getting pretty chilly here at night and really windy, but besides that, PEI is treating me well.

IloveyaandImissya!
Eddie

VI
(lest)

Shimi didn't mind that Eddie showed up more regularly at Belladane's house for dinner. He was an interesting man, and after a whole bunch of carefully worded questions the two women could get him talking a bit. She loved the fresh shower smell he brought to the table and his hearty laughter when they said something stupid. She thought he actually fit into their little family quite naturally, but she did miss her random, crazy girl talks with Belladane when Eddie was present. So, the nights he wasn't there, Shimi made good use of her privacy with her aunt.

"I doubt if I will ever find myself a good man," Shimi said out of the blue one evening.

"And I doubt if I'll ever find myself a good woman. What made you think of that, all of a sudden?" Belladane asked.

"I don't know. Maybe it's because I have these two greasy guys staring at me at the market. They give me the creeps. I should just walk up to them and talk to them. Ask them what their problem is."

"Yes, that might work. Worth a try. Or ... you could just knee them in the balls," Belladane laughed.

"Can you imagine? Maybe that would be the easy way to get out of the cheese business. Get kicked out of the market for assaulting customers." Shimi laughed. "You know, I like to think I'm a strong, brave feminist, but at the same time, I'd like to have a man who keeps me safe. Is that so wrong?" Shimi asked.

"Often the only way a woman is truly safe is when she's with a man; and ironically, often the only way a woman is truly unsafe is when she's with a man. So, there you have it," Belladane stared at Shimi.

"Isn't that the truth. How did you get so wise?"

"I'm not that wise, just a good talker and I've been around the block a few times," Belladane confessed.

"Around the block? Did you date many men when you were young?" Shimi asked gingerly.

"Unfortunately, a few. One in particular I'd like to forget," Belladane sighed.

"What happened, may I ask?" Shimi poised her fork in the air and leaned intently towards her aunt.

"Well let's just say, he couldn't hold his liquor. A rather angry drunk. Thankfully your dad was nearby and punched the crap out of him, and he never came back."

"What? My dad punched someone? I can't picture that. He always seemed so prim and proper in his suits and button-down shirts," Shimi said. "What did Mom say?"

"Oh, she definitely approved, and I think she kind of liked her John Wayne cowboy for a few moments. We were young, a little crazy, and thought we were so cool," Belladane said.

"And I bet you were a really cool teenager," Shimi said.

"Me, cool? Ah, I don't think so. I was so uncool, when my parents went away for a weekend, I used to mess up the house, so they thought I had friends over for a party."

"No way! But you were an athlete; that's cool. You were an excellent swimmer, right? And tennis?"

"Yes, I used to be a very good swimmer. Especially diving and breast stroke. Won a few provincial medals, believe it or not. Also, I did a lot of scuba diving when I first moved here. Loved to explore some of the old ship wrecks. There are lots of them around the island, you know."

"Wow, how come I didn't know you were into scuba diving? That's definitely cool. Why don't you still dive?" Shimi asked.

"Nowadays I rarely get wet outside the bathtub. Probably couldn't find a wetsuit to fit me," Belladane laughed. "But when I was young, I did play a lot of sports, because I thought my parents would love me more if I was sporty, since I wasn't a girly girl. I thought it would soften the blow, know what I mean?"

"I bet you were a great athlete. You're tall and strong and coordinated," Shimi said.

"Yes, I worked hard as an athlete. I would sweat so much I could have bottled it and sold it to the Ancient Greeks. They bought sweat, you know. Thought it had medicinal properties," Belladane said.

"Of course, I didn't know that. Your trivia knowledge never ceases to amaze me. You know I guess we always try to impress our parents no matter what age. I think I'm still trying to impress them, even though they aren't here. Weird right?" Shimi asked.

"No, not at all. We all want our family to be proud of us. And that doesn't stop just because they aren't here," Belladane said.

"I feel like I am still guided by their long-lost voices in my head. Even though the actual sound of their voices is fading. They were so full of good advice. And I remember they used to be so proud of my marks in high school and my milestones in life," Shimi reminisced.

"Ah yes, good old high school. Typically, the most horrible time of our lives. As a teen, I was like a pot-bound root. Strangled by the norms of society and heterosexism. Plain and simple, I didn't fit in. I can remember one time in high school, now this was way back in the 70's when everyone was required to do a gymnastics test for our final mark in gym class. Well, a large girl like me is certainly not a gymnast. Give me a basketball or a shot put, but somersaults and cartwheels, not a pretty sight. I tell you, I never slept for about a week before that test. And the day of the test, the girls were all sitting around in a circle, and when your name was called you had to enter the circle and perform your ninety second routine with the music of your choice. I chose "Leave me Alone" by Helen Reddy." Belladane stuck out her tongue and made a funny face!

Shimi laughed, choking on her broccoli quiche. "What a great song for a tormented teen."

"Exactly! It was my stab at rebellion. Anyway, I did the bloody thing and felt like a donkey in a thoroughbred race. And at the end I did my ridiculous required cartwheel, but of course my feet didn't get up very high, probably a 45-degree angle at best. The girls gave me a whimper of a clap and lots of smirks and stifled giggles. But that wasn't the worst part. I plunked myself back down in the circle all sweaty and out of breath, and the fat cow teacher said, 'You still have to do your cartwheel.'"

"What? No!!!! Was that to humiliate you or did she seriously not recognize your cartwheel?"

"I don't know, but she did like to humiliate people. And the irony was she never demonstrated any of the gymnastics stuff. She couldn't. She always had some ninety-pound Twiggy do it."

"So, what did you do?" Shimi asked.

"Well luckily the bell rang, so I got up and quickly left, but as I was walking by the rack of basketballs, I picked one up and tossed it at half court to the net and sunk it with a loud WHOOSH! Then I turned to the teacher and gave her a little salute. Boy, was I afraid to get home that day."

"Did she call your parents?" Shimi asked.

"Oh yes. Called me 'defiant.' But when I told them my side of the story, they roared with laughter. And said I did good. They said the test was stupid, that fish can't climb trees and squirrels can't swim under water. It doesn't make one more fit than the other. I think Mom even called the Superintendent, because it wasn't long after that that they stopped the required gymnastic testing."

"Good for your mom. We both had great parents. We were lucky," Shimi said, as she finished her quiche.

"Yes, despite not getting the whole gay thing, Mom was pretty great. When I was little, she used to buy me story books, and before she read them to me, she would gently colour all the children in the book with her brown pencil crayon, just so I would see kids that looked like me. So sweet. I miss her a lot," Belladane said, wiping a tiny tear from her eye.

"I know what you mean. After all these years, there's times I still find myself feeling sad about my parents' death. Really sad. It never goes away."

"They say grief is the final stage of love," Belladane said. "Which is kind of sadly beautiful."

"Yes. Yes, it is."

Belladane began twisting one of her long dreadlocks and then expertly spun it around several of the braids piled on her head. Shimi watched intently. She loved her auntie's flowing style, her love of colour, her big silver hoops, but most of all, her wonderful hair which was quickly turning grey. And she loved watching Belladane care for it.

"I love that tie-dyed headband you have on. Is it new?' Shimi asked.

"Ha! Now there's a story. I was in a funky shop today and saw these headbands, tried one on and was delighted it fit perfectly. For as you know, I have a humongous head. All brains of course," Belladane laughed. "Anyways, I was parading around the shop looking at my fabulous self in the various mirrors, when this cheeky seventeen-year-old sales girl comes up to me and says, 'Excuse me Ma'am, but that's a top."

Shimi laughed so hard she almost choked on her mouthful of quiche. "Then what did you do?"

"What did I do? I bought six," Belladane roared.

"Well, I can't wait to see all six. You've got such great hair, Auntie." Shimi studied her aunt's hair and noticed that her hair was now predominantly grey. "When did that happen?" she thought to herself. Time was passing too quickly.

Shimi suddenly felt a pang of melancholy for their parents lost so many years ago, mixed with a new fear of losing her aunt. The curse of coming from a small family: not having a sibling, not even a cousin. Perhaps some day in the future she would be all alone. Shimi tried to push that thought out of her mind.

"God, I love your hair. Wish I had hair like yours, instead of this curly, ginger stuff. So many women would think you're just lovely. You need to get out more. Meet more women," Shimi smiled at her aunt.

Belladane began to rub her mouth and chin. "I think I was reincarnated from a cat. Meadow, am I one of your long-lost ancestors?" The cat who had been lounging on a kitchen chair jumped down, walked within inches of Darcy's nose to torment him, and jumped onto the windowsill.

"What?" Shimi chuckled.

"I have these moustache and chin hairs that grow exponentially like whiskers. And they are symmetrical around my mouth. Just like cat whiskers. What would a middle-aged girl do without her trusty tweezers?" Belladane pondered as she continued to feel around her chin.

"Oh you! You're hilarious! Just remember..." Shimi wagged her finger at her aunt. "Cat Woman was sooooo sexy!"

"Maybe, but these whiskers definitely aren't sexy or cool."

"Yes, you're cool even with your cat whiskers," Shimi said.

"Sometimes I wish I was Benjamin Buttons, that guy who grew younger as he grew older," Belladane pondered.

"Ah, yes, F. Scott Fitzgerald. Loved that story. Yes, think how the world could change if we had the wisdom of old age, and at the same time the strength, health and beauty of youth." Shimi took a sip of her wine.

"Yes, I think I could do some great things," Belladane said.

"You're already doing great things, just the way you are. So many people are better off because of you. Especially me."

"Ah, thanks Honey. I really hope so. I'd hate to be considered a blight on society." Belladane laughed and then continued, "You know, there's this young girl named Stacey at the Supermarket. I think I've told you about her before. She's worked there for several years now. I always pick her check out, check out number 3 ... she's struggling with being gay. So, I always ask her how her girlfriend is … she smiles and in almost a whisper she tells me a sweet story about the two of them. And then I tell her to tell her mother that story, just the way she told me. And she says, 'I can't. I just can't.' I wish there was more I could do for her. I wish she didn't have to struggle like I did. Forty years later and young girls are still struggling to tell their mothers they love a girl. Crazy, isn't it?"

"Definitely! I was so lucky my parents were accepting of me, no matter what I did. They always went out of their way to make my life special, safe and fun. Do you remember that one time I was sick at Halloween with Strep, an awfully sore throat, and I couldn't go trick-or-treating? I was about seven or eight and was so disappointed I wouldn't be able to wear my Superwoman costume. So, Dad put some scary music on the CD player, which he brought out every Halloween, while Mom had me put the costume on.

"I remember that night well. It was one in a million," Belladane said.

"It was so cool. Dad went out in the gazebo; Mom sat at the garage door; you were at the front door; and Gramma Cia was on the back porch. I went back and forth from the garage to the gazebo to the house, probably about a dozen times, collecting Halloween candies from each of you, pretending I was going to lots of different houses. And each time, before Gramma gave me any candy, she made me sing a different little song, even with my sore throat, or made me answer one of those silly riddles of hers. I got so frustrated with her, but I know now she was just stalling, so Dad had more time, cause every time I went to the gazebo, Dad had on a different hat or shirt and used a different accent. Pretended he was a different person. He was so funny! It was the best Halloween ever."

"Yes, and when you FINALLY got home from trick-or-treating, we all sat around and ate those amazing caramel apples your mom had made. Remember, she had also dipped them in chocolate and rolled them in nuts. Boy, were they good! But they were so sticky! Your poor Gram's false teeth ended up sticking together, and your mom had to help her take them out of her mouth and pry them apart with hot water from the kettle. I thought we all were going to choke with laughter, including your Gram. I was picking that caramel out of my own teeth for two or three days," Belladane laughed.

"When I think back on that now, I realize how special my parents were. I was so lucky. I wish they had had the opportunity to get old. I miss them so much." Shimi put her fork down. "So much."

"I know," Belladane said. "So do I."

VII
(violently)

THE CRIPPLING BLOW to the back of Shimi's skull came suddenly, like a brick through a window. Her head was thrust forward and her forehead slammed against the metal shelves in cheese room number two. She grasped the shelves to try to stay upright, but could feel herself losing strength, feel her legs crumbling beneath her. She tried to turn and look at her attacker, but the light from the main room created a dark silhouette in the doorway. Strong hands grasped her neck and forced her forward onto her stomach.

The Gregorian monks kept chanting-chanting their loud, mournful echoes in the small, frigid room. She could hear nothing else but the chanting and her heart pounding behind her ears.

His hands tightened around her neck. Her head was lifted and then banged against the concrete floor. A pain shot through her nose and blood began to smear into her mouth. It tasted metallic and warm. Shimi thought she was going to pass out, but she knew despite the fear and pain, she must try to keep awake. That much she knew. She thought of all her Wen-Do self-defence moves in her head, and she knew the first rule was to scream as loud as she could.

She screamed!

Nothing came out.

She tried to crawl along the floor, scraping her hands back and forth, but she could not take hold of anything that would help her get up. She could barely catch her breath before he banged her face into the floor one more time. Pain radiated across her forehead, and she could feel the blood begin to wet her eyelashes and sting her eyes. He straddled her back, but when he moved a hand away from her neck to fumble with his clothing, she twisted with all her might to grab onto something. Her left cheek stayed glued to the floor, but with a dramatic lunge and stretch her right hand found his neck, felt a high neck wool sweater and under that she gained a quick touch of his sweaty, warm skin. Her fingers felt a large raised bump. He grabbed her hand away from his neck and twisted her arm until she thought it would break.

Finally, a scream left her blood-soaked lips.

Then he was upon her again, pulling her neck up, choking her, then forcing her head down again with a bang onto the floor. She was sure her nose was broken.

The bottom section of her long wool coat was tossed up over the back of her head, which enveloped her in even more darkness. She felt like she would suffocate and tried to breathe through her mouth. Her lips scraped against the concrete floor and the floor's grit stuck to her gasping tongue. She desperately clawed, arm over arm at the concrete, as a swimmer frantic to escape a shark. Suddenly, she could feel the pressure from his foot on her back and then her nightgown being ripped. Despite the pain and fear, she stayed conscious throughout the violence, but barely. She knew she was easy prey, since she had worn her flannel nightgown under her long winter coat, for her last check at the barn before bed.

The rape seemed to last forever. As the seconds passed, he became more impatient, agitated and violent. He didn't utter one word. Finally, he stood, then once again put his boot on the back of her neck to hold her down. She continued to claw the floor with her bare hands, even though she knew all her movements were futile. He grabbed the edge of her coat and she could feel a tug on the fabric. The dark shadow gave her a violent kick to the groin which crippled her with a new type of pain. Only then did she stop moving her hands. His shadow over her disappeared. The exterior barn door slammed.

All that was left was the darkness and the chanting, chanting, chanting... the monks forever chanting.

She lay curled on her side for several tormented minutes. She simply tried to focus on her breathing. After she was able to take a full breath, she crawled on her hands and knees to the shelving unit. She reached out and grasped the shelves with hands raw from scraping across the concrete floor. She pulled herself up to a standing position and rested her forehead on the edge of the shelf for a moment. Her head was spinning. Finally, she looked up. Inches away, in front of her face were rounds of cheese. Dozens of them, staring back at her. They had sat there during her violent attack, in their perfectly controlled world of temperature and humidity that she had created for them, all of them indifferent to her pain. They had borne witness to her vile attack and done nothing. She hated the cheese!

She hated the chanting monks.

She hated it all.

But the monks kept chanting, chanting, chanting...

She felt dizzy, nauseous and longed to lie down again, but she steadied herself against the shelf and continued to take deep breaths. Every fibre in her body hurt. She wanted to scream, rage, kick and bite, but she was too exhausted. Too afraid.

What if he heard and came back?

As she went through the door, she grabbed the speaker off the wall and smashed it at her feet.

She could hear Darcy barking in the house. He sounded angry and aware of what was happening. He must have heard her scream. He was sound asleep with his funny, quivering snore when she quietly left the kitchen only moments ago. She wished she had awakened him, brought him with her, but then she wondered what price her loyal Darcy might have paid in his attempt to protect her.

She stumbled out of the barn and ran, but not towards Darcy and her house. She ran down her lane and across the road to Belladane's. It was all she could think about.

From Belladane's bright yard light, the trees that lined the lane cast long looming shadows across the gravel. Her eyes lost sight every time she passed through another shadow. Several times she stumbled, but regained her balance. Midway up Belladane's lane, she doubled over and vomited between her sheepskin slippers. The concrete grit in her mouth made her gag again and spit. Grit was lodged in her throat, but she wiped her mouth with the back of her hand and started moving again.

The short distance seemed to take forever.

"I must get to her porch light. Get somewhere safe." These thoughts kept repeating in her head.

Belladane always kept an unlocked door. "Locks only keep the honest person out," she had said for years.

Shimi entered the darkened kitchen and knew her aunt would already be in bed, sound asleep with her CPAP machine, which helped her breathe at night, tightly over her face. The mermaid lamp on the kitchen counter cast a beam of light across the wall clock: 11.47 p.m. Meadow, who was typically not allowed on the counter, lay beside the lamp and stared at Shimi with her yellow, reflective eyes. Shimi could feel her own eyelids fluttering and her hands beginning to shake uncontrollably. But she knew now she was safe. Her legs felt like they were going to give out beneath her, but she kept moving.

With her hand running along the wall, she made her way down the hall to Belladane's bedroom. She could make out the image of her aunt sound asleep under a large, white duvet. The air from her CPAP machine on her bedside table made a small, whirling sound. The moonlight coming through the bedroom window cast a long, yellow glow across the bed.

Shimi dropped to her knees and crawled under the bed, pulling her long coat around her stomach. She curled herself into a ball and with her raw, bloody hands held her knees to her chest. She shook uncontrollably. In her mind she continued to hear the monks chanting, and in the distance she thought she could hear Darcy's anguished bark.

For an instant she wondered why she had crawled under the bed and not awakened Belladane. But ever since she was an imaginative child, under a bed had always meant safety to her, plus she didn't want to face the reality of it all. Not yet.

She wondered whether she had locked the kitchen door when she closed it. Did she even close it? It didn't matter. She was not leaving this safe space.

Her head throbbed and the pain in her back from the gruesome kick kept radiating up her spine. The gash on her forehead and bloody nose had stopped bleeding, but now her nose was clogged with dried blood. She opened her mouth wide, then realized her front teeth had cut through her bottom lip. She breathed through her mouth and tried to clear her throat of the bits of concrete grit. She needed water, but knew she couldn't risk going to the kitchen. She focused on counting her breaths … in slowly 1, 2, 3, 4 … and out slowly … 1, 2, 3, 4 … like in yoga class.

Meadow came silently into the room and lay down on the mat by the bed. She stared at Shimi with her big, night eyes and began to purr. Shimi longed to touch the cat, but kept her trembling fingers clasped under her chin. It was a long time before Shimi finally stopped shaking and fell asleep.

VIII
(honestly)

"OH! OH, MY God! Oh, my God!" Belladane was on her knees, her face peering under the bed, her big warm hands grabbing at Shimi's small, cold ones. The early morning sun was coming through the bedroom window. The large, strong woman pulled her niece out from under the bed, sat down on the floor and held her in her arms.

Shimi opened her bloodshot eyes. She tried to say something, but her face felt too swollen and her lips were stuck together with dried blood.

"Shimi. Shimi. Oh my God! My poor baby!"

Shimi allowed herself to be cradled by her aunt. She was cold and stiff and could not straighten out her back. Her head lay on Belladane's thigh and her aunt wrapped her arms around her. Shimi could feel her cheek getting warmer, and could feel the heat through Belladane's flannel nightgown. There was dried blood in her matted hair and on her forehead. It felt hard and tight. Eventually both women were able to stand up and Belladane gently guided Shimi to the edge of the bed. As they lowered themselves to sit, Shimi winced in pain. Belladane kept her arms wrapped tightly around her.

Belladane eased Shimi back onto the mattress and pulled the duvet over her. "I'm calling 911. Don't move," she said.

"Don't leave me," Shimi stammered in a whisper.

"I'm here. I'm here." Belladane grabbed her cell phone from her nightstand and dialled 911.

"911. What is your emergency?" The voice was female and strong.

"I need the police immediately. There's been a violent assault on a woman," Belladane said. Then she gave her address and hung up the phone. Belladane lay down beside Shimi on the bed and wrapped her arms around the small, shivering woman.

"I need to wipe my face," Shimi finally said.

"We are not going to touch or change anything. Just hang in there for now," Belladane said.

Within thirty minutes, two police officers were in Belladane's bedroom. The female officer, Melanie Malone, gently questioned Shimi while the male officer, Ted Chen, took notes. Shimi recounted the moments in the barn as best she could.

"What did the attacker hit you with?" Sergeant Malone asked.

"I don't know," Shimi said. "Maybe his fist."

"Did you get a look at him? Anything at all?"

"No, it was so dark. He came from behind and started choking me."

"Do you remember anything more? Any smells? Or did he say anything?" Malone asked.

"No, he never spoke. Not that I can remember. Plus, the music was loud. But no, he didn't speak," Shimi said. Then she saw Officer Chen raise his eyebrows and give Malone a look.

"What?" Shimi asked. "Is that weird that he didn't speak?"

"Do you know of anyone who would want to harm you?" Malone asked.

"No," Shimi said.

"The reason why I ask is because often rapists speak. It's part of their control, to scare you with their words as well. If he didn't speak, then maybe he didn't want you to hear his voice. Maybe you would recognize his voice, if he spoke," Malone explained.

"No, he didn't speak," Shimi repeated. The thought that someone she might know would do this to her was even more horrifying than thinking it was a stranger.

Sergeant Malone continued to question Shimi, but her memory was blurry. The officer assured her that in time she would remember more details. She handed Shimi her card so she could call if any further details came back to her. "Call me anytime," she said. "You're not alone in this." She also gave her card to Belladane.

Officer Chen excused himself from the room, while Sergeant Malone took photos of Shimi's head and face wounds, the bruises on her neck, her hands, and her inner thighs. Then she made a quick phone call.

When the officer was done with her call, she turned to Shimi and said, "You must get to the Charlottetown Hospital immediately for a rape kit exam. I've told them you are coming, so you will be taken right in. I need you to take off your clothes and give them to me. I will give you some privacy," and she turned to leave the room. 'Please don't touch her clothes anymore," Malone said to Belladane, as she closed the door.

Belladane handed Shimi a grey tracksuit of hers. The tracksuit swamped Shimi and she felt like a frightened child wearing the rolled-up pants and sweatshirt that went almost to her knees.

Sergeant Malone came back into the room and held out an open transparent plastic bag. Shimi placed the coat and nightgown into the bag. The officer zipped the bag closed.

"I want my coat back," Shimi said.

"Yes of course. You will get it back after any DNA evidence has been taken from it," Malone explained. "I notice the buttons on the coat are unusual. And it looks like one is missing. Did you know that?

"No. All the buttons were there yesterday," Shimi mumbled.

"Good to know. Now, like I said, you must go to the Charlottetown Hospital immediately. It's important you don't wash or bathe. Try not to pee or have a bowel movement. If you can wait a bit to go to the toilet, that would be great. And don't drink or eat anything. Do you understand?"

Shimi nodded her head.

"Do you want us to take you there? Or would you rather go together?" The officer nodded at Belladane.

"I'll take her. We'll go right away," Belladane said.

As the officers were about to leave the room, Shimi looked up and said, "I don't want my name in the paper."

"Don't worry Ms. Montray, we will file the report, but your name will not be made public," Officer Chen said.

"We will be on your property awhile. We will look for any evidence in the yard, the barn, and in the cheese rooms. We will also be taking photos. You don't need to come with us, unless you want to, but I know that may be too soon, too difficult. Is that okay?" Sergeant Malone asked.

"Yes," Shimi said. "My goats …"

"Don't worry. We won't interfere with your goats. We will be very careful," Chen replied.

"Does anyone else live on the property? We will be checking for footprints," Malone asked.

"Yes, my friend, Eddie, he's been visiting me, and he helps Shimi with her goats, so his footprints may be around the barn," Belladane said.

"Great. We will also have a chat with Eddie, if he is there," Officer Chen said. "What is his last name?"

"Savenko," Belladane said.

"How long has Eddie been here?" Chen asked.

"About four months," Belladane said.

"Four months, that long, eh?" Officer Chen continued to write in his book. "That's quite the houseguest."

"Well, he's more like a housemate," Belladane corrected.

"Where is he from?" Malone interjected.

"Well, he's from California, I believe," Belladane replied, with a concern creeping into her voice. She wished you could take the "housemate" comment back but knew it was too late.

"I see," Malone said, and a look was exchanged between the two officers.

Officer Chen made another note in his book. Then both officers left the room.

Moments later, as Belladane drove slowly down the lane, Eddie stepped out from behind the line of trees. As Belladane passed, she put down her window and quickly said, "Shimi was attacked. Please hold down the fort, Eddie. And the cops want to talk to you. I'm sorry, I had to tell them about you staying here. I hope I didn't mess things up for you. I'll call you from the hospital, or we'll talk when we get home. Okay?"

Shimi sat motionless in the front seat with her head leaning against the window. She couldn't look at Eddie. She closed her eyes and inhaled a deep breath.

Eddie held Darcy close to his leg, on a bit of rope. The dog twisted and whined when he saw Shimi. Eddie held him firmly and rested his other hand on the side of the car, leaned low to the window and took a quick glance inside at Shimi.

"No worries. Take care," Eddie whispered calmly, but his face held the contours of guilt and fear.

IX
(voluntarily)

THE OFFICER WAS right. At the hospital, they were waiting for Shirley Ann Montray. She was quickly ushered into a private examination room. Belladane stayed close by, often touching Shimi's back or rubbing her shoulder. A nurse named Agnes Lee explained how the rape kit worked and all the samples they would need to take. She explained that the procedures needed to be slow, timely and sequential, but she would do her best to be as quick and sensitive as possible.

Nurse Agnes was extremely conscientious and caring. Throughout the procedures, Shimi was offered food, drinks and heated blankets, but she accepted nothing.

Shimi kept saying, "I just want to get this over with and go home."

Over a period of four hours, the nurse drew Shimi's blood, took samples of saliva, urine, pubic hair, and scrapings from under Shimi's fingernails. She took photos of Shimi's bruised neck, the lacerations on her forehead, broken lip and nose, her scraped hands, and her bruised inner thighs.

Nurse Agnes recorded Shimi's pulse, blood pressure, and did a thorough wellness check. As Agnes was finished with her sample taking and examination, she gently washed Shimi's face, neck, and hands.

Doctor Mary Cummings then entered the room and gave Shimi a thorough examination. She was professional, but kind and gentle. Shimi barely uttered more than one-word answers to the doctor's questions. It was determined Shimi's nose was not broken and surprisingly she did not have a concussion. Doctor Cummings gave her a bottle with a dozen Codeine pills for her pain and some antiseptic cream for her abrasions. She encouraged her to bathe in Epsom salts and eat nutritious foods. 'Your body has been through a terrible trauma. You have a lot of shallow and deep bruising. It will take time before your body heals. But it will heal. Try to go for a walk every day to keep your muscles from seizing up. And get good rest as well," she said. She added that her medical report would be sent to the police within a week.

"You're one brave woman, Ms. Montray. You did right by coming in. Take care of yourself," Doctor Cummings said, as she exited the room.

A knock came to the door and a psychiatrist, who introduced herself as Doctor Mary Watson, came in. She asked Shimi some questions.

"How are you feeling, Shimi? Are you in any pain?" Doctor Watson asked.

"I'm fine."

"If you're in pain, I can give you some pain medication and perhaps some sleeping pills to help you get some rest for a few days," the doctor said.

"The other doctor gave me Codeine."

"Good. Will you be staying alone when you go home?" Doctor Watson asked.

"Shimi will be staying with me," Belladane piped up from her chair in the corner. "For as long as she needs. We live next door."

"Great. Shimi, you may have some flashbacks. Or you may see things in your dreams, or your nightmares. Some memories. It's important you keep a notebook by your bed and jot things down as you remember them. Often these memories are fleeting, as if your brain doesn't really want to remember them. But the more information you can give to the police the better."

"Okay," Shimi said, looking at Doctor Watson with a stare as unshakeable as death.

"I'd like you to come and see me next week when you get back on your feet. Or I can come to see you, if you like. What about next Thursday afternoon around four? How does that sound?"

"I'll see," Shimi said. Her response was curt, bordering on hostile. She didn't seem able to focus.

Belladane raised her eyebrows and gave the psychiatrist a questioning look.

"It's normal for you to feel overwhelmed. And angry. And whatever else you might be feeling. Your feelings will be complicated for quite a while. You're still in shock. When you get home, get rest, good nutrition, and it's best to stay away from alcohol for a few days. Don't bottle up your feelings. You need to talk. I'm giving your friend, Belladane, a medication to help you sleep. Then you will have them, if you need them. There are only seven pills in the bottle. We can reassess your needs when I see you next week. Okay?" She handed these to Belladane and also tucked her business card into Belladane's hand. "Call me anytime if you need to talk, Shimi, and I hope to see you next Thursday," Doctor Watson said. Then she left, closing the heavy metal door quietly behind her.

Just before leaving, Nurse Lee gave Shimi a Levonorgestrel pill, often called the morning-after pill. She said, "This should be taken within 72 hours. If so, it has an 87% efficacy."

Shimi swallowed it down immediately, before the nurse could hand her a small paper cup of water and said, "Thanks. Are we done?"

"Yes. Take care Shimi," Agnes said. "I hope you come to see Doctor Watson next week. She would be a great support person for you."

Shimi remained silent, staring at the floor.

Nurse Agnes touched Belladane's arm as she left, and the two women nodded to each other.

Shimi was quickly driven back to her Aunt Belladane's spare bedroom. As per Belladane's earlier phone call, Eddie had the room ready. He had gone beyond Belladane's instructions. He had vacuumed, put a cozy duvet on the bed and nestled a heating pad under the fresh sheets to warm them. Meadow, immediately, situated herself on the warm spot. On the bedside table sat an old milk bottle of water, a glass, a tea mug, a pot of green tea with honey, wrapped in a tea cozy that looked like a turtle, and a small notebook with a pen attached. The room was welcoming, warm, and tidy. Eddie made sure he was out of sight when Belladane's car came up the lane. He stood nervously in the backyard in the shadow of the barn and secretly watched as Belladane led Shimi into the house.

Despite Belladane encouraging Shimi to have a hot Epsom salt bath and change into something more comfortable, she crawled into the bed in Belladane's old, oversized sweatsuit and lay curled up on her right side for two days. Darcy lay by her on the floor and he rarely moved. He went for a walk with Eddie several times a day, but the loyal dog immediately came back to Shimi's side. He tenderly licked her hand whenever she draped it over the side of the bed.

Belladane and Eddie did a lot of whispering in the kitchen, discussing the best way to help their dear friend. Belladane prepared delicious meals that never got eaten, played Shimi's much-loved music, and offered to watch her favourite movies with her. Eddie continued to milk the goats, store the milk, and just be as close as possible in case the two women needed him. But he tried not to be too intrusive or noticeable. After all he was a man, and a man had just raped Shimi. He felt disgusted and angry at his gender, the meanness that he knew existed in some men. The uncontrollable need for power and control over others, especially women.

"I knew something was wrong when I heard Darcy barking," Eddie said, "but I got over there too late."

"It's not your fault, Eddie," Belladane touched his arm.

"Fuck! I'm so pissed at myself. I had a few drinks that night, even though I promised myself I would stop. And as I was coming across the meadow down by Mrs. Lorhan's house, I thought I saw a person rushing along the road and then I heard a car start up in the distance, but it was so dark and windy. If I had been sober ... I'm so sorry Belladane. I'm not totally on the wagon yet. I'm so sorry. If I had been sober, things might have been different for Shimi. Once again, I let my friends down."

"Look it, Eddie. Sobriety is often not a straight line, so stop beating yourself up. This was not your fault. We've got to hold it together for Shimi's sake. She will get over this. She's strong and so are you! Just keep dating and storing the goat's milk for now. We'll dump it later if we have to. We'll all just do the best we can, my dear."

On the third day, upon Belladane's insistence Shimi dragged herself out of bed. A warm luxurious bath was awaiting her. Belladane had lit candles scented with eucalyptus oil and had thrown lavender sprigs into the hot water. The lights were dimmed and soft Vivaldi music played. Shimi let Belladane undress her like a child, pulling the sweatshirt over her sore neck and tender nose, and helping her step out of the sweatpants. Belladane was shocked at the appearance of Shimi's rib cage. It looked like she had dropped ten pounds in just three days. Shimi carefully stepped into the deep tub and sank down with a sigh into the hot water. She opened a new bar of lavender goat's milk soap that Belladane had set on the side of the tub. She held the soap under the water, rolled it between her hands and brought it to her nose. Then it hit her. The smell.

When she reached for his neck that night, she had smelled something. A familiar scent from her past. What was it?

Irish Spring Soap. That's what it was. Her dad had always used that soap and its smell was so familiar. How had she forgotten that until now?

Belladane insisted they call the police. She dialled Sergeant Malone's number and held the cell phone up so Shimi could be heard. The officer seemed pleased with the new information and Shimi felt a little hope creep into her despair.

The hot water and the bit of memory seemed to bring Shimi a touch of new energy and life. "When will the kit's DNA get processed?" Shimi asked.

The officer hesitated for a few seconds. "Shimi, often the kits don't get done for a long time. Sometimes months." And then Malone whispered, like she didn't want colleagues to hear what she was saying, "Sometimes never!"

Belladane smacked her lips and looked incredulous, but continued to hold the phone out so Shimi could speak.

"What? What do you mean, never?" Shimi couldn't believe what she was hearing.

"Unfortunately, it all depends upon budgets. Processing the kits is expensive. Some departments don't allocate enough money to do the processing. It's not a priority, unfortunately," Malone said with regret in her voice.

"I can't believe I'm hearing this," Shimi said. "What was the point of even reporting it, going through the whole hospital ordeal, if the police do nothing about it?"

"Also, sometimes the kits aren't processed if the victim is not sure whether they want to go ahead and press charges. If you want to really pursue this, I will push the case forward, but it seemed when we spoke you weren't certain. And if the perpetrator is caught and charged, of course we would need you at the trial and your name would be in the news. How do you feel about that?"

"I don't know. I'll have to think about it. Can I do that?" Shimi said.

"Of course," Sergeant Malone said. "Just know I am not giving up on this, and neither should you. Don't let this violence erode you, Shimi. You did so well today when you remembered the soap. We'll talk again soon." Malone then hung up the phone.

"I know you'd probably rather brush your teeth with a cheese grater, Shimi, but perhaps you should push for the rape kit to be analyzed," Belladane said carefully.

Shimi stood up out of the water and grabbed a towel. She stepped out of the tub.

"Hey, why don't you soak for a while longer? It would be good for you," Belladane coaxed.

"I'm done," Shimi said, in a matter-of-fact tone, as she pulled on a night gown.

Shimi went down the hall and climbed back into the bed. She wanted to stay there forever, even though her body was beginning to invent new aches from lying down so much. But the aches she could handle. It was her thoughts that were beyond painful. She was emotionally incontinent. At any moment, she would feel rage, disgust, sadness or fear ... they would come rushing out and she couldn't control them. She couldn't hold any of the feelings at bay. And now she had added another slice of anger to her pile. The police may never analyze her kit and solve this case if she wouldn't push for it. She was not a "priority." The word repeated itself over and over in her mind.

It was all too much. When she slept, she dreamt about that night; when she was awake, that's all she thought about. She felt dirty, alone, and frightened of any sound in the house or yard. When Eddie walked up the lane, with the gravel crunching beneath his big boots, she cringed. When Meadow scratched at the bedroom door, wanting in, Shimi instantly tensed. When Darcy barked, she flinched. If Belladane closed the back door of the kitchen with a thud, she jumped. And then there was the constant chanting of the monks ... the chanting, the chanting. It haunted her dreams and the slow ticking hours of her mind.

Would she ever feel safe again?

She hated how the rapist had taken a big part of her with him. He had stolen her feelings of independence, her strength, her confidence. He had taken so many good qualities that Shimi had been proud of, and now she felt like a wounded bird, who could barely flutter one wing.

She wondered if she would ever get her old self back.

X
(secretly)

When Shimi heard the clear clanging of the bell, she sat bolt upright in bed. She jumped into some of her clothes Belladane had brought from her house: a sweatsuit, a big sweater, and her winter clogs. She stumbled through the kitchen and out the door. Despite her throbbing cracked ribs, she rushed down the lane, with Darcy jumping alongside of her, leaving Belladane in the doorway, yelling, "Shimi Honey? Where are you going? What's going on?"

Shimi ran to her backdoor, but she found it locked. She quickly retrieved the key from under the rock that looked like a faerie beside her sedum plant. She hurried into her kitchen, grabbed all the knives out of her knife block, clutched them to her chest, and ran down her lane again, yelling, "Wait! Wait!"

A slow-moving, white panel van came to an abrupt halt. And within seconds the back door swung open. An elderly man, looking like a summertime Santa Claus, with his long white hair and beard and his brown, canvas apron, stepped out and greeted Shimi with a big smile.

"Hi, Harold," Shimi said. "Glad I caught you. Can you sharpen these, please?"

"Hello Shimi. All of these? Sure thing! Cutting up lots of cheese these days, eh?" Harold ran his finger along the edge of each knife. "Some are already quite sharp."

"Still, I want them all done. Nice and sharp," Shimi said.

Harold gave Shimi a slow, gentle look. "Are you okay, my dear? You look a little busted up."

"I took a tumble, but I'll be okay," Shimi said. "I'll go get my wallet."

"Okey dokey, my dear." Harold got to work and carefully sharpened each knife.

Within twenty minutes she had eight newly sharpened knives, which she carefully placed in her knife block, running her finger over each blade like they were a sacred family heirloom.

"She's been curled up in bed for days and it's the roving knife sharpener who gets her out of bed. That can't be a good sign," Belladane said to Eddie, as they both watched from Belladane's verandah.

"Well, at least she has a purpose," Eddie said.

By the end of the week, Shimi finally had enough confidence to leave Belladane's house and get back into some semblance of a routine. She knew she had to snap out of it. She knew she had to stop wallowing in her imagination, her flashbacks, her fear. Darcy was happy to see her dressed in the morning and walking across the yard to the cheese barn. He jumped and twirled beside her, licking her hand that swung from her side. Her goats stuck their heads through the fence, also happy to see her. She touched their noses and scratched behind each of their ears. Rhoda played shy and held back, but then Rhoda often did. Shimi kept softly saying, "How's my girls?" over and over again, as they pushed against each other for her attention. She realized she had missed their sweet energy and their beguiling eyes. The goats injected a tiny bit of joy into her mind full of misery. For this she was grateful.

She stopped at the corner of the barn and wondered if she could really go in. She would take a moment. All in good time. At her feet were a tall clump of Blanket flowers, and she leaned over to touch their blossoms. She thought how wonderful it was to still have some flowers blooming in early November. She stood with the flower between her fingers and she stroked the softness of the petals. Clutching the top of the stem and pushing her fingers up through the petals, she felt the powdery pollen on her fingertips. A vision flashed in her mind. Suddenly she couldn't breathe. She tightened her grip on the flower's throat and choked it tightly between her fingers until the head snapped. She coughed and gasped for air and then came back to the reality of her day: the flicker of light on the flowers, the smell of the goats behind the fence.

She looked in her hand and saw the crushed, fragile flower. She dropped it and pushed it into the ground with her boot. She moved her foot back and forth, over and over, grinding her fear under the toe of her sturdy boot, pressing down for a very long time.

When she entered the barn, she stopped. There was a small bit of yellow police tape still stuck to the door. She heard a soft rustling from the back of the barn. Shimi froze.

Often criminals return to the scene of the crime.

Eddie entered the room from the back door that led to the goat's stall, holding an empty feed bag. Shimi bent over, put her hands on her knees and breathed a huge sigh of relief. Eddie looked up and saw the look on her face.

"Oh! I'm so sorry Shimi, I didn't know you were here. So sorry to have startled you." Eddie neatly folded the feed bag and put it on a shelf.

"It's okay. I've got to get a grip, Eddie. I can't live the rest of my life, jumping at every sound."

"Give yourself time, Shimi. You'll get there," Eddie assured.

"You haven't," Shimi said, with a curt edge to her voice.

Eddie looked as if he had been punched in the gut.

"I'm sorry, Eddie. That was rude. I don't know what I'm saying or doing anymore. These memories in my head are like a giant living beast."

"No worries, Shimi. You're right. I know that beast. I still have memories that seem so real, like they're happening right now. And I know you do too. Maybe we can help each other ... somehow. Maybe we can set our own world right."

Shimi nodded, took a deep breath and then walked past Eddie. She opened the door to cheese room number two, the room of her nightmares, and stepped inside. Even though the music had long been silenced, the haunting sound of the monks chanting, chanting, chanting, hit her in the face like the blow to her head. She could feel the pain from that blow again, like it was new, so she stood there in the dark, in the silence and stared straight ahead. Every horror of that night returned to her. It replayed in her mind with grainy flashes of darkness and light, slow motion movements, and the horror of it made her right eyelid begin to quiver and her knees shake.

Eddie hovered in the main room, not certain what to do. He wanted to leave, but knew he shouldn't. He wished Belladane was here. She would know what to do, what to say.

Shimi stood in the room for a few silent moments. Then she carefully picked up a round of cheese, felt its beautiful smoothness in her hands, held it to her nose, and then to her forehead for a few seconds. With a gesture that shocked Eddie, she held it above her head and then dramatically hurled it onto the concrete floor. Great chunks of cheese splattered at her feet and up the wall. Then she smashed another, then another, then another ...

Darcy began to jump and bark. Eddie grabbed his collar and stood in the doorway and watched. He was conscious of the light from behind him casting a huge shadow across the cheese room floor. He stepped aside and hoped Shimi hadn't noticed.

Shimi grabbed the entire shelving unit of cheese and pulled on it. It hesitated at first. She pulled again with all her strength. The screws that fastened it to the wall finally released. She jumped back into the doorway, as it came crashing down at her feet. Dozens of rounds of cheese worth thousands of dollars and months of work lay destroyed on the concrete floor.

Eddie didn't know if he should touch her, but he reached out and gently pulled Shimi from the doorway, guiding her to sit down on the bench. "Let's just sit here and breathe for a while," he said.

"It would have always been The Rape Cheese," Shimi said, and she began to cry.

"Yes," Eddie replied. "Yes."

They sat silently for what seemed like a long time. Then Shimi said, "I used to love the night. I mean, I don't walk around in the dark like you, but I loved it. The quiet. The long shadows. The moon and stars. How everything looks different in the night. Like you're seeing another side of the tree, or the house, or the yard. It's like you're seeing its metaphor ... its quiet, moody, lonely side. Does that sound crazy?"

"Not at all."

"And now I hate the dark. I'm afraid of the dark. Shit, I'm afraid of sunlight as well. I think that's what kills me the most. Even worse than the violence I endured. He took my courage away, my love of the dark, my joy."

"I know how that is. I was so lost when I came here, so afraid of everything, especially myself and how I was feeling about life. I so needed an unoffending world. I was so tired of the world of war, of muscle, guns, and agony. I didn't think I would ever feel confident again, or feel needed, but here I do. You and Belladane gave me that. And the goats. Even Darcy. I love doing my little night walks around the neighbourhood. I feel peaceful, content, and maybe like I'm appreciated. Have a purpose. So here, everyday I try to focus on the good stuff. On all the things I'm grateful for."

"Like what?" Shimi asked.

"Well, like little things. Like the way Wilma leans into me when I milk her, and she sighs and constantly tries to nibble on my shirt sleeve. How Darcy knows his treat is always in my left pocket, so he stares at it, until I give it to him. How Belladane is the most wonderful person I have ever met and we can't forget she makes the most fabulous peach pie. And you, and how hardworking, smart, and brave you are. And if you can be brave, so can I."

"I don't know about that," Shimi said. "I don't think I'm brave anymore."

"Look, he didn't take away your courage. You probably weren't that brave before. I mean I know your folks died when you were young and I'm sure that was scary, but maybe you didn't have any big experience with terror or something that made you afraid for your life, like you just did. So, you didn't need to be brave before. But now you do, so now just putting your one foot in front of the other every day … well that's brave. That takes courage. And you're doing it. So, he didn't take away your courage … yes, he left you with a shitload of fear, but he didn't steal your courage. You still have it. I can see it. The fact that you're out here today, well that takes real courage."

"Thanks. I never thought of it that way. I hope you're right. One thing I was thinking a lot about, while I was curled up in a ball for a week, is joy. I thought he had taken away my joy forever, but then I got thinking, was I really so happy before? Did I really love my life that much and now it is totally messed up? Maybe not."

"Happiness. Such a tricky thing, isn't it? We often tell ourselves when we accomplish this or that, we will be happy. When we buy our dream home. Or when we land the perfect job. Or when we find the perfect partner. But maybe we have happiness everyday right in front of us. Maybe the little things are what makes a life happy. Not the next big thing."

"You're right Eddie," Shimi said. "I was like that as a kid, always ready for the next big accomplishment. The next milestone, the next adventure, thinking it would make me happy, but then I stopped. I stopped when my parents died and I just clung to routine, comfort, and certainty. And I even stopped exploring happiness. Even in the little things."

"You know they always do these United Nations surveys every year about happiness, to discover which countries in the world are happiest. And you know who always comes up on top? Poor African countries where the people have so little compared to us. What's with that? It blows my mind."

"Maybe if they live in poverty or war-torn countries, they are just happy to be alive," Shimi pondered.

"Yes. They don't expect any grand life. They are happy to have what they have. I know it's no big, new philosophy. We know all this stuff. It's just remembering it that is hard sometimes and practising. Maybe we can help remind each other," Eddie said. "Maybe this horrible thing that happened to you is a chance at a new beginning? Like those Kensho moments people talk about. After something painful we change and grow into a new life. Maybe even a better one? I don't know, maybe I shouldn't comment. Maybe I'm just talking shit."

"No. No, you're not, Eddie. I appreciate your advice, but sometimes I just feel so overwhelmed with the fear, the anger, sadness," Shimi said. "It's like there is this detour in my body. I don't feel at home in my own body anymore. Now it holds this huge, piercing sorrow. Know what I mean?"

"Sorry to say, Shimi, I don't think those feelings are a detour. I think this is your new life now. You're not on a detour. This is your new path in life, accepting this new reality. And finding the strength to both overcome and enjoy this new reality."

"A new reality? Are you saying this won't get any better? But I really miss the old me," Shimi sighed.

"Yes, I miss my old self too, but maybe our new selves will be better, if we give them half a chance. Maybe we will be wiser, more empathetic, maybe feel more deeply. And to be that way, we need to feel all our feelings. I know this may sound trite, but maybe we should allocate a certain amount of time each day to simply feel angry, afraid, and sad. Just wallow for an hour or so ... let it out ... and then get on with our day. Find something to be happy about. Do you think we could do that?" Eddie asked.

"Wallow time. Sounds doable. Although some days I may need more than an hour," Shimi said.

"Nope, we just have an hour of our choice, any time throughout the day. Let's try it, shall we?" Eddie stared intently at Shimi.

"Okay, I'll try. So, I guess you're going to say that this here was our official wallowing time for today. Right?"

"Right," Eddie smiled. "That's all we're getting for today."

There was a quiet ease about Eddie, and Shimi drew comfort from it. She had noticed that about him the very first day they had met. An ease and a strength. She knew her new fear would be a hard master, and it would take all her strength to keep it from overwhelming her. But she hoped with Eddie's guidance, she would be able to put one foot in front of the other and move through each day.

"So now ... let's get out there ... and milk those girls. Wilma is waiting for us." Shimi fixed a small smile upon her face.

"Yes, and I put on my tastiest shirt today just for her," Eddie said, as he gave Shimi a playful wink.

Shimi smiled again, and suddenly, Shimi realized she had just genuinely smiled. Also, a small spontaneous chuckle had escaped her lips.

And it felt good.

XI
(and then)

A FEW WEEKS passed and Shimi tried to put her life back in order. She tried to embrace the shapeless moments of everyday life. She thought surely her routines would help her move forward. Her obligations would give some predictable rhythm to her days. But then, out of nowhere, a secret door to a tunnel in her brain would snap open and she would remember a quick, flashing detail of that night. A click of a memory would come to her at the most insignificant of moments.

She was walking up the lane from the mailbox one day, when she heard Belladane coming along behind her. "Wait for me," Belladane called after her. Her rubber boots squeaked against the gravel. Shimi stopped and froze!

"Lots of interesting junk mail today, Honey?" Belladane asked when she saw Shimi stop and stare at the mail in her hand.

Shimi turned to look at her aunt. "Your boots! Your boots!"

Then without another word, she rushed to the house, grabbed her cell phone off the kitchen table and dialled Sergeant Malone. Belladane came huffing and puffing through the doorway. She bent over with her hands on her hips, heaving like a racehorse.

"What's the big rush?" Belladane groaned.

Shimi shushed Belladane by holding her finger up to her mouth. The phone rang six times before Malone picked up.

"His shoes squeaked when he turned and left the cheese room. I remember it now," Shimi said, not even identifying herself.

"Good work, Shimi. Did it squeak like a leather shoe or like a wet running shoe?" Malone asked.

"I don't know. I just know one of them squeaked really loud."

Malone said every detail was important and she'd add it to the case file. Shimi hung up the phone.

Belladane said, "I knew these old rubber boots would come in handy someday. Glad I didn't throw them out."

Shimi collapsed into a kitchen chair and rolled her eyes. Then she stood up abruptly and said, "I'll see you at supper. I'm going to take a shower."

XII
(remembering)

SHIMI DRAGGED HERSELF out of bed every morning. She fed her birds, ate her bowl of granola and oat milk with a handful of blueberries thrown on top, took a walk with Darcy down to the stream, and cared for her goats. She spent hours making her cheese in the barn, even though her heart wasn't in it anymore. Every evening she walked across the road and ate dinner with Belladane and Eddie. After dinner, Eddie always insisted on walking her home. Her life fell back into its predictable pattern which gave her great comfort. Yet, at the same time she felt resentful of its predictability, the moments of mundane.

Often, she thought about her conversation with Eddie about happiness and courage. She tried to find joy in every day, making it her mantra. Tried to limit her anger and malaise to one hour. Their "wallowing time" as Eddie had called it. But the memories of that night would strike to her core at the most insignificant of moments: stretching for a glass on her shelf; pulling up her pyjama pants; or pouring kibble into Darcy's dish.

Her brain had built solid walls and the images of that night bounced and echoed off each wall. Sometimes when she became fixated on a memory, she would turn on her stereo full blast and sing and dance wildly to the music. After a few moments, the images would die away and she would be left breathless, sweating, and clear headed. Other times when the images haunted her, particularly at the middle of the night, she would scream into her pillow as loud as she could. She didn't want to awaken Darcy. And her pillow was her assurance that if Eddie was roaming close by, he wouldn't hear her, come crashing through the door, and perhaps be triggered to relive his own memories of screams and horror. After she exhausted all her screams, she would grab her pillow, climb under her bed, curl up, and shake until she eventually fell asleep.

These moments imprisoned her with their certainty and haunted her with their violence. When this happened, sometimes she would remember more details of that night. Flashes would come from the museum of that night, like a camera click in her brain. It would last for only a few seconds, but if she sat down and thought hard, she could often recall the vision in more detail.

She was taking a nap one afternoon on the sofa, with her head lying on her hand. She could hear her watch tick in her ear. She sat bolt upright and stared at her watch. A gift from Belladane years ago. She grabbed her cell and dialled Sergeant Malone's number. It went immediately to voicemail.

"It's Shimi Montray calling. I remember another detail, another memory. He wore a large loose-fitting watch on his right arm. I can remember hearing it tick in my ear as he held his hands around my neck."

Shimi put her phone on the coffee table and stared at her watch for a very long time and then she threw it across the room. It bounced off the wall and landed on the pine floor with a SNAP.

Shimi undressed and stepped into the shower. The hot water and steam swirled about her body. She turned her thin, bony face up to the shower head. The hot water struck her cheekbones that were now pronounced, her hollow cheeks, her thin lips. Then she scoured her skin with a coarse brush, frantically scrubbing her arms, stomach and thighs until the flesh was red and raw. She stepped out of the shower, stood in front of the mirror and cried great, gasping tears into her towel.

Back in the living room, once again she sat down on the sofa and stared at the beautiful watch from her aunt, now smashed into pieces across the floor.

She didn't care that it was broken.

XIII
(perhaps)

During the afternoons, Shimi started taking long walks down Gooding Road and then along Belladane's stream. Darcy was delighted and pranced along ahead of her, a cheery majorette leading a parade. He would constantly turn and check to make sure his best friend was coming, and this made her smile. She had never been into long walks before, but getting out in the cold air of December and feeling the wind bite against her cheeks made her feel alive. Maybe Margaret Atwood was right ... maybe when you're so cold you can think of nothing but the cold, you are happy.

Even in the cold December wind, she often would find herself standing still for long periods of time, lost in thought. Sometimes imagining the worst, other times simply enjoying watching the crows foraging in the bay bushes by the stream. Or the mourning doves hunkered down by the bird feeder, always looking a little sleepy and forlorn. She loved the birds. They were one of her favourite things in life and Eddie was right ... they gave her simple pleasure and made her happy.

Shimi knew her rape kit would probably never be analyzed. She knew the rapist would probably never be caught. And she knew this wasn't right. Yet, she also knew this was partially her fault. He would probably rape more women. She probably wasn't his first, his only. She wasn't that special. And she also knew there was nothing she could do about it. She could not make herself move forward with the case. She found that hard to accept, so she practised telling herself a white lie … it's because of the police. It's all their fault. Lack of funding. Inequity for women. She told this to herself every day. And hoped someday, she may totally convince herself it was true. Meanwhile she felt guilty and weak.

Two months had passed. She felt she was adapting to her new life. Her new courage. Her new outlook. She was grateful she was now sleeping through the night, but she knew she had lasting trauma. Her flashbacks were a living memory that nipped at her unexpectedly. The raw red skin on her thighs and belly were the secret evidence of her constant fear. When she stepped into the shower, she used a large coarse fingernail brush to scrub her skin, searching for a cleanliness she wondered if she would ever find. She wondered if she would ever feel clean enough or in control of her own body. Three hot showers a day had become a self-punishing ritual. She had always wanted her life to be intentional or at least appear that way. But she no longer felt in control.

She was starting to get out with some new friends she had made through her cheese business: a quick lunch or an afternoon movie. Simple things like that. Always during daylight. She felt proud she could walk to the barn and into the cheese rooms without getting the shivers, sometimes even in the evening. She felt she was doing great. Time was the healer, they say. Then she threw up in the toilet one morning, fainted the next afternoon, and the smell of Belladane's once divine dinners made her stomach turn sideways.

"I'm pregnant," Shimi announced at the dinner table, her voice heavy like a stone in the back of her throat.

"What?" How can that be? You took the morning-after pill." Belladane put down her fork.

"They said it wasn't 100% and just my luck, I'm the exception."

"Are you sure? Maybe you're just perimenopausal."

"Yes, I know that. I am, and that's why I wasn't too weirded out last month when I missed my period. With all the stress and my age, I thought it normal. But I took a test ... twice. I'm pregnant. I'm pregnant with a rapist's baby," Shimi said, in a tone that was flat and hard.

Eddie lowered his eyes to his plate. He didn't say anything, but released a huge sigh. His broad shoulders slumped forward.

"Oh my God! My God! Haven't you been through enough?" Belladane's voice was strained and breathless.

"I guess not. Now I'm looking at either an abortion, or carrying a baby I didn't plan on. Having a child who everyday will remind me of that night. Those are my options." Shimi held her cloth napkin over her face and began to weep. "It's all so fucked up."

"Well, let's get to a doctor and see what they say. One step at a time."

"I'm so sick of one step at a time."

"It's going to work out. You'll see. You'll see." Belladane gave Shimi a big hug.

The next day, Belladane accompanied Shimi to a walk-in clinic in town. Shimi didn't have her own doctor, as they weren't plentiful in Prince Edward Island and she had never felt the need for an annual checkup. Luckily all of her forty-three years had been free of any health issues. The attending doctor was efficient and friendly, but the entire hospital room gave Shimi flashbacks to the day of the rape kit examination. When she peed into the tiny bottle, she remembered handing Nurse Agnes her urine sample that day. The rape kit that would never be analyzed and now this unwanted pregnancy. When she had to lie back on the examination table, and "skosh down a bit" and "open your knees wide," she wanted to rage, scream and cry. It made her want to break things.

She could picture herself breaking the mirror on the wall. Ripping down the diabetes poster. She could squeeze the shit out of the smug tube of lubrication jelly. She could put a knife through the cheery blue, vinyl examination table. But she didn't.

She lay there and tried to focus on the poster that showed the entire digestive system. When she was dressed, she had to sit on the chair and listen to the doctor explain that she was two months pregnant. If she wanted an abortion, she must make the decision immediately. Shimi thought it was rather humourous that the doctor told her the length of her pregnancy. Oct 15th was a day she would always remember. And now 59 days, 12 hours, and 3 minutes since that moment, she didn't need any no-name doctor to tell her that.

She left the doctor's office, with a huge lump in her throat and a fist grip that hurt her left hand.

When would fate stop tormenting me?
What have I done that warranted all this heartache?
Now what on earth am I to do?

Once in the car, Belladane suggested lunch at their favourite sushi restaurant.

"Or will the smell drive you crazy?" Belladane asked.

"I'll manage," Shimi replied. "I am really hungry."

They ate their lunch in silence. Despite Belladane's attempts at conversation, Shimi was deep in thought.

"What do you want to do," Belladane asked. "I'll support you in whatever you want to do."

"What would I like to do? Well, I'd like to go home and curl up in bed for a month or so, but unfortunately, I don't have time to do that, do I?"

Belladane leaned forward and angrily whispered across the table, "I'd like to hunt down that guy and cut his balls off."

"I read that most rapists have an inferiority complex, because they were either sexually abused as a child or neglected," Shimi said, while pushing the sushi around her plate with her chopsticks.

"I'd still like to cut his balls off," Belladane reiterated.

"Me too."

XIV
(viciously)

THE SCREAMING STARTED in the middle of the night. Shimi sat bolt upright in bed and thought she was dreaming. Then she heard it again. Darcy started barking and lunging at the kitchen door. Shimi grabbed a big sweater hanging over the back of the kitchen chair and pulled it on over her pyjamas. She jumped into her winter boots and switched on the three huge yard lights that Eddie had installed a few days after her attack. Like the night lights on a baseball field, they lit up the entire laneway, all around the house and barn yard. It was one of the many thoughtful things Eddie had done without being asked. At first, she thought he was being overly conscientious, but he seemed to know exactly what she needed and now she was grateful.

She froze for a few seconds with her hand on the doorknob. Could she go outside in the dark? Something horrible was happening. Was she brave enough to investigate? Was she brave enough to solve the problem? Shimi took a deep breath, pulled open the door and raced towards the barn. Darcy bolted ahead of her. The glare from the lights bouncing off the snow showed the trouble was in the goat pen. She could vaguely make out two goats on the ground and dark shadows above them. The snarling and growling became more apparent as she raced closer to the yard.

Darcy barked and growled ferociously with his head stuck through the rail fence. The two Pitbulls stopped their attack for a few seconds and turned to growl at him. Just as Darcy was about to crawl between the two lowest rails, Shimi caught up to him and grabbed him by the collar. With great difficulty she dragged him to the side door of the barn. He fought her the entire way. Eventually she got him locked in the main cheese room. She knew she had probably already lost at least two goats. She couldn't bear the thought of losing Darcy as well.

She ran back to the rail fence and jumped onto it. But she knew by the look of the Pitbulls, there was nothing she could do. She wanted to run back to the house to find a walking stick or ski pole to hit the dogs, but she didn't want to leave her goats. She also needed her cell phone, but she stood frozen in place, unsure what to do next. Her other six goats were clustered in one corner of the yard, pushing against each other for inner safety. Two terrified goats screamed out in pain, as the Pitbulls continued to clamp down on their necks. The goats kept kicking out their hind legs, trying to raise themselves off the ground, but the dogs kept their jaws locked, pinning the goats beneath them. Ernie, the male goat, charged at the dog that was attacking Wilma, but was soon run off. He had no chance to save the females against the two deadly dogs. He took refuge with the other goats in the corner of the yard. Soon blood was splattered across the snow.

Shimi screamed and flailed her arms at the dogs, but they ignored her. The dogs were fixated with insane viciousness. She was terrified to go into the pen, as she knew she would be attacked as well.

One dog released his hold on Wilma's neck. Blood spurted out from her throat and began to pool around her head. The Pitbull started biting huge gashes in her stomach, and within a minute a section of flesh and hair gave way, and her intestines and small organs were yanked from her body. Shimi could see that Wilma was still alive, but barely. Shimi wondered how she could endure such pain. Her heart grieved for her sweet, charismatic goat.

"Shimi! Shimi, stay there!" Suddenly Eddie was there, and instantly up and over the fence. He had a crowbar in his hands and he began beating the dog off Wilma's body. The dog lunged at him while the other dog instantly stopped his attack on Ethel and circled behind him. But with a swiftness Shimi had never seen in Eddie, he continued to swing the crowbar out at both dogs, keeping them at bay. As he struck out at one, the other would lunge at him from behind. Their attack was synchronized, methodical, working in tandem like they had done this many times before. Shimi didn't know how much longer Eddie would be able to hold them off.

Shimi didn't notice the far-off siren until the police car came racing up her lane, lights flashing, and two officers got out of the vehicle. They walked to the fence like they were on coffee break.

"Shoot them! Shoot them," Shimi screamed, pointing at the dogs circling Eddie.

"I know who owns these dogs. I'll go get him," one office said, as he ran back to the car and quickly backed down the lane.

The other officer leaned against the fence and kept yelling at Eddie, "Get out of there. You need to get out of there!"

"Shoot them. They are killing my goats and they are attacking Eddie," Shimi screamed at the officer. "Shoot them! Can't you hear me? Why aren't you shooting them?"

Eddie was able to back up a few steps. As one of the dogs raced at him, he bent down low and swung the crowbar as hard as he could. He made contact with the face of the dog. There was a loud crack, and the dog screamed the most agonizing yelp, then hit the ground and lay quivering. This gave Eddie the minute he needed to get on the fence and away from the other, who turned, raced back to Ethel's shaking body and continued to bite down on her neck.

"I don't understand why you don't shoot? At least put my sweet goats out of their misery. Please!" Shimi pulled on the officer's arm.

"Too much paperwork when you discharge your firearm," the officer said. "Just wait! Look, the owner is here now."

A scruffy, young man with a ratty beard and crazy eyes, jumped out of the police cruiser and up onto the fence. Shimi knew of him as Harvey, who had moved into a broken-down property a year ago, at the end of a long dirt lane off Gooding Road. He gave a loud, sharp whistle and the dog attacking Ethel stopped, turned, and came cowering to his side. He attached a chain to its collar and looped it around the fence post. Then he went into the yard and picked up the other dog. It was barely alive, taking short, gasping breaths.

"Your fucking dogs killed two of my goats!" Shimi yelled at the man.

"I always have them chained, but I guess they got loose. It's the coyotes. They entice them to roam at night."

"Why do you even have these dogs in this neighbourhood? Look what they've done to my goats? Just look at them," Shimi yelled, pointing at her two dying goats.

"They're my pets, just like you have pets."

The man climbed over the fence with the dying dog over his shoulder, and then he encouraged the other dog to climb under the fence. He held the dog on the chain close to his knee.

Shimi ran after the man as he walked towards the police cruiser. The dog began to growl at Shimi, but this didn't stop her.

"Some fucking pets they are. Why do you have these vicious dogs in this neighbourhood?" Shimi shouted practically in the man's face. Shimi continued on her tirade. "It's because you're a fucking drug dealer, that's why!" Saliva from her angry words sprayed across the man's cheek.

Eddie came and stood beside Shimi and gently grasped her elbow, trying to get her to step back. Shimi yanked her arm away from Eddie, but he stayed by her side.

"Look it lady, you don't know what you're talking about."

"I know exactly what I am talking about and so does everyone else in this neighbourhood. Why don't you take your fucking drugs and dogs someplace else? You are going to pay for this. You are going to pay," Shimi shook her finger in the man's face. Her face was bright red with anger and tears.

"You'd better watch who you're threatening, Cheese Lady," the man said.

The officer who brought him, stepped forward and said, "Now! Now! Let's all just simmer down. I'll drive you home, Henry." The cop and Henry loaded the dogs in the back seat of the cruiser and then the cruiser backed slowly down the lane.

The other officer turned to Shimi and said, "Well, I'll write up a report on this and we can talk tomorrow morning, when you've had some rest and things have calmed down a bit."

"Ya, right! You'll write up a report! I've heard that before. I need you to shoot my two goats. It's not right! You can't leave them in agony like this." Suddenly Belladane was by her side with her arm around Shimi's waist.

"What is your name, Ma'am?" the police officer inquired.

"Shimi Montray, and this is Eddie Savenko, and this is Belladane Johnston. So, you can write all that down in your stupid little book, but you won't do anything useful, like shoot my goats." Shimi glowered at the officer, as he scribbled down the names.

"I'm sorry Ms. Montray, but I can't do that. It's not my responsibility. You need to get a vet to euthanize your animals or do it yourself. You could come back at me tomorrow and accuse me of killing your animals needlessly. I'm sorry, but you'll have to take care of your goats yourself."

"This is all so pathetic. I don't know how you can call yourself a police officer. You should be ashamed of yourself. Those dogs come onto my property in the middle of the night. They terrorize us. They kill my goats, which is totally against the law, and the culprit and his fucking dogs get escorted home like he is the victim here. What's going to happen with Psycho Boy and his deadly dogs? Probably nothing, right? He'll get off Scot-free, right?"

"It will be up to you to press charges, if you wish," the officer said, and he started to walk toward the lane.

Shimi followed him and continued, "Oh, so you're saying, he didn't break any laws? So, I have to press charges for YOU to do YOUR job? Great! Just great!"

With that, the officer was silent. He handed her his card with his name and number. The police car came back up the drive behind him. As he was about to get into the car, he added, "Take care now. Best put your goats in at night." Then he got into the car and slowly backed down the lane.

"Fucking police! Fucking useless police!" Shimi yelled at the cop car. As it backed out onto the road, she bent over in rage and screamed into the night air. She pushed off Belladane's comforting embrace and raced back to the yard. She climbed over the fence. She knelt down beside Ethel, who was bleeding profusely from her neck. The blood was pooling in the snow around her head. Their eyes met, and Shimi wept as she scratched Ethel's ears lovingly. "I'm so sorry, Ethel. I'm so sorry."

She then moved to Wilma and sat down beside her on the ground. Wilma was barely alive. Her stomach and intestines lay on the ground beside the slash in her abdomen. Shimi wept beside her for several minutes. Belladane and Eddie kept encouraging her to get up and go back to the house, but Shimi couldn't move. She wanted to stay with her animals, her friends, her "girls." Then she noticed it, a tiny movement in the sac next to Wilma's back right leg.

It was a red bulging sac, about the size of her fist. Wilma's uterus. As Shimi stared at it, it moved again. Then another rhythmic movement. A tiny fetus. With each hopeful heart beat, it moved in the cold night air.

"Her baby!" Shimi screamed, covering her face with her hands. "I can see her baby."

"Oh God!" Belladane exclaimed, as she stood on the first rail of the fence. Eddie stood several steps behind Shimi, his head bent down, silent, still. His eyes were distant, preoccupied. The rage he felt was a crashing waterfall roaring in his ears.

Shimi bent over to take another close look at her dying goat and Wilma's unborn fetus. She reached out her hand and carefully picked up the small pulsating sac of blood. She held it in both hands and watched it for several seconds, then holding it to her chest, she gagged, bent over and vomited next to the pool of blood that was draining out of Wilma's head. Then she placed the sac carefully back beside Wilma's stomach.

When she finally left the goats and climbed over the fence, Belladane grabbed Shimi's shoulders and ushered her to the house. Darcy continued to steadily bark in the barn.

Eddie stood in the yard, staring at the goats for several minutes. Just thirty minutes ago he was sitting by the stream, looking at the stars, simply breathing. Now he is killing Shimi's wonderful goats. His friend Wilma. He realized that life is often only the appearance of normalcy, a tightrope walk that can change at any moment ... with one misstep of intention or fate, then a fall to the depths of despair. Eddie raised the crowbar above his head, then with both hands brought it down upon the skull of each goat. A thud and shattering sound as metal met bone. A single merciful blow. They were at peace, but the blood continued to flow.

Eddie rolled Ethel's body up in a blue tarp, and then he turned to care for Wilma. As he pushed the tarp underneath her, he realized her tiny fetus was still moving. He stared at it in disbelief, took a deep breath, and then placed his boot over it. He hesitated for a second, then bared down with all his weight. The tiny, pulsating sac burst and was stilled. He turned to the fence, squatted down, covered his face with his bloody hands and wept like a lost child. Wilma's screams echoed throughout his mind. The bloody, pulsating sac was an image he would never forget. Instantly he could see the bullet wounds in the chest of his friends. The blood that was always on his hands. The screaming of bullets, the taste of the hard, dry dirt, and the weight of his uniform and gear. He could feel the way the helmet pinched his chin, and the desert dust scratched his eyes. The look of the small child right before the bomb blasted behind her. All the chaotic screaming and the repulsive spray of bodies and death. He knew he would continue to wander throughout his life haunted by the horrific images he had seen, the things he did, and the things he could not do.

Eventually he stood up and began to tie the tarps tightly around each body. It was an act of strange intimacy. The preparation of the bodies. The tender touching of their heads, the correct placement of their ears, the proper slant of their necks. He had to get it right.

They were heavy but he liked the effort it took to load them into the back of Shimi's truck. He liked the pain that radiated up his back as he twisted to get the goats over the tailgate and into the bed of the truck. Once he had both goats in, he didn't know what to do next.

He sat on the bench in the barn for hours and hung his head like a scolded dog. Eddie thought about his soldier friends, the blood, the screams, the horror, and he cried, great gasping tears. He could feel that familiar pull into nothingness. The vast, brooding bulk of memory. The haunting flashbacks were the dictator of his nightly dreams and his daily visions, but he also knew he had to put one foot in front of the other and practise living. Yet every enjoyable thing within each living day held a glisten of guilt and a twinge of unworthiness.

"One day at a time" he said out loud … yet all he desired was a stiff drink, one right after the other, and a long, dreamless sleep.

Darcy sat by his side and licked the blood from his hands, but Eddie didn't notice.

The dawn was beginning to cough up a new day, but the horror of the night remained as Belladane gently helped Shimi lower herself into the deep, hot bathtub. The older woman knew that often the recipe for sanity after trauma is found in one's bathtub. Everywhere else can be madness. She hoped a hot bath would calm her niece's nerves. Shimi slid down into the tub and lowered her head under the water and stayed there for a moment. Watery silence. Calm. The blood from her hands and face made thin, red swirls in the water. The warm water enveloped her, and she wished she could stay like this, in this watery womb, peaceful and safe.

Belladane sat on the toilet beside the tub and kept folding and refolding the towel on her lap. She had no words of wisdom or comfort. She simply had no words. She knew she was also on the cusp of overwhelming tears or a raging outburst. So, she bit her lip and stayed silent.

Eventually Shimi's head came up out of the water. Her long, curly auburn hair hung dark and straight over her shoulders. She pushed the hair back from her face. She looked pale and withered like a plant locked away in a dark room. As she held onto the sides of the tub, she kept her eyes closed and released a huge sigh.

When Belladane looked at Shimi's quivering fingers, she wondered how much pain this strong woman could endure. She knew with this additional grief, this new pain, the ache in Shimi's heart would grow to an even greater depth. Belladane feared Shimi's rage over her brutal rape and now the murder of her goats would fossilize and birth a deep hardness that would coat the rest of her life.

Belladane stared at Shimi's trembling fingers. Then she realized that under the towel, hers were also trembling.

XV
(towards)

SHIMI PARKED HER car at the end of the long dirt lane. Ahead of her, the dune grass poked up through the skiff of snow on the sand. The sky above her was sunny with great billowing clouds that warned more snow could arrive at any time. She followed the narrow path over the dunes and onto the beach. It was low tide, but the water was slowly advancing onto the shore.

The ice crystals were creeping along the edge of the water, moving in with the tide. They crackled and popped and appeared alive. She remembered the first time, years ago, when Darcy had seen the shifting ice. He had stopped his chase of the gulls and stared at the ridge of dancing crystals. He had then jumped over it and on it, as if in an attempt to stop this mysterious flow, and then he had simply lifted his head and taken off after the seagulls again. She wished she could stop her concerns that quickly, accept the inevitable and, like Darcy, simply ignore what she could not change, and take off in a different direction.

Shimi realized that she was so focused on trying to change the world and how she felt about it, that she was jumping on flowing ice that could never be stopped. The young woman knew she had to change herself and how she reacted to this new reality that she was now living. As Belladane had so eloquently said at dinner the night before, "You must be like a cork in water. You have to learn to float above the fray."

Shimi wished she had the capacity to ignore people and negative situations easily and guilt-free like her aunt. But the fear, the anger, and the indecisions constantly weighed on her. They were a page that wouldn't turn. She wished she had amnesia ... to be able to forget it all, for a while ... for a lifetime.

She was tired. So very tired. But today she knew she needed to come to the beach..

Shimi loved walking the shore in the winter, if the wind wasn't too strong. It helped her breathe. Helped her clear her head. Often while walking, she took a quick inventory of her life, and came back from the sea feeling better than when she had set out. More positive. More grateful. But that was before she had really big problems. A panoply of sorrows and fears. She hoped this walk today would help her as it did in the old days, when life was less complicated.

The wind was coming from the north. It bit into her face and with each breath it filled her nostrils with tiny, sharp, pin needles of pain. She pulled her scarf higher over her chin. "The warlocks of winter, the warlocks of winter," she kept repeating to herself. She had read that phrase in a poem somewhere and now it came to mind, like a mantra in the whirling wind.

She slowed her breath and concentrated on the light bouncing off the ice. The focus on light and sound became her meditation. The glimmer of light on her feet as she stepped over the stones disappeared with each lift of her foot. She tried to focus simply on the light and her breathing, but questions swirled relentlessly in her head.

Should I have the abortion? She wondered if perhaps in some weird twisted act of fate, that the rape was an opportunity to have a child, which she never thought she'd have? Maybe this was meant to be ... if you believe in that sort of thing. A grand plan of sorts.

Should I take the owner of the vicious pit bulls to court and ask for compensation for the value of my goats? Maybe the judge would demand the Pitbulls be euthanized. What if they attack a small child someday? She would be angry if she didn't do something when she had the chance. If she takes her neighbour to court, will he simply breed more dogs? He probably was breeding them for fighting and making big money on them. If she sues him, will he retaliate? Will she feel safe in her own home after that?

Safety: now there's a poignant concept to ponder. Never before had she felt unsafe in the world. On the evening TV news, she had regularly watched catastrophes happening to other people throughout the world: wild fires or floods tearing down beloved family homes, hurricanes devastating entire towns, or a deranged shooter killing innocent shoppers in a mall. She had tried to empathize, but she always felt entirely removed from this kind of fear. Now she understood the meaning of fear, and she could not seem to shake it.

What if the rapist rapes again? Will the police discover the connection and finally realize they have a serial rapist on their hands? Perhaps he has already and is getting bolder and more violent each time. Should she press the police to investigate her rape case more thoroughly and agree to aid to the fullest degree in his prosecution? She would have to tell her story of that vile night publicly, in a courtroom full of people. See her name and perhaps her picture in the newspaper. See the change in the way people look at her. Hear their whispers behind her back at the market, tolerate their sympathetic smiles. And how would this sordid family history affect the baby, who may be born next summer? How could she handle all this? These thoughts filled her with a new sense of nausea.

How could this definitive violence create such ambiguous arguments inside her? How could such rib-cracking, larger-than-life decisions be now part of her once normal, content, boring life?

Shimi stood gazing at the frigid water. It mesmerized her. It beckoned. She could hear the gulls out over the water and the slop of the waves at her feet. She released a great sigh. It would be so simple to walk out into the water and let the watery womb wash all her troubles away. It would rise over her head. It would welcome her with heavy arms, let her sink down to its primordial floor with its silence, darkness, where there is nothing but peace. Shimi pondered this solution. Here ... now ... it was so appealing. She wondered whether she would ever completely heal from her rape. The grinding hours of sleepless nights ... all those nights that gummed at her sleep. She would toss and turn like a restless dog who forgets how many times she has rounded her tail. She was tired, so very tired. And during the day, there was no relief from the turmoil. All the over-the-shoulder glances when she was awake, would also finally come to an end. There would be no more fear. No more questions. No more daunting decisions to make.

As she was about to step across the icy ridge of crystals, she saw all her loved ones' beautiful faces. They jumped in front of her own frozen face like wavering images in the wind. Her mother. Her father. Belladane. Eddie. How would her dear aunt and new friend cope with her drowning? Their faces haunted her the most.

Suddenly tide crystals flowed over the end of her sneakers, with a frigid, stinging wetness that bit her toes. Shimi looked down at her feet. Darcy grabbed at her hand. He snatched her mitt, held it in his mouth and backed away. There was a glimmer of mischief in his eyes. He lowered his front paws playfully and encouraged her to chase him, dared her to take the mitt from him. When she turned again to look at the water, he dropped the mitt onto the sand and came back to her. He grabbed her sleeve and this time didn't let go.

Shimi lowered herself onto the sand and held onto Darcy. He playfully fell onto her lap, where he relaxed for a few moments. They both took big deep breaths and watched the misty, winter cloud of breath float from their mouths. Shimi looked at her breath hanging in the air, the life force within her. She watched it slowly drift off and disappear in the sunlight. Darcy jumped up and then he was gone again chasing the gulls. He knew his work was done. Shimi would not be giving herself to the deep water.

Shimi tried to clear her head. She was here to make an uncrowded decision about her pregnancy. She was not here to end her life. No matter how appealing the idea was, she knew it was not acceptable. She would survive this time. She would keep breathing. She would make the decisions she needed to make. And she knew she had two wonderful friends in Belladane and Eddie who would stand by her, no matter what. Aunt Belladane was extremely supportive and always willing to talk things through, but she knew her auntie was hoping she would terminate this unwanted pregnancy. Perhaps that would be the best for her psychologically. Without the child, perhaps she could, in time, forget about that dreadful night.

Shimi tried to simply focus on the beloved beach that surrounded her, wrapping her in its solitude and beauty. Few people ever walked this part of the North Shore. She loved the great sweeping sand dunes with their tall beach grass that swayed and beckoned in the wind. The piles of black seaweed that lay upon the sand until the next tide swept it to a new resting place. She loved the gnarled and twisted driftwood that washed up from far-off places and lay scattered across the ground.

The lonely beach was a place that kept nothing waiting; it was as straightforward as sunrise and sunset. It was loneliness in motion. Yet, even with its crashing waves and icy December wind, there was still a permanent tenderness to the sea. A comfort that Shimi could always take for granted. And despite the frantic questions that choked her mind, she was able to once again start breathing deep breaths of calm. Eventually, she stood up.

She walked for about an hour, longer than she had all fall. She knew she should turn around soon, as she had to walk all the way back to the truck with her red face bent into the wind, but something propelled her forward. She had momentum and an emptiness of mind that she hadn't felt in days.

From a distance, she could see a jagged scar in the beach and a branch-like frame rising into the air. She thought of the Fata

Morgana mirages that people who live on warm oceans talk about. The distant boats or castles they see above the waves—that aren't really there. As she kept walking, it looked like a pile of sculpted driftwood, but as she walked closer, she came to the place where the storms had cut back the sand right up to the dune grass. Her jaw dropped, and she froze in place. She stood perfectly still, like a castaway who had finally spotted a far-off ship, and for a split second had no idea what to do.

Layers of sand had been eroded, and there lay a great arching skeleton of a right whale. Shimi could tell it had been there for a very long time. Darcy, sensing her wonderment, ran around the rib cage, barking with delight. He finally simply sniffed the dried-out bones, then lay down for a rest. Shimi was glad she walked this far, to this remote area of the shore. The discovery felt like a magical, once-in-a-lifetime experience.

She crouched down to examine the whale. It was fascinating in its entirety. The bones were bleached clean from the sun and the surf. She ran her mitt along the spine and the neck. Part of the skull was missing. The baleen was no longer there; the mouth was a great gaping hole. She touched the smoothness in the space between the eye sockets and tried to imagine the life that once was in these mammoth bones: the intelligent brain, the family-oriented heart. She walked slowly around the skeleton and down the other side, examining it closely. She looked at the whale from all angles. Its great backbone came down to a point where its tail would have been. The flutes still had a few tiny bones attached, but most had been lost over time. She crouched down and dug back some sand. It was almost frozen, but with a little effort, she was able to move some back from the lower ribs until she had exposed most of the cavity.

And that's when she saw it.

Tucked deep within the rib cage. It must have moved forward with the pushing sand and surf. Shimi was amazed it was still there, safe within its mother's bones. The skeleton of a whale fetus lay on its side, entirely intact.

The discovery of it made Shimi quickly stand up and step back. How could this be? How could she be the one finding this? Why hadn't these bones been picked up by some local biologist or secured by a marine museum? Perhaps there were too many right whale skeletons now? If that was the case, it was a very sad commentary on the plight of the whales around the Northumberland Strait. A sudden pang of sadness now clouded her initial delight.

Shimi knelt down by the mother whale again. She stuck her hand through the great rib cage and touched the small skeleton within. With her bare hands, she began to clear the sand away. Despite her hands beginning to burn with the cold, within a couple of minutes, she could see the entire skeleton of the fetus. There was sadness in this moment, yet there was also a rare beauty within the bones. They echoed protection, motherhood, life, and death. Tragedy. Loss. She wanted to keep digging and bring the baby skeleton home. It just seemed like the right thing to do. Perhaps she could preserve it somehow. Perhaps this is why she had been drawn to this place. Perhaps she was supposed to find this ... maybe no one else ever had. But she resisted pulling the baby from its mother. They should stay together ... as they were, in this moment, half buried within the sand and snow, with only the wind and the gulls as their witness.

Shimi sat down onto the sand and pulled her knees up to her chest. Darcy came and lay by her side. Instantly, his body radiated warmth along the leg of her jeans, so she ran her hand along the side of her dog to warm them. She stared at the whale for a very long time, and she cried deep, gasping tears that froze to her cheeks and made her scarf wet and cold. Darcy lay his head upon her knee and closed his eyes. She continued to pet his long, brown coat. In time, she pulled herself together and knew she must leave.

Shimi took her phone from her coat pocket and took three photos of the mother whale and her unborn calf. Then she turned, and with her head bent low to the wind she made her way back to her truck. She looked back several times and wondered if she would ever see them again. But perhaps that was not necessary. This one time was perfect.

At dinner that night, Belladane, Shimi, and Eddie shared a great pizza Belladane had made. It was laden with practically every vegetable imaginable and had a cheesy goodness that left each bite with a great stretch of cheese dangling from their lips. Shimi was starving from her long, cold walk and couldn't eat fast enough.

"Slow down! You're not shovelling coal into a furnace," Belladane laughed.

"I'm just so hungry. I ate nearly an entire box of crackers before I came over," Shimi said.

"Are you sure you should have walked in such cold, my dear. Your face is now as pale as an old man's knees," Belladane touched her niece's cheek.

"It was wonderful," Shimi said.

Meadow moved around Shimi's legs and then raised her front paws onto the side of her chair. Shimi picked some mozzarella cheese from her pizza and fed it to the cat.

Belladane smiled, and playfully said, "Don't feed her at the table."

"Oh, be quiet," Shimi exclaimed, and pulled her phone out from her pocket.

"No phones at the table," Belladane chirped, with her mouth full of pizza.

"I know, I know, but look at this."

Shimi showed them the photos of the mother whale with her baby enclosed within. They gasped and marvelled over the beauty of it all. The astonishing luck that was hers. Eddie stared at the photos for a very long time.

"I can't imagine discovering such an extraordinary find. Such a beautiful ... sad ... profound sight," Eddie said.

Shimi was pleased. She knew this wonderfully, damaged, introspective man got it. He really got it! Got the beauty and the horror of it. Just like she had.

Putting down her slice, she announced, "I've made my decision. I am going to have the baby."

Belladane and Eddie also put down their slices. Belladane looked shocked, but tried to stay composed. Both women remained silent much longer than a simple dramatic pause.

Finally, Belladane asked, "Are you sure?"

"Yes," Shimi replied, in a determined and curt tone.

Both were quiet again. Shimi looked at her plate. Belladane released a deep sigh.

Eddie broke the uncomfortable silence. "Well then, this deserves a toast," he said, raising his glass of Ginger Ale. "To Shimi and her baby."

"To Shimi and the baby," Belladane repeated, with a serious look on her face.

"To the baby," Shimi said under her breath, still looking at the photo of the baby whale.

And they all clinked their glasses together.

"Thanks, guys. I haven't gotten everything figured out, but I do know I'm going to have this baby. That mother whale and her sweet baby helped me make this decision today."

"I see," said Belladane.

"To the North Shore," said Shimi and she raised her glass of Ginger Ale again.

"To the North Shore," they all shouted.

Belladane smiled, but her jaw was clamped and tight.

XVI
(lovingly)

As promised Eddie moved into Belladane's house by Christmas. He had very few possessions: a couple of canvas bags of clothing and a few books, so the move didn't take much effort. Belladane bought new flannel sheets and a cozy duvet for the room that was to become his, and she hung up a few abstract paintings that looked less like breasts and more like sunrises. Eddie drained the water in the trailer, so it was safely prepared for winter and locked up the old barn.

"Thanks so much for this, Belladane. But if you're not sick of me by spring, would it be alright if I moved back into the trailer? I really like the small space," Eddie asked.

"Of course, Eddie. Shimi and I love having you here. I appreciate all your help. You've become a good friend," Belladane said.

"Great, thanks," Eddie said. Then he dumped a wad of money onto the table. "Here is four thousand, sixty-three dollars. I want to pay rent."

"What? Do you think you've moved into the Ritz? You can contribute four hundred a month for room and board," Belladane responded. "That's all I'll take. Oh, and FYI, we do have these things called banks here in Canada." Belladane cast him a playful smile.

"Yes, I'm sure you do," Eddie said, and then he continued. "I get a US veteran pension, a little bit each month, and I want to pay my way while here. I will keep a bit in the bank to pay for my cell phone, but besides that I am giving the rest to you. And four hundred a month is not enough."

"Look Eddie, you're more than helpful around here. I'd like you to take care of the snow shovelling. Bring in the firewood, stuff like that. And I have that old snow blower that I can barely get running. Maybe you can tinker with it and get it going and keep my lane cleared. And please clear Shimi's laneway and doorstep as well. All that is such valuable help. And if I had to hire a guy, it would cost me a lot more money."

"Sure, no problem. But I still want you to keep the money. I want to give you my pension every month. Maybe you can save it for me?" Eddie put his hands in his pockets.

"I don't get it, sorry," Belladane said, sitting down on one of the kitchen chairs. "You just said you have a bank account."

"Well, here's the thing. I'm doing okay with not drinking, and you're right the AA meetings two nights a week are really helping, but I still have some pretty bad temptation. So, you see, if I don't have money, I can't buy booze. Know what I mean?"

"I don't know whether I should keep your money, Eddie. I don't really want to be your mother and police your spending." She gave Eddie a hard look, but then continued. "Ok, if you think it would help. I will hide the money for a couple of months for you. And I'll tell Shimi where it is, just in case I choke on an éclair or something," Belladane laughed.

"Thanks, Belladane, you're the best."

"No. Just the best you've got."

Christmas was a week away, so Belladane and Eddie kicked it into high gear. Eddie brought down the huge box of Christmas lights from Belladane's attic and strung them up on both Shimi's and Belladane's houses. He hung them along the eaves and spiralled them around the bushes. Shimi said that Christmas lights were her favourite part of the season, but she never would have done it herself. Since she had decided to have the baby, she was trying to be more careful and not take as many physical risks. Eddie was more than happy to help out.

All three friends agreed they didn't really want to cut down a perfectly healthy fir tree and then watch it slowly dry up and die for two weeks in the house, so they decided to pass on the Christmas tree. But during the afternoon on Christmas Eve, the two women were banished from Belladane's living room while Eddie brought in Shimi's old, six-foot wooden step ladder. He placed the ladder beside the fireplace and wound a long silver garland around it. Then he attached a strand of red lights and a strand of twinkle lights around it.

"Ta-da!" he said, when the two women were allowed into the room that evening.

"That's the weirdest Christmas tree I have ever seen," Belladane laughed.

"Yes, but considering the weird year I'm having, I think it's perfect," Shimi said. She walked around the ladder tree and added, "Let's hang some ornaments on it as well. I'll go get Mom's box of Christmas stuff. Be right back."

Eddie got a fire going in the fireplace and the living room became a crackling cocoon of warmth. The women decorated the tree with Shimi's vintage ornaments. Shimi took extra care with the one that read, 'Baby's first Christmas.' It had a tiny picture of her inside the glass globe. She put it front and centre on the tree, hanging it from the string of lights. They stood back and decided it was a magnificent tree. Meadow came into the room, walked around the old ladder, crawled under it, and began to chew on the lowest garland. They sat by the fire drinking copious amounts of eggnog and cinnamon spiced chai tea, until late into the night, simply staring at their creation. And the old, rusty step ladder tree sparkled in its radiance.

Later, when Eddie walked Shimi and Darcy home, he stood behind her as she fumbled with the door key. She opened the door and turned to face him. He gave a warm smile, and said softly, "Merry Christmas, Shimi. Sleep well."

"Merry Christmas, Eddie." She noticed how his eyes looked in the yellow light. They appeared like new denim, flat and dark, soft and troubled. She loved Eddie's eyes at night, but also wondered if they would ever stop looking at her with concern and pity.

When she entered her bedroom and began to take off her clothes, she could feel the old terror closing in on her. The first sign was always the flutter in her right eyelid. It took all her strength to hold it together when she was with Eddie and Belladane during the day. But at night, when she was home and alone, she would often succumb to the flashbacks. The geography of fear. The way she moved around the house, turning lights on and off. Pulling curtains closed. Not knowing whether to lock bathroom or bedroom doors behind her, or leave everything open so she could hear completely throughout the house. Every action became an intentional movement and a slave to her memories.

In the scalding, hot shower she scrubbed her skin violently, especially her thighs. She put on a turtleneck sweater, some flannel pyjama pants, grabbed her duvet, then crawled under the bed. Darcy lay on the mat beside the bed, peering in at her with his face on his paws, and despite her "shushing" he continued to whine.

She lay there for a long time. Thinking. Shaking. Trying to rationalize her thoughts. Trying to boost her courage. Belladane's words at dinner last week came back to her. "You're not broken; you're merely scratched. Do not lie down on the train tracks, Shimi. You've got too much living to do." She played these words over and over again in her mind, and then with all her courage and willpower she pulled herself out from under her bed and jumped on top. Darcy jumped up beside her and instantly fell asleep, quivering and making tiny yips in his throat. Shimi placed her hand on his warm side, feeling his heartbeat and his shallow breaths out and in. Within minutes, she too fell asleep.

On Christmas morning the three got together and opened some presents that had magically appeared under the tree. Eddie received a soft, flannel shirt, heavy wool socks, and warm coveralls from Shimi.

"For all those cold night walks you take," Shimi smiled.

Eddie beamed, red-faced with embarrassment.

Belladane presented Eddie with a huge box of apartment goodies: a toaster, coffee maker, electric kettle, a Kuradori hot plate, some small pots and pans, cutlery and some mismatched dishes. "It's amazing what you can find at the thrift shop," she laughed. "These are for the other upstairs room, for when you feel like being by yourself. A tiny fridge is being delivered next week, and I have a plumber coming to put in a sink as well."

"You don't need to do that, Belladane. I can get water from the bathroom," Eddie said.

"I know you can, but I've been meaning to do that for years, so it's no trouble. I've always wanted to make a little self-contained apartment up there, so now's the time. You've got your own front staircase and your own privacy now. That's important. You can make your own breakfast and lunch, but you're to be down here for dinner every night, understand?"

"Wouldn't miss it," Eddie smiled. "Maybe some night I can cook for you two ladies. I make a mean eggplant lasagna and also a tasty vegetarian chilli."

"You're on," Belladane roared. "And oh, I haven't been called a lady in a very long time." She laughed hysterically.

As Shimi smiled at Belladane, she realized her aunt's crazy sense of humour and raw laughter was a true blessing. And more than that, it was actually quite contagious.

Then the attention turned to Shimi. Belladane took a present from under the tree and placed it on Shimi's lap. Out of the colourful gift bag, Shimi pulled a pretty sky-blue diary, a snazzy red fountain pen, and a small bottle of navy ink.

"You may not always be able to get to the beach in the cold weather, so this is for your thoughts, both good and bad," Belladane said. "I know you have lots of them. Maybe it will help you figure things out on this complicated journey called life."

"Aww, thanks Auntie. I love it. It can also be my gratitude journal, right Eddie?"

Eddie nodded, "Excellent idea."

"Well, it was either that, or that damn book, *What to expect when you're expecting*. I saw five copies at the thrift shop."

"Thank goodness you didn't buy me that. I prefer the journal. I'm going to try to write happy thoughts inside. Eddie and I are fetishizing happiness, however small or obscure it may be at times," Shimi told Belladane.

"Well, that's probably the best fetish I have ever heard of," Belladane laughed.

Shimi hugged the diary to her chest, and said, "I look forward to starting it tonight," and then playfully added, "Now don't you go snooping in my journal."

"But of course, I will," Belladane smirked.

Then it was Belladane's turn. From Shimi, she opened a prettily decorated shoebox filled with acrylic and oil paints of every colour; some markers, a bottle of mineral spirits, and three small canvases.

"Sorry it's so practical, but I couldn't find any more of those tie-dyed tops you like to wear on your head," Shimi smirked.

Both women laughed, while Eddie looked confused.

"It's a long story," Shimi said. Then she added, "I know the gift isn't that imaginative, but I was thinking maybe you could create some little paintings for the baby's room? Preferably not vaginas." She made a funny face at Belladane and stuck out her tongue.

"Aw shucks! Well, how about Winnie the Pooh, is that tame enough for you?" Belladane laughed.

"Perfect," Shimi agreed.

Then Eddie presented an envelope to Shimi. She opened the card and inside were two blots of blue paint that looked like a blurred Rorschach smudge. Now it was Shimi's turn to look confused.

"It's Ethel and Wilma's hoof prints. I did it before I buried them. Sorry, but the snow, the mud, and I was kind of crying so hard, I kind of messed them up. My hands were shaking so bad, they're kind of smudged. But I thought you still might like to have them. Is it too weird? I know often folks do that for their dogs and cats when they pass," Eddie said.

"No! No, I love them, Eddie. It's very thoughtful. And unique. And I don't think I ever really thanked you properly for all you did that night. You were amazing, as always," Shimi said, wiping a tear from her eye. As she folded the card and placed them back into the envelope, she said, "I'm going to put these up on my fridge door. I will treasure them. Thanks."

"Have you decided what you're going to do about all that?" Belladane asked.

"Yes. Yes, I have. I'm going to take crazy drug dealer guy to small claims court. I think I need to do that," Shimi said. "I'm filing the complaint next week. I'm tired of feeling helpless about stuff that happens to me."

"Good. Good for you," Belladane said.

Eddie handed Belladane a box. "I know how you hate heating up your old car in the winter for your evening art classes."

Inside the box was an electric car starter. Belladane was thrilled. "Eddie, you think of everything. Thanks so much. But you know it will be your job to hook the damn thing up."

"No problem," Eddie said.

"What a great idea," Shimi said. "I've been pretty self absorbed lately. How are the art classes going? And the AA meetings? Is the driving to Charlottetown becoming too much in the winter?"

"As long as I don't play the radio too loud, it's fine," Eddie laughed.

"Yes, I can't see the road if the radio is too loud," Belladane chimed in cheerfully. "I guess I'm getting old."

Shimi picked up some Lindt chocolates from a huge box on the coffee table. "Wow, where did these come from? My favourite."

"They're a little thank you from Alice, a wonderful woman in my art class. I'm getting to know her a bit better each week. Hopefully you'll meet her someday. She's lovely," Belladane said.

"I like Alice already," Shimi said, as she popped another chocolate into her mouth.

The three of them spent the afternoon preparing a marvellous turkey dinner. They turned up the CBC radio's taping of *The*

Nutcracker, and they moved about the large country kitchen like graceful ballerinas. Eddie said he loved Tchaikovsky.

Shimi laughed and said, "Tchaikovsky? I had you pegged as more of a Shania Twain kind of guy."

"Well, I am in some ways," Eddie winked.

Once dinner was cooked, Shimi carved the turkey, eating the crunchy, greasy pope's nose even before they sat down at the table. Eddie mashed the potatoes with lots of butter and heated milk, and Belladane made the gravy from her mother's secret recipe. For Eddie's sake, instead of a generous splash of rum, Belladane poured in some coffee, and everyone agreed it tasted just as good.

The week passed quickly and on New Year's Eve, the three decided to watch some feel-good lovey-dovey movies. Belladane voted for *Love Actually*. Shimi wanted *About Time*, and Eddie said, "How about *Alien*?"

"Noooooo," both women yelled, and Eddie laughed.

They ate fish and chips from Belladane's air fryer, she had bought herself at a Boxing Day sale, and made heaping bowls of popcorn. They watched *Love Actually* and *About Time*, and all agreed that they cried more in *About Time* than any other movie they'd seen.

"Well, maybe except *Steel Magnolias*," Belladane interjected.

When the clock struck midnight, Belladane broke the awkward moment and yelled, "Group hug!" and they all stood up and hugged each other. Shimi loved the warmth of her friends' hands against her back. She felt safe and loved, so she held onto Belladane and Eddie with all her might until Belladane finally said, "Ok. Ok. I can't breathe!"

The next day at dinner, Belladane said she had big news. She threw her hands up in the air and exclaimed with great joy, "Elmer and Lima just birthed their little one!"

"Who did what?" Shimi asked, giving Eddie a bewildered look.

"The gay penguins at a zoo in New York," Belladane said. "They hatched their first egg this morning."

"Oh, my nerves! Now how in the world did they get an egg? Did they steal it?" Shimi asked.

"Of course not! The egg was donated to them from a straight couple who were bad parents," Belladane said. "This is the second egg to be incubated and hatched by gay penguins. The first was good old Roy and Silo in 1998, who were a great couple until Silo left Roy for a penguin named Scrappy."

"Well, that goes without saying. How could anyone resist a mate named Scrappy?" Eddie grinned.

'I think I could," Shimi said dryly.

And they all laughed.

Shimi looked at Belladane and Eddie around the table. They were all so different, yet they had formed a bond that was well beyond friendship. They were a true family. Shimi loved that their simple everyday actions created their own unique equation of care and happiness. The very medicine they each desperately needed.

December 2022
Dear Elsa,

    Merry Christmas to my darling, Elsa. I hope you are having a wonderful holiday, and your grouchy old boss has given you extra time off. Will you be going to Alex's house for Christmas dinner? I remember what a good cook she is. Please know that I will be with you in spirit.

    Things have been rather horrific here for Belladane and Shimi over the last couple of months. Shimi was violently assaulted while in her barn one night. What a horrible ordeal for her and now to make matters worse, she is pregnant. I try to help her however I can. I have taken on doing the milking of the goats, which lightens her work immensely, but she still has to deal with her trauma, make the cheese, and then sell it. I'm becoming quite fond of her, and we both understand each other's recurring traumatic pain. Wish I could help her more.

    I haven't had a drink in over a month. I am hopeful I am on the right track and can keep the booze at bay. Still having some nightmares and visions of Afghanistan, but I am dealing with it. I can't think of a better place to work through all this. Belladane and Shimi have been a God-send.

    I have moved into the upstairs of Belladane's farmhouse. The trailer was getting quite cold. From the attic I salvaged an old record player and some great albums. I have fallen in love with Leonard Cohen, a Canadian songwriter from Montreal. His songs speak to me. I will play them for you someday. My favourite has become Sisters of Mercy. Belladane and Shimi have become my very own Sisters of Mercy, but don't worry they won't replace you!

    Happy New Year! You deserve it. Will think of you at midnight! Take good care!

IloveyaandImissya!
Eddie

XVII
(kindly)

BELLADANE LOVED TEACHING her adult art classes at East Side High School, Continuing Education Program. It was her ninth year teaching the non-credit course. She could teach whatever she pleased, and she could be as wacky and wild as she wanted. Her biggest goal was to make it fun and non-threatening. She wanted to incorporate some life drawing classes into her course, where students would draw a nude model, but for the life of her she couldn't find anyone to pose for her class. Three ads in the local newspaper and social media sites had come up cold.

Belladane smiled to herself and was reminded of the strip club that had to close on Prince Edward Island, as the owners couldn't find any exotic dancers who weren't related to their late-night smirking clientele. Belladane playfully imagined the club manager coming into the dressing room, telling the exotic dancer, Candy, "There's a full house tonight. So, get your moves on!" Candy would parade out, swirling her tassels, and begin to spin at warp speed around the metal pole, winking at her Uncle Allister in the audience, or blowing a kiss to cousin Bill hunched at the bar. Uncle Allister would be saying to his friend, "I always knew that girl would make something out of herself." Probably not a scenario any exotic dancer would enjoy, but Belladane got a kick out of imagining it.

Belladane assumed the nude modelling job had the same issues. Small town embarrassment. Six degrees of separation? No. More like two or three!

So Belladane made a sarcastic proposal to her class. If they really wanted a life drawing class, perhaps all the artists could be naked and the model clothed. That might be an interesting experiment. The students looked at her like she had three heads. One student, Stan, agreed that might be a fun idea.

Everyone else said, "Ewww!" So, she took that as a definite "NO!"

Since Eddie was a stranger in town, Belladane asked him if he'd be interested in the nude modelling job that paid $25 an hour. "Not bad money for doing nothing," she said. "All you really have to do is stand on a platform, naked, for an hour, and change your pose every 10 minutes. It needn't be hard." Belladane looked sheepishly at him to see if he picked up on her raunchy joke.

He raised his eyebrows and said, "Oh, just shoot me now! I've already got PTSD. I don't need a double dose of it."

Belladane laughed and had to admit to herself that it was wonderful to see Eddie was coming out of his shell. Also, she thought it was a very good sign that he could make a joke about getting shot. As well, he was spending less time alone and seemed less anxious as the winter months passed. The drive into Charlottetown gave them a good opportunity for private chats, and she was learning a little more about him every week.

Two nights a week she dropped him off at his AA group. Eddie had his meeting, then went out with a couple of folks for coffee afterwards or picked up a few groceries. Belladane learned he devoured Frosted Flakes for breakfast and preferred a boiled egg and bagel for lunch. His shopping bag also included some Arrowroot biscuits, apples, oranges, dried figs, tiny cans of spicy tuna, peanut butter, bananas, and chocolate milk, lots of chocolate milk.

Several other evenings in the week, when Eddie was craving a drink, he would join an online meeting on his cell phone, in his bedroom upstairs. The first time Belladane heard Eddie murmuring upstairs, she stood at the bottom of the stairs to listen. She thought he was either reading aloud or talking to himself. Then she realized he was zooming with an alcoholic support group. This made her happy.

Belladane's students were a motley crew, all in different occupations by day, but all wannabe artists by night. Belladane enjoyed them all and loved getting to know them: Maureen was a potato farmer from Hunter River; Jerry was a truck driver who missed every other class due to his schedule, yet always had his homework done; Gloria was a high school music teacher who liked to draw portraits on old sheet music; Maeve, a young woman stuck in the Goth era with her jet black dyed hair and nose piercings, did very fine tattoo art; Edna was an elderly woman who couldn't hear a damn thing, but had a great eye for colour and perspective; Rodney liked to pick up roadkill and do portraits of the dead animals, which were quite poignant; Sylvia loved to paint sunsets and waves, which are always tricky to do; and then there was lonely, old Stan who was simply looking for company, and who kept crushing on Belladane, no matter how many lesbian comments she made.

There were three other students who staggered in and out periodically. Despite Belladane's best effort, they continued to have an undernourished enthusiasm for the class. She wasn't sure why they stayed, but thought perhaps it was the donuts.

When Belladane asked her class one night why they wanted to do art, most agreed it simply made them happy. Belladane knew that was as good a reason as any. Most simply wanted to get out of the house, have a laugh with some paint and wild music. They had no real expectations to improve their artistic ability.

Then there was Alice.

In any class, there is often one student who stands out to a teacher. They are not necessarily the smartest or most talented. It's something more intrinsic, perhaps a vibe they give off, or a personality that is hard to forget. For Belladane, Alice was that student. Alice was a registered nurse, but also spent much of her time being a midwife. Belladane knew she was married, although

Alice rarely spoke of her husband. She sometimes came to class late and seemed rather quiet when she did. One time, Alice had a slight bruise under her left eye. Belladane wanted to mention it, but she couldn't find a private moment with her. She firmly believed women needed to support women and sometimes ask each other the tough questions, so staying quiet about the bruise was painfully difficult for Belladane.

Alice radiated warmth and empathy and took an interest in every topic introduced. She was a keen student and had a natural talent for art. When Belladane asked if she painted at home, Alice replied, "Oh no, not at home. But someday I'd love to have my own little studio tucked away somewhere."

"Why tucked away?" Belladane asked.

"Oh, I just meant, not out in the open. My husband likes things kept neat and tidy. My art would clutter up a room in our house and that wouldn't go over too well. He's a bit OCD when it comes to tidiness." Then Alice looked rather uncomfortable like she had revealed too much.

Belladane immediately understood Alice's complicated home life and said, "I hope someday you can do your art wherever you want," and then she let the conversation drop.

One night as Belladane was leaving the class, she noticed that Alice was still in the parking lot sitting in her car. Everyone else was long gone. The snow was swirling under the street lights, and the temperature was rapidly dropping.

As she was driving past, Belladane rolled down her car window and yelled, "Alice, is everything okay? Will your car not start?"

"No, unfortunately, and I can't reach my husband on his cell. It keeps going to voicemail," Alice replied.

"Jump in with me. I'll give you a lift," Belladane said, as she cleared her clutter of art supplies from the passenger seat.

Alice grabbed her purse and got into Belladane's car. "Thanks so much. I'm not that far away actually. I probably could have walked."

"Don't be silly. You're not walking on a night like this."

As Belladane drove slowly through the dark, wintery streets, the women answered each other's typical get-to-know-you-questions.

"No, I don't have any kids," Alice confessed, "although I've always wanted one. I've had some difficulty in that department. And now my husband says I'm probably too old."

"Too old? How old are you?" Belladane asked.

"Thirty-eight," Alice admitted.

"Well, that's crazy. You've got lots of time. Or have you ever thought of adopting?" Belladane asked.

"No, my husband is not into that," Alice said. "I love babies. And being a midwife, I get to be part of many babies' first few days, and that is so cool. Helping a woman bring her child into this world is a miraculous thing, and I never tire of it."

"But at the same time that must be hard," Belladane said. "When you don't have your own baby."

"Yes. Yes, it is," Alice softly said.

"My niece is pregnant. Quite early on still, just four months, and I'm not sure what she plans for her delivery. Would you be available to help her?" Belladane asked.

"Yes, of course," Alice said. "I've got space on my roster for her. When is she due?"

"Well, she got pregnant, Oct 15th, so I guess that makes her due mid-July."

"Wow! That's amazing that you know the exact date like that," Alice commented.

"Well, it's rather hard to forget. It was a significant night," Belladane said.

"Here we are. That's my house right there." Alice pointed to a sweet little bungalow with buttery yellow siding and a red metal roof. The front door was painted a cheery teal colour. "Thanks so much, Belladane." Alice fumbled in her purse in the dark, until Belladane turned on the interior light. Alice continued, "Here's my business card for your niece. Have her call me if she wants. We can always chat and see if we're a good fit. Thanks so much, Belladane, for the lift. See you next week."

"You're welcome, my dear. Hope it's nothing too serious with your car. Till next week," Belladane said.

As Alice walked up the driveway in the headlights of the car, Belladane waited until she unlocked her front door and stepped inside. As the large living room window became ablaze with light, Belladane could see a charming painting of a sand dune beach above the sofa, which she was sure Alice had painted. Before Alice closed the door, she turned, tilted her head to the side and waved towards the dark car. Belladane thought that was a sweet thing to do, but there was something about the wave. A loneliness? A longing, perhaps? Belladane again switched on the car's interior light so Alice could see her and enthusiastically waved back. Alice smiled and closed the door.

When Belladane backed out of the drive, she touched her horn twice, in a cheery little goodbye beep-beep.

XVIII
(courageously)

THE WINTER MONTHS passed slowly. The snow was heavy and unrelenting, but Eddie took it all in stride. He split and carried firewood for both Shimi's stove and Belladane's. He loved the satisfaction of a wood box by the stove, piled full and ready. He carefully arranged the wood so there were larger logs on the bottom, small logs above them, then the kindling on top. Everything ready to build an easy, perfect fire each morning.

Also, Eddie ploughed snow; he shovelled snow from the walkways and rooftops; and one afternoon while he was tossing snowballs at Darcy, who attempted to catch each one, he realized something. He was happy. Sometimes without thinking, he would stop his work outside and raise his face to the sun and appreciate the apricity that was his. He didn't have a job; he didn't have his own place; he still had bad nightmares periodically; and he still felt like an illegal alien in this wonderful country, yet he felt a true pang of happiness. It was happiness on a strict diet, but it was definitely happiness.

"So, this is what it's like," he said to himself. "I had almost forgotten."

There were times when he was in combat that he never thought he would feel happiness again. Every day was a nightmare of thoughts and actions. Every time he looked into the eyes of his fellow soldiers, he saw only a tangle of pain, regret, and ruin. And any moment of happiness seemed to eventually float away on a raft of fear.

But here ... here on this tiny island in the North Atlantic with these two unique, kind women he felt his life was slowly becoming as perfect as the winter snowflakes that floated down around his face. And he was as ravenous as the whirling March wind for more bits of happiness, so he kept shovelling, carrying firewood, milking goats, and embracing the happiness that he had been miraculously granted.

While working, he constantly thought of Shimi and how she was handling her life. He tried to use her as his own inspiration. In many ways, his problems seemed to pale in comparison. He liked imagining her as a Kintsugi object, perhaps a beautiful vase or slender jug. She was a broken piece of pottery mended with gold or silver, only to make it more beautiful than before. And he knew with care, time, and acceptance, he could be a Kintsugi as well.

At dinner that night, Shimi eased herself into a chair and said, "I'm getting fat. I feel like a busted can of biscuits. You know, those Pillsbury ones."

Eddie and Belladane had to laugh, which motivated Shimi to continue. "Yes, I'm not simply a muffin top any longer, I'm a bonified busted can of biscuits."

"Oh, Shimi stop," Belladane laughed, bending over and holding her stomach. "When you're my age, every sneeze or unexpected laugh is a gamble. Could result in a squirt or a fart. So please stop."

"Sadly, I now know what you mean. Yesterday I peed my pants while picking up a pail in the barn. And don't get me started on the bed farts. Who knew pregnancy could be so much fun? But seriously, I can't fit into any of my clothes, so I bought this housedress and leggings at the thrift shop. It's rather vintage, don't you think?" Shimi said.

"Why when an old woman wears outdated clothes from her closet, she is considered old-fashioned, but when a young woman wears old clothes, it's considered vintage-trendy?" Belladane asked, as she pulled the quiche from the oven.

Eddie brought the salad to the table. "How does one describe the taste of a kiwi or a passion fruit?"

"What?" both women said in unison.

"My point exactly," Eddie said, "Let's eat."

Both women laughed.

As Belladane carefully brought the quiche to the table she knocked into Darcy laying by Simi's side. "Darcy, get the heck under the table," she scowled.

The dog instantly slid under the table and rested his chin on Shimi's feet.

"He is so clingy these days. Gosh, I've never had so much help putting on my underpants. This morning, I managed to get my leg through one leg hole, and he had his nose struck up through the other. It's hilarious." Shimi rubbed Darcy's back with her foot.

"Darcy is more like your psychic companion. He knows what you need even before you do. Pretty soon, you may need help stepping into your underpants," Belladane laughed, as she dished out the quiche and sweet potato spoon bread. In a sweet voice, and a glance under the table she playfully added, "Ah, yes, Darcy is a helpful boy."

"I went to court today," Shimi said as she started to eat her broccoli cheese quiche. "And it's all done."

"What? I would have gone with you. Why didn't you tell me?" Belladane asked.

"That's exactly why I didn't tell you," Shimi said. "I wanted to go by myself. I have to stop relying on you two so much. I'm slowly getting my confidence back, and I want to keep getting stronger, so today was kind of a test of that. I did okay."

"Great! So, how did it go?" Belladane inquired.

"Of course, those two dedicated police officers didn't show up, but the judge was great. She read my account of the night and asked crazy drug dealer guy why he is breeding these dogs. He said he wasn't selling them to fight, but I think she doubted that. Then she asked him if he had any character witnesses, and he said no. She looked at the photos Eddie took of that night. That was a good idea, Eddie, to take all those. Then she asked about the value of Wilma and Ethel and the milk that I got from them daily. He has to pay me $2500 in five instalments over one year. $500 every two months. He pays it to the court, and then the money comes to me."

"Good. Hope he learned his lesson," Eddie said. "Although I do kind of feel sorry for those dogs. Pitbulls can be great dogs with the right owner." Eddie pushed his empty plate away from him, bent down and picked up Meadow who had been tormenting Darcy under the table. Immediately she settled herself, hanging over his left shoulder like a fox stole. Shimi smiled. She realized that this was something they probably did often upstairs in Eddie's room at night, but she had never seen this before. They looked so comfortable together, so relaxed. She felt an instant pang of fondness for this special man. She continued to stare at Eddie and Meadow, but finally brought herself back to the conversation.

"Yes, I agree Pitbulls can be good dogs, but sadly, that leads me to another thing. She ordered the dog that is still alive to be euthanized. He said he would do it soon, but she said, 'No, you will do it today.' Then she had her clerk person phone a vet right then and there and book the appointment. She was really slick, didn't mess around with this guy. I was impressed."

"Such good news, Shimi. Good for you. Glad you pursued this. I'm sure it wasn't easy," Belladane said.

"Well, I doubt if I will ever see any of the money, as he probably won't pay it, but I'm glad I went through with it. It's too bad things weren't moving with my other case. I guess that's a lost cause."

"Maybe that monster won't go to trial, but maybe karma will get him. Know what I mean? Really get him in the end," Eddie said.

Belladane burst out laughing again, and Shimi raised her eyebrows in horrified amusement.

Eddie said, "What now? What'd I say?"

"Nothing! Nothing! She's just being rude," Shimi laughed. "You could be right, Eddie, but I'm not too hopeful."

"How are you doing, Shimi, with your memories? Your nightmares?" Eddie asked.

"I'm still haunted. I won't lie. The memories come flooding back at the weirdest times. Like today at the courthouse, I was in the elevator alone and then this guy got on, on the third floor. He nodded his head and smiled at me. Just a normal look, but I felt like I was going to panic and punch him in the face ... but somehow, I held it together. Now I feel like my creepy imagination triumphs over logic, but I'm trying to have 'starch in my spine' as Belladane says, and just breathe."

"Those horrible memories may always be attached to you. You may drag them around like toilet paper stuck to a shoe, but they don't need to drag you down. They don't need to control your every thought. Don't let that one night cancel out all the other good stuff in your life, my darling. All the other happiness you have felt and the new ones that are yet to come." Belladane stroked Shimi's hand.

"Just mine that inner strength that's in your DNA and turn it into gold bullion," Belladane added.

Shimi and Eddie nodded and looked at each other, but kept quiet. Belladane was always a glass-half-full person. Shimi loved that about her aunt, but she sometimes felt her aunt was getting impatient with her. Perhaps deep down inside, despite all her beautiful language, Belladane really wanted to simply say, "Snap out of it!" Shimi wished she could snap out of it. She wished she could be that calm, and forgetting could be as easy as all her auntie's wonderful metaphors on life.

Shimi's clambering emotions were the product of brutal mathematics, their total often divided and multiplied without reason or a logical formula. And these emotions continued to appear with resilience and fortitude, despite her attempts to "snap out of it."

Belladane drank her tea and didn't say another word. She was afraid she had already said too much. She wished she could make everything right for Shimi, but she knew even her powers were limited in this case. And feeling helpless and not in control was not a feeling she enjoyed, or for which she had any patience.

Eddie put the dishes in the dishwasher and washed up the pots and pans. Then he said, "Thanks for a great dinner, Belladane" and left the room. Within a few minutes, they could hear his little television set upstairs. He liked to watch all the classic comedies from the 90's. *Fraser* and *Seinfeld* were two of his favourites. He said he tried to never watch the American news. "I don't want to know who they are bombing this month," he would say with a sigh.

"He thanks me after every meal. Every single meal. That man is a class act," Belladane said.

Shimi continued to sit quietly at the table nursing another cup of green tea. Belladane leaned across the table and whispered, "He's in love with you, you know."

"What? Eddie? No! No, he's not! You're crazy," Shimi replied, a redness coming to her cheeks.

"The way he looks at you. All his actions say so."

"Well, he's in love with you too then, as he's just as kind to you," Shimi whispered.

"It's not the same and you know it. You didn't know this, but that horrible night, he rescued Darcy from your house who was barking his face off, and the two of them sat outside my back door all night. He didn't know what was going on, but he knew something was wrong when he saw you run here. And then ... then he stayed outside your door every night for over a month, in the cold, just keeping watch over you. Bet you didn't know that, did you?" Belladane looked earnestly at Shimi.

"No, no, I didn't know that. Wow! You know, I don't know what I would have done without Eddie. He was so great taking over everything with the goats. He just stepped in and did it all. We're really lucky he came to us, Belladane. He has become such a lovely part of our little family," Shimi said.

"Well, just don't take him for granted, my dear. And if you have any feelings for him at all, you best tell him before he's gone. We don't know how long he is going to stay. Don't miss out on a good man who is right in front of your face, Shimi."

"I'm not really in any state to be starting a new relationship ... now, am I? My life is pretty complicated right now." Shimi rubbed her baby bump.

"You certainly could do a lot worse," Belladane urged.

"That certainly says a lot about his character, doesn't it? When you think about it, he's an unemployed, broke, alcoholic, illegal alien with PTSD. Yet you think he's a good catch. And you're right, he is," Shimi whispered.

"Eddie is a mailbox that produces a sweet love letter every single day. Just think about it." Belladane gave her niece another serious look.

"Yes, Mother! Come on Darcy, let's go home," Shimi got up and Darcy came out from under the table and stood by the door. "You're right though. He is lovely in a dozen ways previously unknown to me."

Shimi flicked on the yard light switch and picked her coat off the hook by the door.

Before Shimi had buttoned up her coat, Eddie came bounding into the kitchen, pulling on his own coat. "I'll walk you home, Shimi."

Belladane raised her eyebrows as if to say, "I told you so."

"Thanks Eddie. But I'm okay. Got to get back on the horse, know what I mean? I'm not feeling that afraid anymore," Shimi said, as convincingly as she could. She opened the door, turned and chirped, "Thanks for dinner, Auntie BellaBell! Night night, my lovelies."

"Sleep tight, my darling," Belladane said. She picked up a wicker hamper and started folding laundry on the kitchen table.

Little did Belladane know that Shimi would count every step as she walked down her aunt's lane, across the road, and up her own lane to her back door. 117 steps. She would count every single one. And she would rush straight ahead, like a person afraid of heights crossing a wobbly, rope extension bridge. The counting helped her wrestle her persistent fear of the night. Yet, as Shimi rushed home with her heart beating rapidly inside her chest, she wished she had taken Eddie up on his offer to walk her home, like she had done all the other nights. The beech trees that lined the lane rose up like tall slim ghosts, and some of the branches scraped against each other with deep groans. But Shimi kept moving. She wanted to run, like a drunk who is afraid he will fall over if he doesn't keep moving, but she knew she was probably being watched, so she walked. Painfully, she walked. She knew if she ever wanted to truly be brave again, she must start by pretending to be brave. The one begets the other.

Halfway across the distance between the two houses, Shimi felt like turning back. Running back to the comfort and security of Belladane's kitchen and Eddie's smile. Holding his arm as they had crossed through the night on all the other evenings had made her heart beat slowly and steadily. Now it was wild and racing. Shimi thought, perhaps this wasn't the time for her stubborn tug of pride and independence. Perhaps she should accept all the help her friends offered her on a daily basis. But Shimi marched on, intentionally, deliberately. She tried to imagine she was wearing a suit of armour – the indelible steel stitches of courage propelling her forward.

Shimi was getting tired of being a burden to her friends. Belladane was constantly clucking over her and Eddie was always taking care of her. She had definitely become what people call "high maintenance." She felt like a fragile science project. One mounted on a piece of Bristol board that takes over the entire dining room table. Her fears. Her growing belly. Her unpredictable moods. An exploding volcano.

After Shimi's departure, Eddie immediately left the kitchen to go back upstairs, but Belladane knew he would be standing in the dark stairwell by the front door, watching Shimi walk safely to her house. She knew it and she smiled. What Belladane didn't know was something Eddie knew all too well ... something of which he was painfully aware. Just because Shimi would reach her back door safely, didn't mean her fear would be over. Her fear would be there inside her kitchen, waiting for her, as reliable as the sunset. The fear would be there when she turned on the light. When she poured dog food into Darcy's dish in the corner of the kitchen. When she walked down the dark hall to her bedroom, her footsteps the only sound in the sickening, sudden silence. When she plugged in her cell phone for the night. When she dropped her clothes to the floor and stepped into her pyjamas. When her inside voice screamed curses to the silence, and her mouth found the courage to whisper: "I wish he was dead."

Eddie knew all the everyday fears. He knew all too well the courage it took to lead an ordinary life.

March 2023
Dear Elsa,

    Happy Birthday Sis! Hope you had a great 39th birthday for the umpteenth time! Ha! Sorry for the long delay, but I have no excuse really, other than I have been busy being happy! You read that right. I feel I am getting stronger and happier all the time. Thanks to my new life here.

    As Shimi gets bigger in her pregnancy, I am caring for the goats now full time. We have become good friends. They are such cool animals. They greet me every morning and love to nibble my clothes. I bring them treats of arrowroot biscuits and apples. If I ever do come home, I might just buy myself a goat. I wonder if a goat can be classified as an emotional support animal? Ha!

    Shimi is thinking of stopping her cheese business and selling her goats. That will be a sad day for me, but with the baby on the way, maybe it is a good time for her to lighten her load. As you can probably read between the lines, I am becoming very fond of Shimi. She is a lovely person, and we seem to really get each other.

    To tell you the truth, I think I'm falling in love with her. I haven't told her that, of course, wouldn't want to scare the poor woman. After all, I'm not the best catch in the world, now am I? But time will tell. Will keep you posted.

    I told Belladane I was going to write to you, and she said to say hello, and that she hopes to meet you someday! Her exact words were, "Any family of yours is a friend of mine." That's our Belladane.

    I hope you like the package I sent. One of Belladane's breast art paintings. I knew you didn't believe me. Just another interesting thing about her. She is outrageously real! Hang it up and think of me, and wish me luck!

IloveyaandImissya!
Eddie

XIX
(instead)

BY LATE APRIL, Shimi was six months pregnant and feeling great. Belladane said she glowed, and Eddie agreed. The bouts of morning sickness were over and the weight she had gained was still bearable, so she tried to enjoy her second trimester, knowing the next stage might not be quite so easy. She had already had one ultrasound at the hospital and was told the baby was developing nicely. Shimi was eating healthily (Belladane made sure of that) and taking her prenatal vitamins. She was getting good exercise with her daily walks, and she was sleeping well at night. Although she was trying to stay calm, her mental health remained her biggest concern.

She tried to live in the moment and not worry too much about down the road, but she still hadn't made a decision about keeping the baby or putting her up for adoption. She also continued to have some flashbacks and nightmares which left her feeling rattled, a feeling which often stayed with her for the rest of the day. These, she never talked about to her friends, as she didn't want to dwell upon that night anymore. She was tired of them always asking her, "How are you doing" with a concerned look in their eyes.

Plain and simple: she was tired of being a victim.

She liked Eddie's comment, "Keep one step ahead of your past," and she said it to herself often, but in reality, keeping that one step ahead of her past was very hard to do.

Despite the nightmares, Shimi realized she was no longer afraid. She could cope with each day and night and not feel that residual fear strangling her every thought and action. She realized that most of her emotions now fell under the category of anger. Why did that evil man get to violate her in such a gruesome way, then go off on his merry way in his fucking squeaky shoes and enjoy the rest of his life, whereas she would be saddled for the rest of her life with a constant reminder of him and the care and expense of a child she never wanted? Or if the baby was adopted, then a child would be in the world who would never know her biological parents and why she was given up for adoption. And that would not make for healthy self-esteem. So, the rapist gravely damaged her life and quite possibly the future life of the child. That's what made her angry - really angry. That night was an abhorrent gift that kept on giving, and she didn't know how to reconcile that.

Belladane insisted Shimi go to a clinic for a six-month check-up. At the clinic, she was examined by a middle-aged man named Doctor Abbottsford. "It's good to get a regular ultrasound to see that there is nothing wrong with the baby. After all, you are a geriatric mother."

Shimi flinched at the term, "geriatric." She could feel herself clenching her jaw, as she asked, "Well, if there was something wrong, could you fix it before the baby was born?"

The doctor pushed his shoulders up in a gesture indicating he didn't really know.

Before he could add anything, Shimi said, "Exactly. And if there was something wrong, I wouldn't terminate at this late stage either. I don't need to know the sex, or the possible health issues of the baby. Why would I want to worry about that before I need to? So why have another ultrasound?"

"Most mothers want as many as they can get," said Doctor. Abbottsford.

"Well, as you've said, I'm not most mothers." Shimi knew her comment was curt, but she didn't like Doctor Abbottsford's manner.

Why did he have to call her a "geriatric mother"? She thought that was more than slightly offensive. On one hand, he talked to her like she was a rare bird calling her a "geriatric mother," yet on the other hand, he expected her to be like all other mothers and want as many ultrasounds as possible.

Doctor Abbottsford asked Shimi several times about the father, and she was vague each time. He kept pressing the topic until finally she said, "I don't know anything about the father's medical history or genetics. Quite frankly, I don't know who the father is."

Doctor Abbottsford said, "Oh, I'm sorry," in a tone that Shimi could not quite interpret. Then he was silent, which filled Shimi's mind with a slew of questions.

What the hell was he "sorry" about?
Was he sorry he pressed me for the information?
Was he feeling sorry for me, that I don't know who the father is?

Any way she looked at it, the comment grated on her nerves. She knew there was a great deal of judgement involved when a woman says she doesn't know who fathered her child. She also knew she should tell the doctor the circumstance of her pregnancy, yet she didn't want to elaborate. She couldn't form the words in her mouth. Six months later, she felt she was slowly healing from that night ... but she would be happy if she didn't have to repeat the word "rape" again for the rest of her life.

Shimi wondered if she should take Belladane up on her offer and meet the midwife in her art class. Her aunt had only mentioned it about sixteen times, but Shimi was tired of always following Belladane's advice. She liked to think she could make her own decisions and manage her own problems, but deep-down Shimi knew she was simply being stubborn, as usual.

That night at dinner, after hearing about the doctor's appointment, Belladane suggested, once again, that Shimi might consider Alice, the midwife.

Shimi tried to look indifferent even though she knew she had been leading up to the conversation on purpose. "I thought I'd just use any doctor who was at the hospital when I go into labour. I'm not picky."

"Not picky? You already don't like Abbottsford. Look, you wouldn't go to a dentist with bad teeth or a fat weight loss doctor."

Eddie smirked, but he kept his mouth closed and kept eating his dinner. He was getting quite used to the pregnancy banter that occupied the dinner conversation each evening.

Belladane continued, "So why not get yourself the best care possible and I think that care comes from a knowledgeable woman, whose sole job is to deliver babies."

"How on earth do you come up with some of these comments?" Shimi laughed. "Okay! Okay! I'll meet your wonderful midwife. You're right. I'd rather have a llama assist me in this birth than Doctor Abbottsford."

"A llama? That didn't take much convincing," Belladane smirked. "You were just being difficult, as usual. Weren't you?"

Shimi chuckled and finally agreed even though she felt annoyed that Belladane had so much control over her life and was always right. "I suppose, but don't tell anyone I caved that easily. I have a reputation to keep, you know, of being independent and stubborn."

Belladane nudged Eddie's foot under the table and they both looked directly at Shimi and nodded their heads in agreement.

Belladane invited Alice over for dinner the next week. Like Belladane had predicted, Shimi liked Alice instantly. The tall, blonde, wholesome-looking woman didn't bring any Lindt chocolates, but she did arrive with a jar of naturally-made hand cream for Belladane, and a long, supportive body pillow for Shimi.

"I thought an artist can always use hand cream, and well I knew you were about six months, so I thought you might really enjoy this pillow. It's great for back and hip pain." Shimi was thrilled and hugged the pillow like a child who had just won the biggest, stuffed animal at a carnival.

Then Belladane formally introduced Shimi Montray to Alice Matters. Alice looked shocked and said, "Shimi Montray? Oh, I've heard of you. The cheesemaker. My husband interviewed you last year."

"Your husband is Leon Birkshire?" Shimi asked. "Wow, small world."

"No, just small province," Alice chuckled.

"How is Leon? I don't see him at the market anymore. He used to drop by occasionally."

"Oh, he's fine. Works a lot. I rarely see him either. He is always chasing down some story."

"Yes, I always enjoy his radio show," Shimi said. Then she added, "Say hello for me."

"I will. Now let's get down to business, shall we? I have heaps of questions to ask you and some weighing and measuring to do," Alice said.

Belladane excused herself and said, "Dinner will be ready at six. Don't be late, ladies. It's seafood gumbo tonight and I don't want the shrimp to be overcooked."

Shimi led Alice into her living room, and they sat together on the pretty, blue velvet sofa with throw pillows decorated in bright flowers, one with a vibrant blue bird on it, the other with the colourful face of Frida Kahlo. One of Belladane's huge paintings hung above the sofa, with splashes of vibrant blues, greens, and yellows. Shimi had redecorated several years ago, finally taking her parents' old, dark furniture to Habitat for Humanity. The refresh of the living room was cheery, bright, and more her style. There were two comfortable lime green armchairs opposite the sofa, in front of three massive white bookcases filled with books and the wood sculptures of an elephant, a deer, and a shore bird her parents had purchased during their various travels. Shimi loved the smoothness of the wood and the intricate grain that radiated throughout each piece. She often picked them up and simply held them to her chest.

Darcy curled up on his bed in the corner by the huge sunny window that overlooked the side garden and meadow. Within minutes, he started to snore, whimper, and flutter in his sleep. Both women found the dog entertaining to watch. He was the epitome of everything content in the world.

Alice had such a gentle, kind way about her; Shimi felt her fear of meeting Alice disperse as quickly as smoke from a cigar. They discussed the symptoms of pregnancy that Shimi was experiencing, and Alice was able to give expert advice on each.

Alice asked, "Are you enrolling in Lamaze or any birthing classes?"

Shimi said, "Definitely not."

"That's okay. I can teach you all you need to know about having a healthy delivery. We can talk about the type of labour you want, positions you can use, your breathing techniques, of course, and any equipment you might enjoy using," Alice said.

"Equipment?" Shimi asked, looking rather confused.

"Don't worry about that now. I just mean things like a large exercise ball which you can sit on during labour, straight back chairs, aromatherapy, simple things like that. I will have everything you need. I will help you through all the final stages," Alice said.

When Alice also asked Shimi what type of birth she wanted, Shimi looked totally confused. Then Alice explained that there could be the traditional hospital birth, a home birth, a tub of water, and so on. The possibilities seemed endless. Shimi hadn't given it any thought.

"I guess having it here at home would be my first preference," Shimi said. "But because I'm older, a 'geriatric mother' as Doctor Abbottsford called me, should I have it in the hospital?"

"Oh, I hate that term. It is so not necessary. And so many women now are having babies in their forties. They practically outnumber women in their twenties, so the medical terminology has to adapt. Geriatric is such a demeaning and judgemental word. We don't call men fathering babies at a later age 'geriatric fathers,' now do we?" Alice said.

"Just another horrible double standard. Thanks, Alice," Shimi said, rubbing her baby belly.

"Shimi, I have successfully delivered many babies at home by mothers in their forties. As long as you are healthy, have good blood pressure, your baby is in the right position, and all that, we can start at home, and if we need to, we can go to the hospital. You're not that far from Charlottetown. What about the father? Will he be helping you with the delivery?"

"No!" Shimi said rather loudly. "I definitely want to have the baby here. I like privacy."

"Yes, of course, and we often feel more comfortable and safer in our own home," Alice said.

Safe. That's a word that Shimi could not say easily anymore. She hesitated for a moment, and then she started to silently cry. Alice put down her laptop where she had been taking notes, turned to Shimi saying, "What is it? Or maybe just crazy hormones?"

Shimi stood up and walked to the large window that overlooked her back garden. She looked at the bird feeder outside. Every couple of days, she faithfully filled up five large feeders in her yard, one outside each prominent window: kitchen, living room, bedroom, her office, and barn. There had been so much snow this winter; Eddie had taken over the task, but she was now happy the snow had almost entirely melted. There were only a few icy patches left in the yard, so she could visit her birds more often. She stood watching the goldfinches flit alongside the sparrows. There were three mourning doves feeding off the ground. They were her favourite. She loved how calm they were and the startled little squeak their wings made when they took flight.

"The songbirds are declining at a shocking rate. Since the 1970's, over three billion breeding adult birds have been lost in practically every species. But especially the small ones, like sparrows, chickadees, nuthatches, and juncos."

Alice came and stood by Shimi in front of the window. "I didn't know that, but now you mention it, I don't hear as many in the morning. Do you remember as kids, the birds would wake you every morning at dawn?" Alice asked. "They were so loud."

"Yes," Shimi said. "The North American forests alone have lost over one billion birds." Shimi rubbed her baby belly. "Perhaps this little one will be walking through a silent forest when they're older. Can you imagine?"

"Awful," Alice commented. "What do you think is the main problem?"

"Well, it's compounded. Agricultural and lawn care pesticides. People say they love birds, and then they spray their yard so they can have perfect weedless grass. It's ridiculous. The loss of habitat, like grasslands, have made ground-nesting birds decline by 53% since 1970. Large cities impact migratory paths. Air pollution. Domestic cats kill a lot. Lights on in high-rises at night kill thousands every night. The list goes on and on. They're all just trying to survive, despite our human nonsense."

"Such a shame," Alice said.

"They are discovering that birds are smarter than we realized. There are sparrows and finches in Mexico City that build their nests from cigarette butts. And the nicotine in the filter stops ticks and fleas from entering their nests."

"That's incredible. And when you think of it, probably the best use of cigarettes, don't you think?"

Shimi was silent for a few seconds, then quietly said, "Yes, the birds have taken something bad and turned it into something good."

Shimi slammed her hand onto the wide window sill. Alice jumped, the birds scattered, and Darcy woke up, stood up, looked around, turned in a circle and then lay back down with a loud sigh.

"I was raped," Shimi said fiercely. Her anger came out of her so suddenly it even shocked her.

"Oh Shimi, I'm so sorry. I'm so … so sorry." Alice raised her hand to place it on the woman's back, but Shimi flinched and quickly stepped aside.

"No, I'm sorry. I don't know what's wrong with me. It's like my emotions are on steroids lately."

"No doubt," Alice replied.

"You know, I've never said the 'rape' word out loud to anyone except six months ago to the police. And believe me, once was more than enough. I didn't even tell dear, old Doctor Abbottsford."

"Shimi, I can't imagine how horrible it has been for you. Just know, you can tell me as much or as little as you like. Never feel threatened by my questions, okay?" Alice said.

"I'm sorry, but I'm so angry, Alice. But I just feel … I just feel soaked in anger. And this anger seems to pile on top of other angers that I have held inside for years. My parents dying. Dropping out of school. Never finding the right guy. Doing a job for so many years that I am so tired of. This rape. This baby! Even the blessed songbirds dying. I just feel marinated in anger." Shimi held tightly to the window sill with both hands, placed her forehead against the glass and let out a deep sigh.

"You are totally justified in your anger. I get it. What happened to you isn't fair. And it certainly isn't fair for the birds! But anger and stress are hormone disruptors, as you probably know. So, for the sake of your baby, we need to work on ways of addressing your anger, helping you decrease your stress and feel more relaxed."

"What I need is a stiff drink several times a day," Shimi said.

"Well, if anyone deserves a stiff drink, it's you. But it's good you aren't drinking," Alice said. "You're doing the right thing. We will work on your stress together. I can teach you breathing exercises, some yoga stretches, and other strategies which might help."

"Sometimes I just want to scream all day long, or cry, or beat something. But I try to hold it together, as I know it would kill Belladane. She tries so hard to make my life perfect. She likes to fix everything. It's just her way. She's done so much for me over the years. She is my aunt, my mother, my best friend."

"We are all blessed to have Belladane in our corner. But I'm sure she wouldn't want you hiding your true emotions. She loves you and only wants you to be happy," Alice said.

"Ah yes, happiness. Eddie often talks about happiness. The elusive happiness," Shimi said in a cold, indifferent tone.

"Eddie?" Alice inquired.

"You'll meet Eddie at dinner. He's another person in my corner who is also trying to grab some happiness."

"I believe it is a worthwhile pursuit ... and sometimes it isn't the conventional ways that make us happy. We have to create a life that works for us," Alice said.

"Thanks, Alice. And another thing ...while I'm being perfectly honest. And we're talking about happiness and all. I don't know how to say this delicately ... so I'll just say it. I'm not even sure I want to keep this baby. I felt I did at first, but as the months go by, I don't know whether I really want to be a mother. Does that make me a horrible person? I know I'm supposed to feel blessed for having a baby."

"Well, you're only blessed if you want one. And not wanting one doesn't make you a horrible person. I will support you, whatever you decide, however you want to handle this," Alice replied with concern and kindness in her voice.

"I want to have a strong, healthy baby, and I know I already love this baby, but I don't know whether I will love being a mother," Shimi said. "I don't know whether I want this event to be the climax of my life, know what I mean?"

"Did you consider termination?" Alice asked.

"Yes, but I was rather late discovering I was pregnant, and then I thought I was given some signs ... a goat fetus, a whale fetus ... it's a long story ... but they all seemed to point to keeping the baby. Sounds stupid, I know."

"Not at all. When I have tough decisions to make, I often look for a sign," Alice said.

"I haven't told Belladane I might not keep the baby. Please don't mention it," Shimi said. "I want to wait until I'm more certain, either way."

"Whatever we talk about will always stay between you and me," Alice assured her.

The two women stood quietly for a few moments. The birds had come back to feed, and a robin began to enthusiastically bathe in a large, ceramic planter tray Shimi had placed on top of a stump to create a bird bath. Since the weather was still chilly at night, Eddie filled it up with fresh, warm water each morning. The robin fluttered her wings with joy and the water splashed around her making tiny rainbows of sunlight.

"I love the birds," Shimi said, almost to herself. "They make me happy."

Alice chuckled, "You want to hear something kind of weird? I don't know why, but I'm kind of scared of birds."

"What a pair we are! You love babies, and they scare me to death. I love birds, and they scare you. We're going to get along just fine," Shimi said, with a chuckle.

"Yes, we will," Alice said. "Now let's get over to Belladane's. It's time for that seafood gumbo."

XX
(intimately)

EVERYONE WELCOMED SPRING by tossing boots and toques to the back of their closets. Daffodils and tulips poked up in Belladane's garden, and tiny purple crocuses came up around the mailbox. As Shimi barely tolerated winter at the best of times, spring always felt like a welcome renewal. A new beginning, more symbolic to her than New Year's Eve. A chance to start over.

Shimi sat in the barn's large room with the glass cheese cabinets where she stored her cheese ready for sale. She had been slowly decreasing her milk production over the winter, and she knew she wanted to stop her business entirely. She had stopped going to the Farmers Market when she began to look pregnant, knowing she would no longer be able to hide behind her big sweaters and heavy woollen skirts. There was no way she could face questions about the baby. For the last few months, an organic shop in town had been selling her cheese for her.

She had CBC radio on and was listening to some lovely Celtic tunes. She rubbed her belly thoughtfully. Alice was coming to see her every few weeks and said she was doing great. The baby was growing and would probably be a big one. That news gave Shimi the chills. She was reminded of some women talking in a yoga class years ago about childbirth. She hadn't really paid that much attention at the time, but now she could readily remember Muriel, a jovial woman in her late fifties who had said, "My daughter had natural childbirth and she was ripped from her ass to her appetite."

All the ladies had chuckled, then agreed that it often happened. Then many talked candidly about their own horror stories. Their stories and the word "ripped" now haunted Shimi everyday.

This pregnancy was already doing awful things to her body: her back hurt all the time; she still was sensitive to some smells; and her gastrointestinal sounds were without compare, sometimes even startling the goats. Now thinking what the delivery may also do to her made Shimi cringe and realize she was more than a little scared.

"I've left one fear behind, just to cling onto a new one," Shimi thought.

Eddie came into the room from the goat side of the barn. He was doing all the goat care now and was very good at it. Shimi secretly loved to watch the way he handled the girls. He never started milking a goat until he had a little chat with her first, and half an Arrowroot biscuit offered from his pocket. The other half was given after milking. He would give the girls a little scratch behind their ears and a sweet pat on their backs. The goats loved him and couldn't get enough of his company. As soon as they heard him walking up the lane each morning, they would call out to him from the barn. If Shimi was sleeping in, the ruckus from Betty and BamBam alone would instantly tell her that Eddie was in the vicinity.

"Hey Shimi, how's it going?" Eddie said, as he plopped himself down on the bench next to her.

"I'm good. Getting fatter every day."

"I think pregnant women look so beautiful," Eddie said. "But then again that's easy for a man to say."

That was one of the many things Shimi liked about Eddie. He seemed like a natural feminist, who realized the unfair double standards between men and women that were still rampant in the world. If she had to put it simply, she would say he was enlightened.

"Thanks Eddie. This is a perfect time to talk to you about the goats. I've made a decision. I'm going to stop making cheese. I think I have enough product for a couple more months, but I am not going back to the market ... ever ... not even after the baby. And once the shop runs out of my cheese, well that will be it."

"Wow! I knew you have been thinking of quitting for awhile now, but it's still a shock. How do you feel about it?"

"I feel kind of scared and sad, but at the same time I'm relieved. I've kind of wanted to stop for a couple of years now, and this seems like the perfect time."

"What about the goats?" Eddie asked.

"I don't quite know yet. I might keep a few and sell a few. That decision will be much harder than stopping my cheese business. As you know, they are sweethearts and friends. I love the goats, well, except maybe for cranky Rhoda."

"Ah, she's just misunderstood," Eddie winked.

"Kind of like me?" Shimi asked.

"Kind of like all of us," Eddie smiled.

Shimi nodded in agreement. "Thank you for all your hard work, Eddie. I couldn't have done it without you. I'm not paying you enough, you know," Shimi gave him a gentle nudge of her elbow.

"Listen, you pay me more than enough. These goats have been my salvation. They've given me a purpose in life. I was so lost before I came here, but you and Belladane and the goats, and I can't forget old Darcy ..." Eddie bent over and touched Darcy on the head, who was curled up beside them. "Well, you all brought me back to life. The goats make me happy when they greet me each morning, and you know how we all need more happiness in our lives." Eddie grinned at Shimi.

"Yes. Yes, I know. I'm still writing in my happiness journal and feeling grateful for each small thing," Shimi said. "Belladane was right; writing it down helps."

"Is Belladane ever wrong?" Eddie asked.

Shimi shrugged, "I guess not yet, anyway. And how irritating is that?"

"Well, it will probably be good not to be so busy once the baby comes. You'll need all the time you can get then."

The baby! Everything always goes back to the baby!

Shimi jumped up quickly from the bench, but her left foot was hooked behind the other and she stumbled forward. Eddie instantly caught her and gently lowered her back onto the bench.

"Whoa," he said. "That was close."

Shimi grabbed her stomach and rubbed it. She could feel the baby moving, adjusting to the jolt. Eddie lowered his head and gently kissed her hand over her stomach. She was shocked at his sudden tenderness, the intimacy of this small but revealing gesture. She wanted to kiss his lips, but instead she grabbed his hand and placed it on her stomach.

"There," she said. "Right there. Can you feel it?"

He hesitated for a moment, then looked at her with wide-eyed wonder. "Gosh, isn't that amazing. Never felt a baby before. If you want, I can help you get a room ready. Build him or her ... or I guess I'm now supposed to say build 'them' a little nursery. These last couple of months will go by fast."

Shimi sat silently. Eddie began to wonder if she would ever speak. He worried that perhaps he had said something wrong. Perhaps making the pronoun joke was inappropriate?

Shimi wanted her own life back. Every conversation now was always about the baby. She wished she could be anyone else but herself. Anyone else but a rape victim. A messed up pregnant rape victim. But everyone has their issues, she thought. She couldn't think of anyone she would want to be, even in her recent state. She thought it might be nice to be nonhuman for a change. A teacup? A bar of soap, perhaps? A book? Yes, a well-loved book.

Shimi felt so angry inside, so confused about every aspect of her life. Her anger was relentless. It now owned her. Was bought and paid for. Individually wrapped.

She swallowed her anger and finally spoke. "I don't know whether I'm going to need a nursery. Know what I mean? Are you shocked?" Shimi asked without looking at Eddie.

"It's your choice, Shimi. No one is going to judge you. No one can begin to understand all the feelings you've had to deal with during this pregnancy."

Shimi knew she couldn't Pollyanna her way through her pregnancy and all the feelings and decisions that were bitterly attached to it. "Thanks Eddie. I'm so uncertain. One minute I feel one way; the next minute I feel the opposite. It's like I have emotional whiplash! Alice calls it hormones, but it's more than that. All I know is I want a simple life, and I want to forget that night. I never wanted a child, but if I did, I certainly didn't want it to be the result of the most scary, violent night of my life. And I don't know how to reconcile that."

"Whatever you need, Shimi," Eddie said, as he gently took her hand in his. "I'm not going anywhere."

"Sometimes I wake up in the middle of the night. And for a second, I wonder why my back aches, and then I remember. And suddenly I panic like a goldfish on a carpet, and I feel like I can't breathe. And then, at other moments, there's a little nudge from inside of me, and I rub my belly, and I feel a pang of love for this little munchkin, this little miracle." Shimi continued to hold her belly, knowing at this very moment the cells in her uterus were continuing to rapidly multiply and take total control of her, both body and soul.

"Yes," Eddie said, turning his thoughts inward. "Miracles! Some you love and other miracles you hate."

Shimi knew Eddie was thinking of his combat duty and the friends he left behind. She clenched his hand tightly and said, "I'm glad for one miracle in particular, that you made it out of there alive."

Eddie lifted his arm up and Shimi tucked herself in beside him, resting her head upon his shoulder. He wrapped his arm around her.

"Oh, how I want to go back to my old life, where I had no real problems, so I bitched about stupid stuff, like the long line at the grocery store checkout, or the price of gas, or burning my toast," Shimi said.

"Everything is going to work out, Shimi. You'll see. It will be as it is meant to be." Eddie's voice was soft and reassuring.

Shimi and Eddie sat silently, and suddenly she realized that for the first time in a long time she felt at peace. This quiet moment with Eddie was a single note of music, beautifully played. And often that is enough.

XXI
(naturally)

BELLADANE WORKED STEADILY on her breast art. She loved the way the paint felt on her skin, the way the canvas seemed to guide her, tell her which way to move to create an interesting effect. She worked in her studio most afternoons, and was able to finish about four paintings a week. Through her online website and various local galleries, she typically sold about two paintings a week. Luckily, she sold four or five paintings a week during the summer months when tourists flooded to Prince Edward Island.

Shimi quietly turned the doorknob of Belladane's studio and stepped into the room. Her aunt's back was to her. Belladane turned around, while she was deep in thought, wiping orange and turquoise paint off her large breasts with a towel.

Belladane gasped. "Jeez Louise! You sneak up like a Prius! Nearly scared the livin' piss out of me." Belladane gave a hearty chuckle.

"Sorry Auntie, I should have knocked. Just wanted to have a chat before dinner tonight."

Shimi rarely ventured into Belladane's studio. She respected her aunt's need for concentration. Shimi was proud of Belladane's commitment to her art and the fact that she could make a decent living from it, something she knew many artists couldn't do.

"What's up?" Belladane asked. She continued to wipe the paint off her hands and breasts.

"Don't stop on my account," Shimi said.

"Ah, time to call it a day," Belladane said. "I'm getting tired. Not a spring chicken anymore."

"You have such beautiful breasts. And you're sixty-six. How does that happen?"

"Well, for one, I've never had kids," Belladane said.

"Ouch," Shimi laughed. "Does that mean mine are going to be ruined like the rest of me?"

"No, of course not, Honey. You've got lovely breasts and they are certainly getting bigger by the month. Are you sure you don't want to help me with some paintings? No one would know the difference," Belladane laughed, as she pulled on her tee shirt. "Now that you've given up making cheese, we could pump out these paintings twice as fast. What do you say?"

"Ah ... that's a hard no! Although I do enjoy watching you. I find it so sensual now. I remember the first time I walked in on you painting with your breasts. Years ago, when you just did it for a hobby. I was horrified. I thought you'd gone totally bonkers."

"Well, most would think I've gone at least half crazy! But who cares, right? So how are you doing these days? How are you coping?"

"Oh, I'm fine. I'm doing okay," Shimi said as she turned her head to look at Belladane's drying artwork.

"You say you're okay, but I know your sock is slipping off in your shoe." Belladane made fierce eye contact with Shimi.

"Oh, you and your metaphors! Okay! Okay! Some days are good. Some days are bad. I still shower too much. Sometimes I still want to sleep under my bed, but today is a good day, so let me enjoy it, okay?"

"Great! And how are your breasts feeling these days?"

"Well, they can be quite painful at times, but they're not bad right now."

"Great! Pregnancy takes its toll, doesn't it? Take your top off and let's paint them. Give it a try. Go wild for once, Shimi. It will help you relax."

"Do you have a friggin' concussion?" Shimi growled.

With her large hands on her hips, Belladane stared at her, saying, "That was pretty good, actually. But no, I don't have a concussion. What are you afraid of, my dear? It's easy ... like pulling carrots."

"Oh, okay, okay!" Shimi pulled off her loose blouse and took off her bra. She used to be a B cup, but had started wearing a C. She felt self-conscious in front of her aunt, and held her blouse up to her chest, but deep down she knew if she was going to make it through this pregnancy and delivery, she would have to lose some of her shyness and inhibitions.

Belladane selected some soothing music: Coldplay, Elton John ballads, music she knew Shimi would enjoy.

"Now sit on this stool and just let yourself relax. Let yourself go." Belladane picked up a jar of green acrylic paint on the window sill that had been warming in the afternoon sun. She dipped her fingers into it, then came over to Shimi. "Just close your eyes and breathe deeply. Allow yourself to relax."

Shimi exhaled a large breath and closed her eyes. "I can't believe I'm letting you do this."

Belladane took her finger and stroked Shimi's chest just below her neck, with the green paint. She made small circles and then began to make bigger consecutive ones. She then took some yellow paint and moved it around the green circles and drew the paint down her breasts. Shimi felt a shimmer of excitement up her spine, but she continued to tell herself to relax. Belladane took more green paint and brought tender strokes up her breasts towards her neck. She made radiant blue swirls around her nipples and splashes of tiny orange dots and streaks along her collarbone. She took great care in her painting. She took even greater care in her touch. Belladane loved this woman. She had loved her since Shimi was six years old. She was the daughter Belladane never had and she was happy that Shimi trusted her enough to let her do this to her aching body and sore bloated breasts.

Shimi continued to revel in the feelings Belladane was giving her. It had been so long since she felt good, felt excited about her body.

"Ok, we're done. Have a look in the mirror," Belladane said.

Shimi turned and looked in the full-length mirror. She looked like a goddess of trees. Green branches and smudges of leaves twirled across her breasts. Just below her neck flashes of blue and yellow sunlight burst through the intertwining branches. Shimi felt as if she were laying in the most magnificent forest, looking up at a radiant blue sky.

"This is beautiful, Belladane. I look like I am sprouting branches. I'm Mother Earth."

"You are a goddess of nature, inside and out."

"And you're right, it did feel good. The paint was so soft and warm. It was rather exciting, really. Can I tell you something?"

"Of course, my dear. Anything. What's up?" Belladane asked, as she wiped her hands on a towel.

"That night … I got excited. I mean sexually. And I feel really weirded out and ashamed about that. Rather disgusted, really," Shimi said.

"Well, Honey, I would think that could easily happen with all that adrenalin pumping. It would be an involuntary reaction of your body. Men can get erections at the least sensual times, so it only makes sense that could happen to women too, doesn't it?"

"But it was gruesome, and I thought he was going to kill me. How could I get excited? And maybe he knew that. It makes me sick to my stomach, that he might have known that," Shim replied. "Maybe he'll come back."

"Oh, Shimi, he's not coming back. And the lubrication was simply your body's way of protecting itself from internal injury. I think that response is totally natural," Belladane said.

"But I orgasmed," Shimi said. "How could that happen?"

"Shimi, I'm telling you. What happened to you was not your fault. You have no control over how your body reacted to that violence. We need to read more about this, but I'm sure this happens a lot."

"I never told the police that part. I was worried they would not take it seriously, if they thought that I enjoyed it," Shimi said.

"Even though I have no doubt your body acted entirely with its own protective reactions, I agree. I wouldn't tell the police. If the creep is caught, the bastard's defence lawyers may use this information. So best to keep it to yourself," Belladane said.

"Yes, you're right. I did Google it, and it did say it can be normal, but it still feels abnormal to me and disgusting," Shimi said.

"Look, he was disgusting, not you. You have nothing to be ashamed of, but if you are writing about this in your journal, be careful. You never know. In the future you wouldn't want it subpoenaed."

"Oh, I never thought of that," Shimi answered, looking newly concerned.

"It's all good. You're in control of the future and how things go from here. And all these feelings and questions you have are normal. And you can talk to me about anything, you know that, right?"

"Yes, Mother," Shimi teased, with a smile.

"I'm very proud of you, Shimi, and how you're handling everything and you know someone else who would be very proud of you? Your mom."

"Thanks, Auntie," Shimi said, with tears sparkling in her eyes.

"Now, let's take your picture. Then you can look at it and remember your beautiful bush," Belladane smirked.

"Really! You make the awfullest jokes!" Shimi said, but she handed Belladane her phone.

Belladane took two photos: one of Shimi's entire body and a close-up of simply the painting on her chest. She handed the phone back to Shimi.

"Now press your chest up against this canvas and we'll see what happens." Belladane handed her a canvas washed in light green paint. Shimi pressed it to her chest and held it there for a moment.

"Voila," Shimi said, as she pulled it from her chest. "Hey, that isn't half bad. I kind of like it. A beautiful abstract forest."

"A keepsake for you. Your first breast art," Belladane laughed. "Now show this painting to Eddie. He likes art. No, better yet, show him the photos."

"Oh my God, would you give it a rest," Shimi said, as she started to wipe the paint from her body and get back into her blouse. "Although I must confess, Eddie did kiss me in the barn the other day. To be exact, he kissed my hand on my stomach. It was very sweet."

"That is wonderful. That Eddie, he does love with his sleeves rolled up. He is one of a kind. What happened next?" Belladane pulled up a stool and looked at Shimi in an exaggerated wide-eyed stare. "I want to know every detail."

"Nothing more happened. We just talked."

"Shimi, try not to let your normal desires get lost in fear and doubt." Belladane put her hand on Shimi's shoulder.

"I don't know whether I will ever be able to let someone touch me again."

"Look, you're too young and vital to be a lonely ship squeezed into a bottle for the rest of your life. And you know, a new touch might help you forget about the horrible touch. I know that's easy for me to say, but just think about it." Belladane gently touched her niece's cheek, leaving a tiny fleck of yellow paint on her face.

"A lonely ship in a bottle? Really? Where do you get this stuff? When your boobs retire, you should write a book on metaphors. Could be a bestseller."

"Ha! Ha! Very funny. When I was a kid and started swearing, my parents said chronic cursing was a sign of low intelligence. They kept telling me to explain myself better with better words. But hey, don't change the topic. We're talking about Eddie."

"I'm trying. I really am. We had a nice cuddle and a really good talk. I confessed I might not want to keep the baby." Shimi looked at Belladane for a reaction.

Belladane didn't look shocked. She hugged Shimi, tenderly rubbing her back and holding the back of Shimi's head close to her chest. "This is your life, Shimi. And you have plenty of time to decide about that. You might feel differently after she's born."

"Oh, it's a she?"

"Yes, she is definitely a she."

"Maybe I should be considering my options now though. Maybe I should be looking into private adoption or talk with an agency."

"All in good time, my darling. All in good time."

"So, maybe you should stop crocheting baby blankets and hats?"

"And how did you know about that?"

"I know more than you think," Shimi said, picking up her bra and the canvas. As she started walking toward the door, she added, "You know, dear Auntie, you are my still, stable point in this wicked, whirling world."

"Who said that?" Belladane asked.

"T.S. Elliot, I think, but I'm paraphrasing rather generously," Shimi replied.

"Well, thank you, my darling. You are my constant, as well."

"Constant pain in the ass," Shimi retorted.

"There, there now. Stop paraphrasing the paraphrases and scram."

"What's for dinner tonight?" Shimi asked as she began to walk out of the room.

"Frog legs in muddy pond water sauce."

"Oh boy! My favourite!" Shimi said as she turned and walked through the doorway, waving her middle finger above her head in a playful salute.

XXII
(solemnly)

SHAWN MORGAN AND Joanne Belly arrived early one June morning with their half-ton truck and double horse trailer. As they backed up the lane towards Shimi's barn, her heart jumped into her throat. Was she really doing this? Selling her sweet goats. She loved her "girls," but deep down she knew it was time. Time for a change.

"Change is hard," Shimi thought, "but even harder when you don't know what you're changing to."

Am I quitting my cheese business to be a full-time mother?
Or a childless mother?
Maybe I should simply move to Bali.

She had always wanted to go there. The documentaries she had watched had fascinated her: the landscape, the Balinese culture, the vibrant colours. Her parents had raved about their trip there.

She exhaled a heavy sigh. She knew she was lucky to have a choice. A choice in creating a new life for herself. She knew most women in the world didn't have that luxury, but it didn't make her decision any easier.

After a long talk with Eddie, she had decided to keep two goats. Betty and BamBam were the oldest and near retirement, so they would stay as pets. Belladane had assured her niece that she could easily care for the old goats, if Shimi ever wanted to travel.

Respectfully, Shawn and Joanne stood back a few steps, while Shimi walked around the yard and touched each of her goats, saying her goodbyes. Shimi talked about the personality of each goat, while Joanne took their photos and made note of names and little idiosyncrasies. Shimi thought that was wonderful. The girls would keep their own names. She was pleased she had picked this young couple and their farm to be the new home for her goats.

As the goats were loaded into the trailer, enticed by Eddie with pieces of apple and Arrowroot cookies, Shimi felt the lump in her throat grow. The end of an era. The end of her amusing goats and her musical cheese. But it was time to move on.

The joy of it all had left her, and she knew because of that night it would never come back. She didn't want that one night to be the touchstone of her life, but she didn't know how to change it. The memory of that night was a key left in a door, a door that could now never be securely locked.

As Joanne handed Shimi a wad of cash, she assured her that the goats were going to a good home. Shimi was welcome to visit them anytime and see their living conditions.

"Drop in anytime you're in the neighbourhood," she said, as she gave Shimi a gentle hug. "You don't need to call ahead."

"Thanks. And you call anytime, if you have any questions," Shimi answered.

Joanne talked about how excited she was to learn how to use goat milk and make her own cheese. Just outside Victoria-by-the-Sea they were making a little homestead, and were thrilled with the opportunity to find such beautiful goats.

As the truck drove slowly down the laneway, Shimi stood in the middle of the lane, watching them leave. She could see her girls clustered together at the front of the trailer. But Rhoda stood alone. She had her face up against the small slit in the trailer's wall, and she was looking directly at Shimi. Cranky Rhoda was the goat watching the only home and owner she had ever known slowly disappear. The image of Rhoda's nose and eyes searching through the small opening touched Shimi's heart. Shimi looked again, to assure herself it was Rhoda. Rhoda, the goat least loveable, was the one looking longingly at her. She couldn't believe it. She wanted to run after them, stop them, and take them all off the trailer. Put them back in their yard where they belonged. Feed them Arrowroot cookies and let them nibble on her sleeve. Tears came to the corner of her eyes, and she wiped them with the back of her hand. Darcy sat by her knee and licked her wet hand.

Shimi was frozen in place. The truck beeped twice in a friendly goodbye, and Joanne stuck her hand out the window and waved. Shimi took a deep breath and waved back.

Goodbye my girls!

Goodbye Rhoda!

Then the goats were gone. Out of sight.

Eddie looked at Shimi, and she knew he had seen the same thing. A final hint of affection from Rhoda, the distant, unfriendly goat.

"Goodbye, sweet Rhoda," Eddie said, and then he took Shimi's hand in his and led her to the barn. They sat down on the bench. Their typical spot. It had been a place of many conversations since Eddie was found washing in Belladane's stream over a year ago. Shimi took great comfort in Eddie's calm. He was a man who didn't need to fill every moment with conversation, yet at the same time one felt like he was still connected, still present. And when he did speak, he got right to the matter, no matter how hard the topic might be.

"Pretty sad to see them go, isn't it?" Eddie said.

"Yes. Have I made the right decision? I felt so anxious watching them leave, so now I don't know," Shimi pondered.

"I think both you and the girls are going to be fine. Better than fine. It's great that they are staying together and going to a great farm. And you ... why, you're starting a whole new exciting chapter of your life. It will all come together in time. You'll see," Eddie said.

"I hope so, Eddie. I finally made a decision about the goats, so now I have to make a decision about the baby." Shimi shuddered to think about it. She rubbed her belly and looked tenderly down at Darcy at her feet.

"All in good time, Shimi. All in good time."

"I hope so," Shimi said. "I just feel so anxious all the time. Believe it or not, I used to be a rather calm person."

"No, you're simply getting stronger and stronger like some kind of super germ," Eddie said.

"What? Did you just call me a germ?" Shimi raised her eyebrows playfully.

"No, that didn't come out right. Never mind. I'm terrible at analogies. I'm just trying to keep up with Belladane and all her crazy comparisons."

"No. Not possible. No one has the creative flare that Belladane has," Shimi laughed.

"True that! But seriously, you are getting stronger even though you feel anxious. Inside I still feel anxious sometimes, but at least I'm able to fake it on the outside a bit better," Eddie chuckled. "I guess you won't be needing my help much anymore, now the goats are gone. I'll continue to care for Betty and BamBam, if you want."

"That would be wonderful, Eddie," Shimi said. "That's if you're going to be here."

Eddie looked at Shimi affectionately and replied, "I'm not going anywhere."

"Great. I'm glad." Shimi could feel her face turning red. She suddenly felt uncomfortable. Was her affection for Eddie too obvious? She felt like her heart was visibly dangling from her chest. So, she quickly changed the subject. "And I was wondering if you could do something else for me."

"Sure. Anything," he said.

"There's an old wooden cradle, looks handmade, with all that other junk in the back of Belladane's barn. It's a bit of a mess, but I was wondering if I might be able to use it ... for the baby... for the time being. Would you mind digging it out for me?"

"No problem. I'll give it a once over and see if it can be salvaged."

"I was going to put her in a deep dresser drawer, use that as a baby bed, but Belladane thought that was too ... too ... something or other," Shimi said, leaving the lost word dangling in the air.

"Oh, we know she's a girl, do we?"

"It seems Belladane does!"

Within two weeks, Eddie walked up Shimi's Lane, his arms stretched up high in the air, carrying the most beautiful antique cradle Shimi had ever seen, upside down over his head. He had dug it out, scrubbed, repaired, and sanded it.

"I put on a coat of non-toxic white paint. I hope you like it," Eddie said.

They brought it to the house and put it in the corner of the kitchen, next to Darcy's bed.

"It's beautiful. Thanks, Eddie." Shimi gave Eddie a hug, and as she held onto his back, she could feel his muscles relax. With her cheek against Eddie's shoulder, she could feel the distance between them collapse, and she wanted to stay like that forever. She wanted to kiss his mouth and tousle his curly hair. She wanted to touch her lips tenderly to each of his sad eyes and bury her face in the crook of his neck, but she pulled away. She looked quickly at the cradle and said, "Now I'll make a little mattress for it, and she will be all set."

"Sounds perfect," Eddie said, with a generous grin. "She'll be here before you know it. Are you getting scared?"

"Terrified!" Shimi said.

XXIII
(becoming)

SHIMI WAS BRUSHING Betty and in the process of giving her right ear a good scratch, when her water broke. Darcy started sniffing around Shimi's legs, like she had just deposited a steak dinner at her feet. Then he started barking and no matter how much she yelled at him to be quiet, he wouldn't stop.

Shimi held her baby belly, waddled through the barn and out the main entrance to the lane. She had never been much of a cell phone person, but Alice had encouraged her to carry it at all times.

"Always have it in your pocket," Alice had said.

"What if I don't have a pocket in my stretch pants?" Shimi had joked.

"Then strap it to your head," Alice had laughed.

As she walked to the house, she took the phone from the back pocket of her shorts and called Alice. She answered immediately.

"My water just broke," Shimi said, trying to sound calm.

"I'm on my way. I'll be about 20 minutes, tops. Just relax and breathe and remember everything we've talked about," Alice said.

"This is really happening," Shimi said, with wonderment in her voice.

"Yes. You're going to do great. Don't worry! We've got this! I'll be right there."

Despite following Shimi closely to the house, the screen door had snapped back to the frame before Darcy could scoot inside with her. Now he continued to bark outside the kitchen door. He definitely knew something was wrong. Shimi often wondered where Darcy got his brains. She knew it certainly wasn't from her training.

Shimi eased herself down onto a kitchen chair, and before she could get herself settled, Eddie came crashing through the door with Belladane huffing and puffing right behind.

"I was just about to call you two," Shimi said.

"Darcy let us know right away," Eddie said. "I told him to." And then he smiled.

"Oh, did you now? Well maybe you can also tell him he can shut up now," Shimi smiled, but then bent forward, wide-eyed with a small contraction.

Belladane flew into action. She put water in the kettle and set it to boil.

"I don't think we need the water hot quite yet," Shimi said.

"Maybe not for you, but I need a strong cup of coffee," Belladane chirped. "But first, let's get you into some dry clothes, shall we?"

She held Shimi's arm as she guided her to the bedroom, helped her get out of her wet things, and got her settled in an oversized pink tee shirt that fell to her knees.

"Comfy?" Belladane asked.

"No!" Shimi growled. She looked up at her aunt with a terrified grin.

"You're going to do great." Belladane patted her on the back.

"That's what they all say," Shimi sniped.

"They also say most women in labour are bitchy, so I see that is true," Belladane quipped.

Shimi scowled, then had to smile.

The birthing supplies were in the corner of the bedroom, carefully planned for several weeks. Everyone knew their responsibilities. Belladane pulled the sheets off of Shimi's bed, and replaced them with a heavy plastic sheet, and then put a newly washed white cotton sheet over top. She put Shimi's favourite calming playlist on Spotify. Belladane brought the pile of towels that were wrapped in plastic to keep them clean, and set them on a stool she placed close to the end of the bed. She also set up a small folding table for Alice to use. Eddie and Darcy were in the kitchen, busy sorting out the water. That was the job they had opted for.

Shimi had asked Eddie several weeks prior if he would like to be part of the birth, and he had said, in a playful way, "I know how to boil water. That's what the helper does in the movies, right?"

"You're welcome to be in the room with me, if you want," Shimi had said.

"Oh, that would be cool, but I don't know, Shimi," Eddie had said.

Feeling a tad rejected, Shimi had quickly added, "No worries, whatever works for you."

Eddie was uncomfortable saying to Shimi what he was really thinking. He knew he owed her a better explanation, but he couldn't speak the words. They hadn't talked seriously about his PTSD for a couple of months and he liked it that way. Not always talking about it, made him feel a bit more normal, a little less wounded. He knew he wasn't entirely healed, as he still awoke some nights to the screaming nightmares, and flashbacks sporadically haunted him at the most inopportune times. He was worried that seeing the blood during the birth might be a reminder of his trauma, his friends, the explosions, the horror. He wasn't sure he was ready for that. He was scared he would freeze up and not be competent the moment Shimi needed him the most. He didn't want anything to mess up the relationship they had, the fondness for each other that was growing with each passing day. Shimi needed competent people to help her, and he wasn't sure he was that guy yet. He didn't want this day to be about him and his issues. This was Shimi's day. He needed to keep it together, and he was afraid he wouldn't be able to if he was in the room with her, watching her cry out in pain and anguish. He understood all of this, but his lack of courage and confidence made him angry and ashamed.

Alice's Jeep wheeled up the gravel lane and came to a crunching stop. She came into the kitchen carrying a small duffle bag and asked Eddie to unload the stuff in the car. She then flew into action, yet in a calm and controlled way. She started timing Shimi's contractions and said Shimi was moving along faster than most first time mothers.

Shimi was relieved, but concerned at the same time. The last nine months had been an agonizing period of waiting, something Shimi was not very good at, but now she wanted to slow things down and delay this birth as long as possible. It was all too real. All too terrifying.

The plan was they would start in the house with lots of walking, rolling around on the exercise ball, and resting on her bed, but once she was dilated appropriately and the contractions were less than five minutes apart, they would move outside to the small swimming pool. It was sixty inches wide in diameter, and held about 26 inches of water. Eddie had set it up on the back patio, situated next to the grapevine arbour, in a perfect location to receive the afternoon sun. He had refreshed the water in it daily for the last week. Shimi secretly watched him from her living room window. His serious face while he tested the water temperature always made her smile.

But sometimes he saw her spying on him. "I'm just practising," Eddie would yell. "And don't worry, I'm not wasting it. I use it to water the flowers and refresh the bird bath."

Now Eddie went to the pantry where he had stored the garden hose he had bought at the local hardware store. He hooked it to the laundry room sink, ran the hose out the back patio door to the pool, and began to fill it with warm water. He pulled the thermometer from his jean pocket. He wanted the water to be the same as body temperature. 36 degrees Celsius. He had to get his job right.

Belladane was going to sit behind Shimi and support her during the delivery. For once she was as serious as an atlas. As Shimi began to double over with severe contractions, she almost wished Auntie BellaBell had a silly joke. They walked about the house for hours, and Eddie kept filling and refilling the pool. He didn't know what else to do, so he tried to keep himself busy, even though he worried about all the well water he was wasting. Alice finally told him to stop, saying she would tell him in plenty of time to fill the pool.

When it came early evening, Eddie walked over to the barn and fed Betty and BamBam. He then refreshed their water pails in the barn and put them in for the night. Since the Pitbull attack, he had been keeping the goats inside at night, even in the summer.

As Eddie did his work in the barn, he reflected upon a story Shimi had told him a few weeks prior that didn't sit right with him. She had been in a supermarket in Charlottetown picking up some groceries, and she had bumped into the drug dealer neighbour, Harvey Quinn. He had glared at her as their shopping carts met in the produce section.

Then he took another long look at Shimi's baby belly and said, "You're pregnant?" with a bewildered look on his face.

"What's it to you?" Shimi had asked, knowing the response wasn't as original as she would have liked.

"I thought you two bitches only liked girls ... or maybe it's your GI Joe boyfriend you've got living there," Harvey sniped.

"I haven't gotten any payments from you lately. What's wrong, the drug business drying up?"

"I don't sell drugs!" Harvey said forcefully, and then he looked around to see if anyone else was listening.

"Everyone knows you sell drugs. All those cars that go into your place and come out two minutes later aren't delivering Avon. And if your dead-beat uncle wasn't a local cop, you would be in jail by now," Shimi said, louder than necessary.

"Everyone knows your GI Joe boyfriend is a fucking US runaway." Harvey pushed past Shimi and reached for a bag of potatoes.

That's when Shimi saw it. A large round metal watch flopped loose on his right wrist. Shimi froze. Harvey growled and pushed past her. Shimi couldn't get that image out of her mind and she prayed she wouldn't meet him again in another aisle, but at the same time she wanted to have a closer look at him and his loose watch.

She had her chance a few minutes later. Harvey was standing choosing a bottle of mustard just as she was turning to enter the condiment aisle. She stared at him with microscopic precision. As he bent to reach for the mustard his dingy shirt collar fell off to the side, and she noticed a large dark tattoo on the right side of his long, skinny neck. His right hand was still on the handle of his shopping cart, and his left hand reached for the mustard. There was a large silver ring on his fourth finger, with a turquoise stone in it. These two details stung like the poisonous memory in Shimi's mind. She turned her cart around and quickly left the aisle, hoping she wouldn't meet him again in the store.

That night at dinner, when Shimi told Belladane and Eddie about the encounter with Harvey, Eddie knew he was probably the culprit, the man who violated Shimi. He wanted to bash the guy's head in, but he knew he couldn't get arrested. He knew Shimi needed him. He would be no use to her if he was in jail.

Belladane was the voice of reason, saying, "I'm sure there are hundreds of men with loose watches on their wrists and rings on their fourth finger. And I would bet he doesn't use Irish Spring soap. He's only smelled of pot whenever I've been near him. Although, I wouldn't trust that guy as far as I could throw him. Maybe you should call Sergeant Malone."

"What's the point?" Shimi had said, as she moved the roast potatoes around on her plate. Her defeat and its acceptance were visible for all to see.

Shimi's quiet comment, 'What's the point' resonated in Eddie's head for a long time. It made him feel useless. He had failed his friends in combat, and now, once again, he felt like he was letting his new friends down.

Eddie tried not to think anymore about Harvey Quinn. He locked up the barn and decided to kill some more time during this long-drawn-out delivery by taking Darcy for a walk down by the stream. Darcy had been in the house most of the day, panting in the heat, never leaving Shimi's side. Darcy was reluctant to leave when

Eddie whistled for him to come, but after being tempted with some treats, he finally agreed to a walk. Eddie threw Darcy's favourite stick in the direction of the stream and they were on their way.

Once there, Darcy eased himself into the cool water, slipping and sliding on the moss-covered rocks at the bottom of the shallow stream. When the cool stream water reached Darcy's belly, he sat down. This was a funny little habit of Darcy's. Eddie thought he could hear Darcy give a sigh of relief. After he was completely wet, he gave himself a gentle shake, but Eddie knew Darcy had also saved a good bit of water for Shimi.

When they came back into the kitchen, Darcy raced up to Shimi, who was leaning against the table, and delivered his second big shake. Water and dog hair splattered across the three women in the kitchen. They all groaned as they wiped off Darcy's moist, smelly greeting.

"Oh great! Labour pains and wet dog smell," Shimi said, but she laughed and when her eyes met Eddie's, he felt a warmth he hadn't felt for anyone in a very long time.

Shimi scooped a coffee can full of bird seed from the large bag kept in the pantry, and made her way to the back patio doors. Her left hand held her lower back as she walked.

Eddie attempted to take the can from her, "I'll do that."

"I'd like to do it. I haven't talked to the birds all day," Shimi said.

Eddie, Alice and Belladane watched Shimi from inside the house. She filled the big feeder that sat on a five-foot post, and then scattered some carefully on the ground for the mourning doves. A single chickadee sat on a low branch and listened as Shimi talked to her. The gentleness of care and solitude of the moment made Belladane's heart grow. This woman gently moving about the garden, talking to her birds, about to give birth to a rapist's baby was truly a wonder.

Belladane was the first to speak. "As Shimi would say, 'As beautiful as the first bird at dawn.' Looking at her out there now ... sometimes there is more beauty in life than the world can bear."

Belladane knew these shapeless moments of an ordinary day, like filling up a bird feeder are often the special ones, keeping one grounded and often sane.

As the day wore on, Belladane made a huge plate of egg salad sandwiches and iced tea. Eddie devoured four sandwiches, while Shimi had some clear vegetable broth, a fudgesicle, and then sucked on some Lindt chocolate Alice had brought in her huge bag. It was a hot evening, and the heat didn't seem like it was going to let up for the night. Luckily a soft breeze was beginning to come in off the bay.

Shimi paced throughout the house, rolled on the huge purple exercise ball, or rested in her bed for Alice to determine her dilation. Finally, Alice deemed Shimi was ready to move into the pool of warm water. Belladane sat behind her on a cushion on the patio stones and gave Shimi support from behind. With every screaming contraction, Shimi pushed herself back against Belladane. Within thirty minutes the sixty-six-year-old woman was exhausted and her lower back radiated with pain.

"Eddie," Belladane yelled, "I need your help." Alice, who was kneeling on the other side of the pool, nodded in agreement. Eddie came and helped Belladane up off the patio stones, and she quickly dropped down onto a comfortable Muskoka chair with a relieved sigh.

"That was as exhausting as a Hollywood stuntman on the fortieth take. And I'm not even the one having the baby," Belladane groaned.

Alice and Shimi had to chuckle and smile. Belladane was quite pleased her comic relief was well received.

Eddie kicked off his Birkenstock sandals. He stepped into the pool with his denim shorts and tee shirt, sat down in the water, spread his legs wide apart and pulled Shimi back against his chest. "We've got this," he whispered into her ear.

As the time grew closer, Shimi turned around on her knees, placed her hands and forehead on Eddie's shoulder, screaming into his ear with each forceful push.

The soldier never wavered.

The baby made a perfect entrance into the world at 9.02 pm, just as the July sun was about to set. The horizon was bright orange with radiant red streaks crossing just above the treeline. The twinkle lights wound around the grape arbour and along the line of the patio ceiling cast tiny shadows across the pool. With each movement Shimi made, the glimmer of the tiny lights across her body sparkled, then disappeared, then sparkled and disappeared again.

Belladane and Alice had never seen anything more beautiful.

XXIV
(boldly)

"It's a girl," Alice chimed as she pulled the new born from the water and rested her upon Shimi's belly. She carefully cut the baby's umbilical cord, clamped it, and placed a small white towel over the baby's back.

"I knew it!" Belladane raised both of her arms up in the air. She beamed from ear to ear.

"Ten fingers and ten toes," Alice added. She rubbed the baby girl rapidly on the back. The baby gasped and then began to howl.

"Well, she's got her mother's lungs," Belladane chirped.

Shimi beamed. She was glad to have some humour injected into the day. Everything had been so serious for the last 9 hours. It was good to see Belladane back to her sarcastic self. Everyone could now breathe a well-deserved sigh of relief.

Alice began to quickly clean the baby, then swaddle her in a soft white cotton towel.

Eddie continued to hold Shimi for a couple more minutes in the pool of water until the placenta was released. He was proud of himself. He had held it together for Shimi when she needed him the most. For this accomplishment, he felt unshackled joy. He knew he would remember this moment for the rest of his life. He had never felt more significant, yet at the same time, so insignificant. He was simply amazed at what women went through to have a child. The entire daunting event both overwhelmed and awed him. He knew he would never be able to put into words his wonder and total admiration of this miraculous event.

Eddie helped Shimi step out of the pool and wrapped her in a new terry robe that Belladane had just warmed in the dryer. She sat down in a lawn chair and Alice handed her the swaddled baby. Only her head was visible.

"Look at her beautiful hair," Shimi said, as she gently caressed the baby's head. Fine hairs were stuck to her tiny skull. "I think she's going to be a ginger."

Eddie stood silently at the edge of the patio, leaning against one of the stoas. He smiled and just kept smiling. It was a night he would never forget, and he felt rejuvenated with hope that he would one day be the reliable and competent man he used to be. The shadows and light from the twinkle lights surrounded Shimi and her baby, and Eddie thought Shimi had never looked more beautiful than she did at that moment holding her newborn in her arms. Shimi's damp auburn hair hung in long massive curls. And her cheeks were rosy like she had just come in from a walk along the North Shore. She reminded him of a Waterhouse mermaid poster he once saw in a gallery in New York City. The curator had said all the originals hung in a British museum in London. He now wanted to own that poster. Perhaps he could order it online, he thought. For him, it would always commemorate this magical night with beautiful Shimi.

Belladane pulled out her phone. She started moving around Shimi and the baby. She couldn't take the photos fast enough.

Shimi ignored Belladane, totally engrossed with the baby on her chest. She stroked the baby's cheeks for several minutes and looked deep into her dark eyes. "Hello Baby," Shimi said over and over again. Then she gently kissed her on the forehead.

Belladane kept taking photos, meanwhile repeating, "Oh, what a beautiful girl."

Shimi smiled up at her aunt and said, "Why don't you take a break from the photos and hold her?" She then handed the baby to Belladane.

"Oh, I thought you'd never ask," Belladane laughed.

Belladane gently cradled the newborn in her arms, and said, "Could she be anymore lovely? A perfect, perfect girl!" Belladane unwrapped the towel and reached in to grasp the baby's tiny fingers. As the towel fell back from the baby's head, Belladane said, "Oh, what's this?"

"What?" Alice and Shimi said simultaneously.

"I think she has something on the side of her neck," Belladane said, as she handed her back to Alice.

"Let's go inside where we have better light? Shall we?" Alice said.

Once in the bedroom, Alice examined the baby more closely.

"Oh, I missed this. I just thought it was a bit of blood. It may be a vascular birthmark. Often as many as 40% of newborns have this type of mark. Nothing to worry about. Some folks still call them an Angel Kiss." Alice hesitated for a moment, continuing to examine the baby's neck.

Shimi snatched the baby from Alice and looked closely at the mark. She ran her finger over the red shape. Suddenly, her face went pale. She was speechless.

Belladane leaned over the baby as well, and said, "It looks like a Merkaba, the joining of two triangles, the ancient symbol of chariots. I think it's a sign of good luck, Shimi."

Shimi remained silent. Alice touched the baby's neck again and then said, "Yes, but this one looks a little different. Could be a hemangioma ... which sometimes are hereditary."

"Hereditary?" Shimi repeated curtly.

"Yes," Alice said.

The room fell silent, and suddenly there was a different energy in the air. Eddie, who had been standing back in the doorway watching the women, stepped forward and looked down at the baby resting on Shimi's chest. Shimi kept running her finger over and over the raised, red bump on the baby girl's neck.

"Hereditary? This must be what I felt that night. He had a patch of raised rough skin on his neck." Shimi's voice escalated with anguish, "He had this same mark on his neck. I remember it now. I bet this is what I felt that night." Shimi looked up at Eddie and Belladane with tears in her eyes. Shock and horror were written across her face. "This is what I felt under his sweater."

Alice looked at her friends in disbelief. "You never told me about the birthmark, Shimi. What side of his neck was the mark?"

"His right side, just like hers," Shimi said. She laid her head back on the bed in exhaustion, cradling the tiny baby girl on her chest. She let out a huge sigh and then closed her eyes. Her lips began to quiver and a few tears began to move down her face. Belladane and Eddie came and stood on either side of her bed.

"It's okay," Eddie said. "She'll be perfect, like her Mamma." He laid his hand on the baby's back and gave her a gentle rub.

"Yes, it's going to be alright, Shimi. You'll see," Belladane added.

Alice stood at the foot of the bed and nodded her head in agreement, but the set of her jaw and the look in her eyes revealed a grave concern.

XXV
(woefully)

ALICE SAID SHE would stay a few days with Shimi and the new babe to help get them settled. She was very efficient with her work: weighing, measuring, filling out the paperwork. She taught Shimi how to bathe the baby, care for her new belly button, and helped her start breastfeeding. She made a footprint of the little one for a souvenir. Everything went smoothly under Alice's guidance and care. Once again, the jitters Shimi had anticipated about going through labour and then becoming a competent mother slowly eased under Alice's guidance.

"Have you decided upon a name yet, Shimi?" Alice inquired, as the two women sat in the gazebo late in the afternoon, the baby asleep on the sofa beside Shimi.

"Oh, gosh I haven't. I don't know if I should name her. I can't imagine giving her up now, as I love her to bits, but I still can't imagine keeping her and being responsible for her for the next twenty odd years of her life."

"What an incredible decision to have to make," Alice said.

"I simply love calling her Baby. But I guess that wouldn't suit her when she's a teenager," Shimi laughed.

"Wasn't the girl in the *Dirty Dancing* movie called Baby?" Alice asked. "I guess that was supposed to be her real name."

"I think so, but no. I will not legally name her Baby. Women get treated like children enough, without having a name like Baby."

"True," Alice said.

"I have thought and thought about Baby ... about what's holding me back ... and I know what it is ... it's the birthmark. That bloody birthmark. A constant reminder of him," Shimi said.

"Yes," Alice said. Then quickly changing the topic, she added, "Don't worry about the name, you have a month to register her ... and even after that you can do it online for up to a year."

"I was kind of thinking of Grace, as she was a bit of a miracle. Although a mighty horrifying one," Shimi said.

"Grace is lovely," Alice said.

"If you had a daughter, what would you call her?" Shimi asked.

"I always thought I'd name my daughter, Zavi, after my mom," Alice said. "She was a great lady. She died a couple of years back."

"Oh, I'm sorry," Shimi said. She tried to quickly change the subject, as she had the feeling that Alice had already been struggling emotionally since the baby was born. There was something not quite right.

"Did you call Leon and invite him over? He's welcome to drop by, you know. You must miss him," Shimi said.

"Yes, I did talk to him this morning. I told him all about the baby. And did invite him over. He said he's too busy, but I doubt that."

Shimi noticed an instant change in Alice's face and she wasn't surprised. There was a definite weight on Alice's shoulders.

"Is there something bothering you, Alice? You've been very quiet today. I thought I was the only hormonal one." Shimi tried to make a little joke.

Alice was silent for a moment, and Shimi resisted the need to jump in and navigate them through the silence. Shimi had learned in life that silence may precede the most difficult of conversations, but often the most necessary ones. Finally, Alice pushed her head back on the sofa and tears started to run down her cheeks. She released great sobs and covered her face with her hands.

"What's wrong, Alice? Oh Honey, talk to me," Shimi said, gently pulling Alice towards her in a warm embrace.

"It's Leo," Alice said.

"What about Leo?" Shimi asked.

"He's everything," Alice cried.

"What do you mean, he's everything?"

"He's Irish Spring soap, a loose watch ... all of it!" Alice cried.

"Oh Alice," Shimi said, not quite sure what Alice was trying to say.

"His left sneaker squeaks. His wedding ring has a large stone and it's loose on his finger. He always wears turtlenecks. And the birthmark! He has the same raised birthmark on the right side of his neck!"

After Shimi recovered from her initial shock, the two women talked well into the night. Between baby feedings, Alice confided about her marriage and who the famous Leon Birkshire really was.

"He became very upset when he first found out that I was thinking of being your midwife. He tried to talk me out of it, and I couldn't understand why. He then became quite threatening about it, so I didn't even tell him for the longest while that I had taken you on as a client. When I finally confessed, he went into a rage and I didn't understand, but then I often don't understand his rages, so I didn't think it was unusual."

Alice continued to explain that Leo was terribly controlling and dictated every aspect of their lives. He was condescendingly rude and sometimes physical with Alice, often forcing himself on her if she was too tired or not in the mood for sex. He was often unaccounted for at night and would never answer his phone when she called. If Alice asked where he had been, he would turn the conversation around on her, accusing her of being suspicious and jealous. He was moody and would often go for days without speaking to her. He was prone to fits of mania and fits of rage. He had a sweet, diplomatic public persona, but Alice was the recipient of his private one.

"Dr. Jekyll and Mr. Hyde," Alice said. "There's many times I'm frightened of him."

"Alice, I'm trying not to judge, but why do you stay with him?" Shimi asked.

"I don't know," Alice cried into her hands. "I feel I'm in control of every other aspect of my life, but my marriage. It's like I'm stuck in this clutch of destructive love and fear. It's illogical, I know. I know I'm not being sensible."

"I will help you, Alice, with whatever you need. You are my dear friend. And you deserve better than what's happening to you. You've helped me so much. Now let me help you," Shimi said.

Alice gave Shimi a rueful smile.

Shimi sat forward and took both of Alice's shaking hands. "But first ... now tell me Alice. Tell me the honest-to-God truth. Do you honestly, 100%, think Leo is the one who raped me?"

Alice lifted up her face and stared squarely at Shimi with her bright blue eyes. "Yes! Yes, I do."

XXVI
(secretly)

When the sun rose the next day, everything felt different to Shimi. The dawn of a new day ... a question that had been haunting her for nine months was finally answered. But what to do with the shocking answer was now a new question. What was she to do about Leon Birkshire?

Alice and Shimi had talked throughout the night, and even though they were both exhausted emotionally and physically, they felt they needed to give this information to Belladane and Eddie. And they needed to do it right away.

Once they read their texts, "Can you come over?" Eddie and Belladane came rushing across the road like the house was on fire. They both looked worried as they came into Shimi's kitchen, so they were pleased to see Alice and Shimi sitting at the kitchen table, drinking a pot of green tea. Baby was lying in a wicker clothes hamper at their feet.

Belladane looked at Shimi's pale, tired face. "What's up?" Belladane asked, as she flopped down into the chair across from Alice. She bent over the hamper and picked up the tiny baby. Belladane beamed as she cradled the tiny, sleeping bundle in her arms. Eddie grabbed the chair across from Shimi, turned it around and straddled it.

The revelations of the night were explained to Eddie and Belladane. Both sat silently and seemed in shock. Sometimes Eddie lowered his forehead onto the back edge of the chair and seemed to be silently cursing. Alice shed tears throughout the conversation, but tried to hold it together. She had done so much sobbing throughout the night, her eyes were already puffy and sore. She didn't realize one human could hold so much humiliation and shame, yet she knew this was only the beginning - she had a long, rough road ahead of her.

"We have to make a decision and consider all the ramifications," Shimi said.

"What's to decide? Go to the cops, and have the bastard arrested this morning," Belladane exclaimed.

"It's not that simple," Shimi explained. "It's like there's a swampland of factors we have to consider. If Alice gets involved, who knows what Leo will do. She's the one in danger now. And Leo will know she's the one who put it all together and told us about him."

"I feel sick to my stomach," Alice moaned. "I just can't believe this is happening ... but no, I guess I can. I have known for a while there was something going on with him. Maybe I should just go home and confront him."

"Not a good idea," Eddie said. "A man like that, who feels cornered ... it wouldn't be safe."

"Maybe we all could go," Belladane suggested. "Safety in numbers. Except you Shimi, you stay home with Baby."

"Maybe we should go to the police, and have Alice stay here at the house where she is safe," Shimi said.

"Yes, but we need more than a suspicion, or circumstantial evidence ... we need DNA proof," Belladane added. "They need to test that bloody rape kit. Alice, do you have anything with Leo's DNA on it? We could take that as well."

"We have to be careful. In most of these cases, the guy is out on bail immediately. Probably not even enough time for Alice to get out of the house." Eddie looked gravely at the three women.

"Yes, and if we go public, this information will blow wide open in this little province. And since he works for the CBC and is a popular journalist, the whole country will hear about it. I don't know whether I want myself, Alice, and Baby to always have this horrible story attached to us for the rest of our lives. I know that is horrible and selfish, but I just don't know whether I can go through with this," Shimi said.

"Oh Shimi. What a mess! I'm so sorry. As for me, I could move away, I suppose. Start fresh somewhere else." Alice then muttered to herself, "No one in this town would want to hire the wife of a rapist."

"I don't want to move away. And I don't want you to move away either, Alice. This guy has already taken so much from me. Fucking Leon Birkshire is not taking away my home as well," Shimi said, slamming her hand down on the table. Baby jumped in Belladane's arms and started to cry.

Belladane stood up and paced back and forth, comforting the baby. All four were quiet for a moment.

"Maybe we don't go to the police. Maybe we don't go public," Eddie said.

"What do you mean?" all three women said at once.

"How do we get this guy, without bringing down the three of you? There must be a better plan," Eddie said. "We need to think."

"Look, this isn't NCIS or the Navy Seals, Eddie. We need to talk to the police and let them handle it. You two women are victims here and have nothing to be ashamed about. Remember, today's news holds tomorrow's tacos," Belladane said.

"I think it's fish," Shimi murmured.

"Whatever," Belladane said.

"I know you want to stay out of this Shimi, and I get that. But we also have to wonder how many women he has raped. You're probably not the only one, and if he is not stopped, he will continue," Belladane said.

"I know. I know. You think I don't know that? That's about all I've thought about these last nine months. How many victims are out there, just like me, and who will be his next?" Shimi raged.

Belladane's eyes filled with tears.

Suddenly there was a scratching at the kitchen door. Shimi looked questioningly at the others. They had heard it too. Eddie jumped to his feet, looked out the glazing and then ever-so-gently opened the door a few inches. In walked Meadow, with her tail in the air and her chin held high.

"Hello, Sweet Pea! What are you doing here?" said Belladane as she scooped up the cat in her arms. "Oh, my nerves! I don't like her crossing the road."

"Curiosity killed the cat," quipped Shimi.

"Oh, don't say that," Belladane growled.

Darcy was instantly interested in Meadow's bum, but she gave him a look and he backed right off. She jumped down from Belladane's lap, then settled on the sunny kitchen window sill.

They talked across the morning. They talked while they ate cold left-over lentil soup and All Dressed potato chips. They talked through a pot of coffee and a huge jug of iced tea. Eddie was holding Baby, when Shimi finally went outside in the mid-afternoon to feed her birds.

As Shimi was pulling open the patio screen door at the back of the kitchen, Eddie said, "Could you please fill up the bird bath as well, Shimi. I forgot to do it this morning."

Shimi said, "No worries. We can't have thirsty birds, now can we?" Then holding her tummy, she gingerly stepped outside.

"Okay, we need to come up with a quick plan while she's outside," Eddie whispered. "This is too much for Shimi to handle right now. She hasn't even been able to make a decision about whether this little one is even staying here, or pick her name for that matter. Now she has to make a gigantic decision about this, as well. She's got way too much on her plate."

Belladane agreed. "Yes, how much more can Shimi endure? I'm afraid she is being pushed to her breaking point."

Alice spoke gently, between the tears, "I agree. I will go along with whatever you both want to do."

So, the three of them decided, with Baby as their witness, that Shimi would not be involved in any plan. They all agreed she had been through enough. And since Shimi wanted it that way, the violent circumstances of Baby's conception would be a secret they would take to their graves.

Finally, they all went their separate ways. Shimi, Alice, and Baby went for a well-deserved nap, hoping their brains would stop spinning and they could get a couple of hours of sleep. Belladane walked down the lane to her house, her face clouded in fear, and a dozen disturbing questions plaguing her mind. She grasped Meadow tightly, all the while gently singing under her breath, "The cat came back the very next day. The cat came back. I thought he was a goner, but the cat came back. He just wouldn't stay away."

Eddie and Darcy walked to the river. While Darcy cooled himself in the shallow water, Eddie sat on his favourite rock. He knew he had an idea, but it was so enormous – so gigantic, it was impossible as yet to wrap his mouth around it and bring it to life, put it into clear, audible words. How would he ever say these words to Belladane? And if she was mortified with his words, he knew he could never take them back, never un-say them. A part of him, that he wasn't proud of, would be out there in the world forever, stored in Belladane's memory. And in the crevices of his own disturbed, revengeful mind. He tried to justify his thoughts by pondering whether revenge and justice were really so different. He didn't actually believe in the whole "an eye for an eye" thing, but shouldn't true justice include some form of retribution? There had to be a plan for Birkshire. It had to be a good one. And it needed Belladane's help.

He sat rubbing his hands together and staring at the dog who was playfully splashing after a frog. He hoped Darcy wouldn't catch it.

XXVII
(supposedly)

Alice's cell phone pinged that evening with a text from Leo:

> What the hell is going on? I'm going out fishing early tomorrow morning and should be back by noon. I want you home when I back.

Alice responded:

> I'm almost done here. Will see you then. Are you taking the boat out of Nufrage?

Leo answered right away:

> What a stupid question. Of course, that's where the boat is!!??

Alice bit her lip with patience and responded with all the dignity and fake enthusiasm she could muster.

> Thought you might be river fishing someplace else. Happy Fishing! Catch a big one!

Alice went immediately across the road and relayed the text message to Belladane and Eddie. Then rubbing her brow, she murmured, "Maybe I should be there tomorrow afternoon, waiting for him?"

"This is the safest place for you to be right now, Alice. I'd think twice before going home. We'd only worry about you if you left," Eddie said.

"I really don't know what to do," Alice exclaimed. "I'm so torn. I want to confront him and I want to avoid him forever. I want him dead, yet I want him to rot in prison forever. And I don't want to drag Shimi through the mud. Oh, how I want to wake up from this horrible, horrible nightmare."

Shimi came through the kitchen door with Baby fast asleep in her arms. "Hey, what am I missing?"

"Nothing much. I was just telling Belladane that I might head back home tomorrow. She said she is ready and able to help whenever you need it." Alice said.

"But what will you do about Leon when you go home?" Shimi asked.

Belladane and Eddie stayed conspicuously quiet.

"He wants me home. He texted me. So, I will go home. It may be rough, but if he hurts me … I will go to the police … have him arrested. But I won't involve you, Shimi. I won't say anything about what we know." Alice stood like a drooping flower.

"Look it, Alice, you can't be a martyr. Don't put yourself in harm's way," Shimi pleaded. "You can stay here as long as you want."

Eddie spoke up earnestly, "And even if you did get him arrested, he'd be out before you know it. Then you and Shimi would definitely not be safe."

"Listen to Eddie, Alice. He's right. Promise me you won't hurry home," Belladane pleaded.

"I promise," Alice said. "Now, Shimi, go have a nap while Baby is asleep. You need more rest." She held out her arms for the baby.

'Music to my ears," Shimi sighed, as she placed the sleeping infant in Alice's welcoming arms.

Once Shimi had left, Belladane spoke up. "I've been doing some research that I don't want to repeat to Shimi. In some states in America, a rapist can file for custody of the child. If there are no assault charges and conviction, then it's fair game for the rapist to ask for shared custody, as it's a civil court trial, not criminal. Can you imagine? It's all so sick."

"No way," Eddie exclaimed, pushing his mop of curls off his forehead. "But I shouldn't be surprised. America has its messed up, sexist laws for sure."

"I'm not quite clear on the Canadian laws, but I've made a phone call to a lawyer friend of mine, and she's going to get back to me within a couple of days. Maybe even today. She's a real estate lawyer, but she said she has contacts and would do some research for us." Belladane added, "I'm also afraid if this came to court, Leon would say that it was consensual and that she enjoyed it. It would be her word against his. What if he won? Then what if he pursued the baby?"

"The fact that we're even talking about this, and that you're afraid Birkshire is the type of creep who might sue for custody is just another reason why he cannot get away with what he's done. And he should never find out about the baby. What do you think he'd do, Alice?" Eddie asked.

"I don't know. Obviously, I don't know my husband well at all, but I do know he likes to be in control at all times," Alice said. "And of course, he does know about Shimi's baby, and I'm sure he knows it may be his." Then, she reluctantly added, "And I know he has always wanted kids, but I couldn't have any."

Eddie pushed his hair back again with both his hands and let out a huge sigh. "So Birkshire knows Shimi is your patient? Well, that complicates things for sure."

"Yes, I told him before I knew any of this other stuff," Alice whimpered. "I'm so sorry. I'm so … so sorry."

Belladane gave Alice a long, reassuring hug. She stared at Eddie over Alice's shoulder and whispered, "This is so messed up."

They agreed they would try to wait for legal advice from Belladane's friend. They would wait until that evening.

But the legal advice never came.

Around eleven that night, Eddie took a walk to the stream. He sat on his favourite big rock and watched the moon rise high above the trees. Just like the haunting words of Gord Downie of *The Tragically Hip*, he watched the constellations reveal themselves one tiny, sparkling star at a time. It had been a while since he had roamed around the neighbourhood late at night and enjoyed the speechless gaze of the moon. He thought about how drastically his life had changed in one year. He loved these women. They were his friends and he felt both an obligation and honour in helping them. He wasn't able to protect his soldier buddies, but he'd be damned if he let anything happen to these three wonderful women and precious baby.

He finally went home and googled rape cases and custody battles well into the early morning. He learned that most victims do not take the crime to the police. If they do, most police don't pursue the crime in court, and if the crime is brought to court, most rapists get acquitted. What horrible statistics to swallow. Eddie never believed in the argument of the dark, but this time he wondered if there was any reason not to take Shimi and Alice's dilemma into his own capable hands. Shimi had already paid for that night with everything inside her. She paid for it by bearing her pain, agony, monster memories, fear, nightmares, and even an unwanted child. And God only knows what Alice has endured. Eddie wished he had half their strength and resolve. His fists were clenched tightly. He was hot with rage. And he knew it could be his most productive fuel.

He dragged himself home, crawled into his bed and tried to get a few hours of sleep. He knew that the new day would be a difficult one and a testament to his own strength and conscience.

At the crack of dawn, Belladane texted Shimi to tell her she would be spending the day in Charlottetown, doing a big grocery shop and lots of errands. She added that Eddie said he had an interview at the immigration office and would be catching a lift with her. He said he was hoping they would get his paperwork started for his permanent residency.

When Shimi wandered into the kitchen, Alice was already up and at it. The midwife said she had to check on another client who was due in a month, so she also would be away most of the day. She asked if Shimi would be okay on her own.

"Of course," Shimi said, as convincingly as she could. "I'm a big girl. Baby and I will be fine."

Shimi's phone pinged. It was a text from Eddie, which she thought was weird. Eddie rarely texted her. He preferred to communicate in person.

> "I'm off with Belladane to "town" today. Immigration needs me. Fingers crossed it is a successful day. Keep Darcy close."

Shimi read the text to Alice. "When is Darcy ever not close?" Shimi joked. Upon hearing his name, Darcy jumped up and put his paws on Shimi's lap and wagged his tail.

Despite her trite comment to Alice, Eddie's text rattled Shimi.
Why would he say, keep Darcy close?
Did he think Birkshire would be dropping by?
If so, why would he be leaving her alone?

Within all the plaguing thoughts of Leon, she hadn't thought about what she would do when she saw Birkshire again. Would her face reveal the truth she now knew about him? Would he then know, she knew? She couldn't imagine how all this would play out, but she knew in time she would have to face him.

Despite being on edge about Birkshire, Shimi enjoyed her solitude and quiet time with Baby. She tied a bed sheet around her shoulder and hip creating a comfy sling and tucked Baby in it. She walked out to the barn to feed the goats. Betty and BamBam sniffed the tiny baby, but seemed more interested in nibbling on the sheet. She sat down on a stump in the goat yard for a very long time. It was comforting to have the sun on her back, the baby on her lap and the goats nuzzling about her feet.

Later that afternoon, Shimi placed a chair pad in the old wicker laundry hamper and draped a small cotton sheet inside. She placed Baby in the hamper and carried her to the gazebo. She put the hamper on the floor by the sofa and then lay down to rest. She dozed whenever Baby slept. Darcy snored by her side. The birds flitted up and down about the feeders, as content as pigeons at the Vatican.

She tried to relax, but also stay alert. Eddie's words, "Keep Darcy close" echoed in her mind.

As Shimi looked at her sleeping baby, she wanted to believe that everything was fine in her world. If only she didn't need anything else in her life. If only this baby was enough. Many women looking at this perfect baby would be completely and utterly happy, despite Leon Birkshire, despite anything else going on in their lives. They could shake off the past and simply move forward, in an attempt to enjoy each simple moment.

Today, everything at this quiet moment could be seen as fine. Yes, this small moment in her gazebo she would accept with full gratitude. She also knew this moment would not last; it was only temporary. Decisions had to be realized. As her father used to say, "There will be a reckoning." All these questions and thoughts buzzed through her mind like a barber's clippers, and no matter how she tried to relax she couldn't make them stop.

Despite her whirling worries, she was glad she had this alone time. She hadn't had a moment to herself in weeks. Although she did think it was quite odd that her three friends had left her alone all at the same time, she was happy they were off somewhere else, living their own lives instead of hers. She realized she had felt agitated lately with the constant attention of her well-meaning friends, their opinions, their questions, their concerned looks ... all of it.

Sitting in the gazebo, suddenly she felt at peace. Perhaps something was happening in the universe at this very moment that brought her this peace. This clarity. Was she having a Satori moment? She didn't know for sure. But she did know she had already made a decision about Baby, but had yet to speak it out loud.

She knew that finally speaking those decisive words out loud would give the decision energy, action, and life. It was a secret she desperately needed to hold in her hands and heart, perhaps for another few days. The timing had to be just right.

She pondered the illogic of love and accepted that love is not always the elusive end of the road where you stay. It is often a moving target that changes like the direction of the North Atlantic wind, similar to the constant spinning of happiness.

She also knew that the night of the rape was a Kensho moment in her life, a turning point. It had set her on a new path of determination, consequence, and love, and in a weird kind of way, she knew at this moment she was happy.

Last night she had read a Rumi poem before bed, as had been her ritual for many years. Belladane had given her a book of Rumi poetry years ago and it had given her many moments of support and solace, but last night's poem resonated with her, leaving her both comforted and confused.

> "When I sit in my own place
> of personal silence,
> what I want,
> also wants me."
> -Rumi

XXVIII
(regardless)

IN THE EARLY evening, everyone got back to Belladane's place, tired, hot, and hungry. Eddie and Belladane brought in bags of groceries and a dozen new canvases for her art. Eddie looked dashing wearing a new pair of beige shorts and a light blue golf shirt. He said it was about time for a new outfit, and when he bought it he wanted to put it on right away. Shimi found this odd as Eddie had never indicated he cared about clothes. Typically, he roamed around in cut off jeans and a plain white tee shirt.

Shimi asked, "Did you wear your new outfit to your immigration meeting?"

Eddie hesitated for a couple of seconds, then mumbled, "Yes." Then he clearly added, "Now let's get this dinner on the table. I'm starved."

Shimi had been hoping he would have lots of good news to tell her about the interview, but despite a few more questions his comments were short and vague. She worried it didn't go well.

Alice arrived back as well. She also looked exhausted and troubled. She said her client was having difficulty sleeping, plus the poor woman was already worn out running after her two preschoolers. This pregnancy wasn't planned and was definitely taking its toll. Alice pulled a bottle of wine from her backpack and proceeded to pour it into a water glass. To Shim's surprise, she filled it to the brim.

Belladane also looked exhausted. Her linen clothes were damp and dirty, and her hair was a soggy mass of black curls. When Shimi pointed to the mess on her tunic, her aunt said, "It's from the back of the car."

"You always have a clean car. What did you do, go off-roading?" Shimi asked.

Belladane quickly replied, "The humidity today could drown a cat. It's so close. I'm drenched." She piled bags of Chinese food on the table and said, "I'll be right back."

She immediately jumped into the shower, threw her clothes in the washing machine, and then came quickly back to the kitchen in her summer pyjamas. Her massive curls lay freely upon her shoulders and sparkled with tiny water droplets. Normally her colourful scarves tied her curls and braids high on her head. Shimi had not seen her aunt look so natural, so casual, since the morning after the attack. Shimi loved her this way. Belladane's flowery pink pyjamas were made of cool, smooth silk, and when her aunt plunked herself down beside her at the table Shimi could not help but run her fingers along the sleeve.

Belladane looked at Shimi with the warmest of smiles and said, "Come on, it's getting cold. I got all your favourites."

They sat around the table eating stir-fried vegetables, yam glass noodles, mushroom dumplings, and garlic shrimp from the white cardboard boxes. Only Alice was an expert at chopsticks. The other three dropped as many slippery dumplings as they grasped, but Darcy who was situated strategically under the table didn't mind. Baby slept in the clothes hamper on the floor. She was like a magnet for the group and everyone enjoyed chewing their food in silence and staring at the little miracle of perfect flesh and innocence.

When Baby began to fuss, Alice quickly picked her up and told Shimi to finish her dinner. Baby immediately calmed in Alice's arms. Alice had a special tenderness for Baby and handled her effortlessly like they had been together forever.

Shimi knew it was Alice's expertise with babies that gave her this grace, but she also wondered if it was more profound than that. Perhaps Alice thought of Baby as the child she and Leon never had. Shimi desperately wanted to talk to Alice about this, but she didn't know how to start the conversation. She would have to find a way if they were to continue their friendship long after their professional relationship was over. Shimi was sure they both wanted that, as over the last few months they had become exceptionally close, and now the revelation about Leon had drawn them even closer.

Alice shared the sparkling wine with Belladane, saying after the stressful day they both deserved to finish the bottle. Belladane said she hoped it would give them a good night's sleep. Shimi and Eddie shared a big jug of iced green tea. Belladane, Eddie and Alice were rather quiet throughout the meal. Then all agreed they were keen to get to bed early and be done with the day.

Shimi was disappointed, as she was eager to talk more about Leon and what they should do. She also wanted to talk to them about her decision about Baby. But looking at her tired friends, she knew that discussion would not happen tonight. She felt like a child who had just lost her grasp on her balloon. She had been keyed up all afternoon, rehearsing in her mind the words she would say, the way she hoped the conversation would go. Shimi sat back and watched her tired family. And like the quiet morning in her gazebo, she felt another pang of happiness.

Before she went to bed, Alice texted Leon explaining that she wouldn't be home this evening as planned. She wrote she needed to support the new mother for another day or two. It was her job.

Leon never responded.

The next morning, Shimi asked if Alice had heard back from Leon.

"No," Alice said, "but that isn't uncommon. He often goes for days without responding. He's angry I'm here and probably wondering what's going on." Then Alice immediately fell silent and quickly busied herself folding the baby's laundry.

Shimi wondered if Alice was giving her the unvarnished truth, or whether she was holding something back. She dropped the conversation and accepted the obvious silence between them.

In the early afternoon, Eddie encouraged Alice to go home and see if he was there. Alice hesitated, but then agreed.

Eddie touched Alice's arm. "I'll go with you." Then he quickly added, giving Shimi a quick glance, "Just in case."

When they reached Alice's pretty bungalow in downtown Charlottetown, she went inside alone. Eddie sat on the front steps.

Alice viewed her home in a totally new light. She was immediately struck by the nothingness of the house. Now that she knew the truth about her husband, she saw her home for what it really was: a vacant space of pretty pretends and blatant lies.

She thought of the last night she spent with Leo, how he had berated her, saying, "You have the personality of a cardboard box," and "With you, I'm intellectually slumming it."

The house now was silent and her sandals echoed down the tiled hallway to the bedroom. To another looking around the house, one might see a shadow of a husband and a wife, the artefacts of a normal marriage: a coffee mug on the counter, a newspaper on the coffee table, a pair of slippers by the bed, but Alice knew that these props did not reveal their real life together Alice thought of all the sad vacancies of this house and her life: no friends, no dinner parties with family, no cuddling together watching a movie, no box of old Valentines stuck at the back of the closet, or pictures of warm Caribbean holidays on the mantel. There was no happiness in this house. And no truth.

Alice looked at Leon's desk in the office, set up in the small bedroom. He had a daily habit of ripping the pages off a Far Side joke calendar. The last two days had not been removed.

As she came out of the house, her neighbour, Mary Evans, was walking along the sidewalk with Benson, her old Cocker Spaniel. Alice smiled, waved, and quickly said to Eddie, "He's not here, and it looks like he hasn't been back since fishing."

"Call his office," Eddie encouraged. Then he too waved at the neighbour.

They sat in the car while Alice called the local CBC office, but Jane, the receptionist, said Leon hadn't shown up for an arranged interview with an Olympic athlete that morning. They also thought it was strange that he hadn't been in touch with anyone.

Alice informed Jane where she was staying, then said, "Please let me know if you hear from him, Jane. You have my number."

Jane, who Alice adored, held the phone close, her hand cupped over the mouthpiece. She whispered, "No worries, Alice. I'll let you know if I find out anything. Are you sure you're okay?'

"Yes, I'm fine, just staying a few days at a client's house, but I am getting concerned about Leo," Alice replied in a straight voice. She desperately didn't want her voice to crack.

When Alice finished her call, Eddie said she should text Leon again, "Just to be safe."

Alice wrote Leon another text, asking him where he was and that she was getting concerned.

There was no response.

Alice looked at Eddie and said, "Do you think we've done everything we should?"

"No," Eddie said. "Next, we drive to Naufrage, and if his boat isn't there ... then we call the police."

"I'm scared," Alice said, staring intently at Eddie.

"You're doing great! Everything is going to work out," Eddie said, as he looked over his shoulder at the empty street. Then he gave Alice a big hug.

XXIX
(presumed)

THE POLICE DROVE up Shimi's driveway around eleven the following morning. Immediately Darcy began a barking marathon, all the while wagging his tail and escorting the police to the side yard. It was an oppressively hot day, so Shimi, Alice and Baby were sitting in the gazebo, resting in the cool shade, discussing the merits of getting an air conditioner for the house. Shimi hated to get an air conditioner that only added to global warming. The Maritimes typically had a cool ocean breeze, but the summers were getting much hotter. It wasn't a conversation Shimi actually wanted to have. She was desperately trying to fake her way through any kind of discussion, any conversation that didn't involve Leon. She knew Alice was anxious and worried.

Instantly, by the way the officers walked, Shimi knew that something was gravely wrong. The two officers introduced themselves as Sergeant McDonald and Detective Gallant. They showed their identification and asked if they could come into the house. They stood with their hat in their hands, while Shimi placed Baby in the clothes hamper in the living room. Darcy scooted to his place under the table.

"Are you Alice Matters?" they asked Shimi.

"I'm Alice," Alice stepped forward.

"I'm Shimi Montray, her friend," Shimi added.

"Ms. Matters, are you married to Leon Birkshire?" Sergeant McDonald asked.

"Yes," Alice said calmly and then her hands began to shake and her knees started to give out from under her. Shimi helped her onto a kitchen chair and asked the officers to sit down as well. Shimi busied herself by getting Alice a glass of cold water. She then placed a huge jug of ice water in the middle of the table and three glasses. The officers said "thanks" in unison.

"We regret to inform you, Ms. Matters, that your husband's body was found in the water near Naufrage by some fishermen, early this morning. His boat was secured by the coast guard about an hour later, adrift near St Margaret's Beach."

"Oh God! Oh God!" Alice cried, covering her face in her hands.

Shimi stood behind Alice's chair. She placed her hands upon Alice's shoulders, and as she looked down at her friend tears welled up in her own eyes. Shimi couldn't believe what she was hearing? Leon Birkshire was dead? How could this be? It was all so sudden. Her mind was rocked with a hundred questions.

"What happened?" Are you sure it's Leo?" Alice asked.

"Well, he had his wallet with his drivers' licence in his pants pocket, but we would still like you to come down to the station and identify him," Sergeant McDonald said.

"How could this have happened?" Alice asked, between her tears.

"We don't know for sure, and we are investigating, but at this point it doesn't look like foul play. Looks like he probably slipped and knocked his head on the side of the boat, then fell into the water," Detective Gallant remarked.

"Was your husband feeling well lately or did he have any health issues?" McDonald asked.

"No. No, not at all," Alice answered. Then she quickly added, "Well come to think of it, he was having some feelings of being light headed lately, but I don't think he had been to the doctor yet." She looked up nervously at Shimi, who was still standing behind her and holding her shoulder.

"I see. And what about psychologically? Did he take any medications or suffer from depression?" Gallant inquired.

"No. He works for the CBC and was happy with his life and his work," Alice said. "Do you think he committed suicide? Is that what you're implying?"

"No. We're not suggesting anything at this point. We simply try to look at every angle," McDonald said.

"Does your husband have any problems with drugs or alcohol?" Gallant asked.

"He doesn't do drugs, but does have a few drinks, like anyone else," Alice replied. "Nothing excessive."

"Has he been in any kind of trouble lately? Perhaps financial trouble or some sort of personal trouble?" Gallant asked.

"Not that he's mentioned. He seemed himself the last time I saw him," Alice said and she put her hand on Shimi's hand on her shoulder. She looked up at her friend in solidarity. Shimi squeezed her shoulder and nodded her head, as if to say, 'You're doing great.'

"When was that? The last time you saw him," the detective inquired.

"I guess it would have been Tuesday. Tuesday morning."

"That was five days ago. Is everything okay in your marriage?" McDonald asked.

"Yes, but I'm a midwife and have been staying here with Ms. Montray since her baby was born on Tuesday evening. There were a few complications." Alice squeezed Shimi's hand once again.

"Have you received any questionable texts from him lately?" MacDonald asked.

"The last time I heard from him, he said he was going fishing. I tried to contact him after that, but he didn't reply to any of my texts, so that's when I contacted the police. I've been so worried," Alice said.

"May I take a look at your cell phone, Ms. Matters? Would that be alright with you? I don't have a warrant," Detective Gallant added.

"Yes, of course. I will open it for you." Alice pulled the phone from her sundress pocket, unlocked it and opened the chat from

Leo. Gallant looked at the texts from the last few days and passed the phone back to her.

"Your husband's texts were rather demanding. Is that typical of him?" Gallant asked.

"Well, he was concerned I was having to spend so much time with Shimi. He worries that I work too hard and don't take care of myself." Alice released a tired sigh.

"I see." MacDonald nodded his head up and down.

"Do you know of anyone who would like to harm him? Any enemies, so to speak?" Detective Gallant pressed a final question.

"Enemies? No, of course not. Everyone loves … loved Leo." Alice's voice cracked with more tears.

"Okay, well if there is anything you can think of, anything at all which might help us figure out what happened to your husband, please give us a call," Detective Gallant said, handing his business card to Alice. He also handed one to Shimi.

"There will be a toxicology report in a couple of days. We will let you know those results. As yet, I don't know whether there will be an autopsy. We will decide that after the toxicology report," Detective Gallant said.

"Would you like us to drive you to the station?" Sergeant McDonald asked.

Shimi stepped forward and quickly said, "I can take Alice to the station. We will get ready and be there in about an hour or so. Is that okay?"

"Yes, of course. At the station, ask for me and I will take you to the coroner's office," Detective Gallant said.

The police officers once again expressed their sincere condolences, then left. Shimi closed the screen door behind them and watched them back down the lane and drive along the road, until they were out of sight.

Shimi put Baby in the bedroom and then walked into the living room. Alice was curled on her side on the sofa. Her arm was swung over the edge with the back of her hand resting on the floor.

"I'm so sorry Alice. How are you doing?" Shimi asked, sitting down at the end of the sofa and placing Alice's bare feet in her lap.

Alice wiped her eyes with the back of her hand and said in a hollow, toneless voice, "Well I guess our problem is solved, isn't it?"

"Oh Alice, don't talk like that. True, there were many times I wished him dead, but now this has happened, I don't know what to think," Shimi said.

"It's a convenient end to a difficult problem," Alice sighed. "But I am kind of feeling weird. I don't know how to feel. Relieved? Sad? Guilty? Confused?"

"How about feeling all those things. Just feel what you feel. But why would you ever feel guilty?" Shimi inquired.

Alice hesitated and said, "Oh, I meant I feel guilty about not helping you. About not leaving Leo years ago. Not exposing Leo now ... all that and more."

"Well, let that feeling go. You have no reason to feel guilty, but we have to be careful when questioned. Please ... please don't mention anything about the rape or Baby. There might be too many questions directed at us, know what I mean?"

"Yes! Yes, of course. I will try to keep my head." There was a bitterness in Alice's voice Shimi had not heard before.

"Thank you, Alice, and once again, I am so sorry." Shimi began to gently rub Alice's feet.

"No, no you're not Shimi, and you don't need to pretend you are. We know each other better than that. Call it karma. Call it retribution, whatever you want. Leo was a bad person, and he got what he deserved." Then, she cried silently into the sofa pillow.

The word "retribution" resonated in Shimi's mind. She was about to ask about it, when suddenly Eddie and Belladane came rushing through the kitchen door and into the living room. Their faces were ashen. They said they had been waiting patiently for the police to leave, but the officers had sat in their car for a few moments on the road, before they finally took off. They wanted to know everything. Shimi stood up, but Alice remained on the sofa.

"Leon was found dead this morning in the water near Naufrage. They think he fell and hit his head on the edge of the boat and then drowned," Shimi said calmly.

Belladane let out a dramatic, "Oh God!"

Eddie stood silently, stoically expressionless.

Shimi continued, "They will do a toxicology report and perhaps an autopsy, but as yet don't suspect foul play. Alice has to go to the station to identify his body."

Belladane sat down beside Alice on the sofa and began to rub her back, "I'm so sorry, Alice. How are you doing? I can drive you to the police station, if you want."

Shimi said, "No, I'm going to drive Alice."

"Do you think that's wise?" Eddie asked. "You're tired, Shimi. You've just had a baby."

"No, I want to do it. I need to do this." Shimi's voice was loud and firm. She didn't say any more, but she knew she wanted to see Leon Birkshire's dead body and that made her feel rather wicked and ashamed.

Shimi softened her voice and turned to Belladane, saying, "Could you watch Baby for a couple of hours?"

"Of course, where is the little angel?" Belladane asked.

"She's sleeping in the middle dresser drawer in my bedroom. Darcy's keeping an eye on her," Shimi said.

"Oh Shimi," Belladane scowled.

"She's safe. It's no different than the cradle," Shimi said.

"It most certainly is," Belladane protested.

The two women drove to the police station. It felt good to be in the air-conditioned car. They sat silently the entire way. Alice leaned her head against the passenger window and every few minutes released a heavy sigh. When Shimi glanced over at her, she was reminded of her drive to the hospital the morning after her rape. She had assumed the same position in the car, the quintessential posture of a woman haunted and afraid.

When they arrived, Detective Gallant was waiting and accompanied them to the coroner's morgue. Walking down the long, white hallway towards the morgue reminded Shimi of her parents' death, and how she never saw their bodies after the car wreck. Belladane had said it was for the best, saying she should remember them the way they were. Yet there were times over the years Shimi wished she had insisted that she see them one last time, no matter what they looked like.

They stopped outside the door of the morgue. Alice turned to Shimi and said, "You don't have to go in. I can do this."

"No, I'm coming with you," Shimi replied. She knew she wanted to see the body. She felt a vindictive pleasure in seeing the rapist's corpse, and this made her feel ashamed. But she didn't care. She would finally look the man in his face, the man who had brutally raped her and fathered her child. She had worried about coming face to face with Leon Birkshire in a courtroom, which would have both humiliated and frightened her, but this was better than any scenario she had imagined. Leon Birkshire was in a morgue, and she would identify his cold, evil body. She would hold his final look in her memory forever. This was both a terror and a satisfying thrill.

When Leon's body was rolled out of the storage vault and the white sheet was pulled back to his chest, Leon's stonelike face stared out at them. His eyes were half open, his face white and bloated.

Alice let out a gasp and turned her face to Shimi's shoulder. Shimi put her arm around her shaking friend.

"That's him," Shimi said, staring directly at Leon's horrific face. She observed, with fascination, the raised, red birthmark on the right side of his long, slender neck. "That's Leon Birkshire."

"Yes, that's my husband," Alice said softly, but she continued to look away.

The two women who hated Leon Birkshire went back down the long hallway, their shoes echoing as they walked towards a new chapter in their lives. The rotting corpse of the man who had terrorized them was rolled back into cold storage, and the heavy metal door slammed closed.

Two weeks later, after an autopsy revealed that the back of Leon's head had struck the side of his metal boat, and he then died of drowning, the pathologist concluded that the death was not suspicious in nature. Immediately thereafter, an intimate memorial service was held for a popular man who no one actually knew. Four CBC colleagues, two neighbours, two of Alice's colleagues and a cousin, Leo's parents, his sister and her two children came to pay their respect to a man who they thought was a hard-working journalist and all-around good guy. Belladane and Eddie offered to go to the service with Shimi and Alice, but everyone decided it was best they stay home with Baby. Shimi pumped milk for the infant and said she would try to be back within a couple of hours. Belladane encouraged her to stay with Alice as long as necessary, saying it was important that someone was with her, guiding her through this difficult time.

At the funeral, Leon's younger sister, Marlene, spoke and told tender and loving stories of their childhood in Nova Scotia: Leon taking her camping and teaching her how to catch frogs; Leon driving to Sackville University and bringing her home when she caught mononucleosis; Leon building his father raised garden beds, when his dad could no longer bend over to weed his prize vegetables. The stories were of an everyday loving man, who touched the hearts of his family in so many wonderful ways.

Many questions flooded Shimi's thoughts. How could such a loving, little boy grow into such a monster? And how could this monster have such an opposing loving side? What had happened to him to make him this way, or did he simply grow into his true self over time with no negative provocation at all?

Shimi had ordered a bouquet of yellow roses on Alice's behalf. The white ribbon read, "A Loving Husband." They looked pretty on a stoa sitting next to a photo of a handsome Leon Birkshire. Sitting next to Leon's urn was a huge flower arrangement that cascaded over the side of the table. It read "A Loving Son." The minister gave a caring commentary on life, death and love. He said he didn't know Leon personally, but had enjoyed his "intimate and poignant CBC stories" over the years. The minister's touching prayer spoke of forgiveness and friendship. Shimi felt guilty that she didn't feel one ounce of remorse over Leon's death and although Alice wept continually throughout the service, Shimi's eyes remained dry.

Leo's favourite song, "Into the Mystic" by Van Morrison, played while his nephew, Craig, carried the urn down the aisle. Alice and Shimi followed and got into the back of a shiny, black sedan. Craig placed the urn on Alice's lap and then closed the door. Leon's family followed behind in their own cars.

Alice's hands visibly shook while holding Leon's ashes. Shimi feared Alice would drop the urn. She envisioned the urn would topple over, the lid would come off, and the ashes would be tossed all over them. That would be a horror she could not endure.

"Do you want me to hold the urn for you, Alice?" she asked.

"No, of course not! I can do it," Alice snapped, with an anger that surprised Shimi. Shimi remained silent and gazed out the car window for the rest of the journey to Sherwood Cemetery, where Leon Birkshire would finally be laid to rest in a family plot.

Alice was very obliging when it came to the family's requests for the funeral arrangements. She was actually happy she didn't have to plan it on her own. She agreed to all the family's requests and arrangements. She only made one decision on her own. She secretly took a cup of ashes from Leon's urn the night before the funeral, carefully placing the grey powder in an empty cookie jar on the kitchen counter.

Throughout the entire day of Leon's funeral, Alice played the grieving widow well, and Shimi never left her side. After the cemetery, seven folks gathered at the Hunter Ale House for some suicide hot chicken wings and craft beer, two of Leon's favourite things. Leon's dad gave a short and tearful toast to his only son, while his bereaved mother rushed to the ladies' room three times. An hour later, Alice paid the bill, left a hefty tip for the waitstaff and excused herself, saying she had to meet a client who was due any day. There were hugs all around, plenty of tears, and although she had never been that close to Leon's family, they made her promise she would keep in touch and maybe even visit them next year in Manitoba . . . a promise she knew she would not keep. She needed to be entirely free of Leon Birkshire and anything or anyone who reminded her of him.

As Leon's sweet mother clung to Alice and wept, Shimi swept away the first trace of her own tears. A mother's son! A mother's most dreadful fear, the death of her child. Leon Birkshire's mother had become a vilomah, without warning, with no chance of saying goodbye. Shimi knew the only consolation of Leon's sudden death was that Catherine Birkshire would never know the truth about her son. She would never have to accept that her son, who was a renowned CBC journalist by day, was an evil rapist by night. She would never have to face that sorrow, that all-consuming shame.

Shimi drove Alice home to her house. She stood in Alice's living room trying to convince Alice to come and stay with her for a few days, but Alice insisted she wanted to be alone. Shimi finally gave up. As Shimi was about to leave, Alice presented to her a white envelope saying, "I remember months ago you said you would like a piece of the man who raped you. So here he is Shimi. Here's a piece of Leo. Do whatever you want with his ashes."

Shimi was shocked and rather horrified with Alice's gift, but she accepted it with the sentiment in which it was given. She stood for a moment looking at the envelope in her hand, wondering what she would ever do with what was left of Leon Birkshire.

Alice stood silently and wept. Shimi took her friend in her arms and tried to give Alice the best hug she had ever shared in her entire life. Alice's body shook within her tender embrace. Suddenly, Shimi began to cry as well, but she knew tomorrow her eyes would not be puffy.

July 2023
Dear Elsa,

    Hope you are doing well. Things have drastically changed around here. Shimi's baby was born this month, and you'll never guess what I did. I helped deliver the baby in a small wading pool in the backyard. It was the most incredible experience I have ever been part of. No words, really.

    She is the most beautiful baby girl and since she isn't officially named yet, we all just call her Baby, which seems to suit her well. Shimi doesn't know whether she will keep the baby or put her up for adoption. A really tough decision, and I'm trying to be supportive either way, but I must admit, I already love that little munchkin, and believe it or not, I'm getting very good at changing diapers!

    Things are very stressful around here, as we discovered the man who raped Shimi. He was the husband of the midwife, Alice, who helped Shimi with her pregnancy. I write "was" as he is now dead, which wasn't soon enough for me. Now Shimi doesn't need to humiliate herself by going public with the long-drawn-out stressful court case. The guy was found drowned after a fishing trip. Couldn't have happened to a better guy! Karma, maybe! Fate! Who knows, maybe retribution. Whatever you want to call it.

    So, there are a lot of different types of grieving going on around here, and time will tell what happens next. I feel badly for Alice, finding out her husband is a rapist, but she has found a sanctuary here with Belladane and Shimi. I am very fond of these three women and I'm willing to do whatever it takes to keep them safe.

    As you can tell, I really feel that this is my new home. I don't miss California much, but I miss you every day. Why don't you come and visit me? Belladane has lots of room in this old farm house. Think about it. Hope you are doing well, Sis!

IloveyaandImissya!
Eddie

XXX
(definitively)

DESPITE IT NOT being hers, Sergeant Melanie Malone was extremely interested in the Leon Birkshire case. Something seemed to nag at the back of her mind. She didn't know what. When most of her colleagues had left for the day, she took the case file from Detective Gallant's desk. She knew this was slightly unprofessional, but she needed to have a look. She carefully went through the enclosed documents and photos, both the hard copies and the computer files.

The coroner's report stated that Leon Birkshire had died of a blunt strike to the back of his head. Traces of Birkshire's blood were found on the edge of his boat. It was anticipated his body had then fallen into the water and been there for approximately twenty-four hours. Toxicity reports indicated there was no alcohol or drugs of any kind in his system. She looked at the coroner's photos of Leon Birkshire and saw the raised red birthmark on the right side of his neck. You don't see those very often, she thought. She was immediately reminded of Mikhail Gorbachev, the Russian leader, who had such a mark on his forehead.

Sergeant Malone pondered Birkshire's fatal head injury. If the back of his head had struck the edge of the boat, how did his body end up in the water? Surely, with this kind of fall he would have slumped forward or simply slid down into his boat. Perhaps he didn't pass out right away? Perhaps he struck his head and then tumbled over the side a few moments later? And with a gash that large, why wasn't there more blood on the bottom of the boat? Perhaps it had been washed away while adrift?

Something didn't feel right.

The evidence file cited the contents of the boat: a rope, power motor, gasoline can, metal fishing tackle box, a metal water bottle, and two life jackets. Inside the tackle box were typical items for fishing gear: hooks, a spool of 30-pound line, a Swiss Army knife, a filleting knife in a leather sheath, lures, a braided turquoise bracelet, the style children make at summer camp; a silver hoop earring with some fish hooks threaded through it; and an old, yellowed bone button. There was a photo that had been taken of all these items laid out on a table. Malone zoomed in on her computer and looked at each item carefully. She could see why he might use a silver hoop earring to organize small fish hooks. And many people get those little braided bracelets given to them by children. But what about the button? It was a unique object. Surely Detective Gallant had looked into these items.

Malone stared at the old, bone button. Why did this resonate with her? She couldn't quite put her finger on it, but she knew she had come across that item before. She was on her way home from work, when she recalled the button. She immediately pulled a U turn and raced back to the station.

She took the case file of Shirley Ann Montray from the evidence room. Opening it, she read once again the contents of the file she had made herself. The victim has stated that she had felt a patch of raised lumpy skin on the right side of the rapist's neck. And he had ripped a bone button from Montray's wool coat. She opened the file on her computer and found the photos of the coat. She zoomed in for a close look at the buttons. They were an identical match to the one photographed in Birkshire's tackle box.

Malone's body went cold. She quickly wrote an email request to Ken Burton, the head of the forensics lab in Halifax, requesting the rape kit of Shirley Montray be processed as soon as possible. She was sending the kit by FedEx tonight, and she would send a sample of DNA to them within 24 hours. She wrote, "Put a rush on it, and once analyzed please send the findings to me directly." Malone knew Ken would do exactly as requested, since he was an old high school friend, and he owed her a couple of favours. She was reminded of the time during a spot check Ken had been pulled over by her partner, while she inspected another driver. Ken had blown over the legal limit and Melanie had quickly nodded at her partner, and then drove Ken home and told him to "get a cab" next time. As well, over the years there had been two cancelled speeding tickets.

She spent the entire night going through all the rape files from previous years. And by 1 am she had what she was looking for. One victim, Corrine Flynn, had been walking home from work one night when a man with his face covered had forced his way into her home when she unlocked the door. He had struck her from behind and had choked her. Just before he fled, he kicked her and ripped a braided turquoise bracelet from her arm. Malone googled Flynn's name and found a CBC archived report, regarding her community garden project in Stratford. The interview had been done by Leon Birkshire three months prior to Flynn's rape. Four years ago, another woman, Donna Dal Santo, had reported a rape that was never solved, and that rapist had taken one of her silver hoop earrings. He had ripped it out of her earlobe. Malone stared at the photo of her bloody right ear for a very long time. She googled Donna Dal Santo and discovered six months prior to the rape she also had been interviewed by Birkshire regarding a Women's Film Festival being hosted by Charlottetown's Independent Cinema. In her quick search, she found one other rape victim who had been interviewed by Leon Birkshire. Malone's spine began to tingle, and she wondered how many more there truly were.

Leon Birkshire was a serial rapist and with the DNA results from these three kits, she knew she would be able to prove it. This was the kind of detective work rarely experienced in quaint Prince Edward Island. No, this was the kind of stuff you see on TV shows, like Law and Order, Special Victims Report. Malone's mind exploded with excitement and pride.

As soon as the lab results from the rape kits were in her hand, this report would be on her Chief's desk. This was exactly what she needed to finally be promoted to Detective. This would be her big break, which was long overdue.

Malone drove home with her mind racing like a run-away train. She fell into her bed, and got four hours sleep before her clock radio jolted her into a new day.

When CBC Administration Offices opened that morning, Malone was at their door. She showed her badge, and spoke with Jerry the security guard, saying she was there to take a look at Leon Birkshire's office. No questions were asked. Janet, the pretty receptionist, volunteered to escort her to the small cubicle near the end of the large open-space room. There were no other journalists at their desks yet, and Malone was relieved. She wanted to get in and get out quickly. And with as few questions as possible. As Janet was about to step away and leave Malone at Birkshire's tidy desk, she turned and quietly said to the officer, "You know, Leon Birkshire was not a good man."

"What do you mean?" questioned Malone.

Janet suddenly looked nervous. "Sorry. I shouldn't have said anything, and I don't really want to say anything more." She turned and walked away quickly.

Malone didn't press the subject any further, as she was sure she already had all the incriminating information and evidence she needed to label Leon Birkshire a serial rapist.

Malone rifled through Birkshire's desk and found numerous other items which typically belong to women: a hair tie, another earring, and a small brooch with a poodle on it. Malone took photos of these, and then placed them in separate evidence bags. She also took the stained coffee mug on his desk, and strands of hair from a brush in his bottom drawer. They would be excellent samples of his DNA. Even though she knew her investigation was not by the book, and the evidence might be inadmissible in court, she was pleased with her findings. It was a start to a much larger investigation that would follow.

Waiting for several days for the rape kit results was torture for Malone, but when Burton finally sent her his analysis, she knew she had the evidence she needed. The DNA of Leon Birkshire matched all the rape kits Burton had analyzed. She also wondered how many other rapes might not have been reported.

For some strange reason she didn't go running, as initially planned, to her Chief with the proof. She was worried that he and Detective Gallant would be angry with her under-handed methods, and her meddling in another detective's case. It also crossed her mind that perhaps these two men knew more than they were revealing. Leon Birkshire was a bit of a celebrity in town. Was there some kind of cover-up going on? All these thoughts worried her. So, she sat on the information for a day.

Then she knew what she had to do.

Melanie Malone drove to Shirley Montray's house the next day. She wasn't sure exactly what she was going to say, but she knew she had to speak with Shimi. The new mother seemed startled and extremely uncomfortable when Malone arrived unexpectedly in her yard. Malone asked if she could talk to Shimi, and if they could sit in the gazebo.

"How are you doing, Shimi?" Malone asked. "And who do we have here?" Malone looked fondly at the baby and gently shook her chubby bare leg.

Malone realized Shimi was very nervous when she asked about the newborn baby in her arms. Shimi quickly said, "I'm okay."

"Are you really?" Sergeant Malone questioned.

"Well, let's say I'm getting better. For the longest time I was just ... just a suggestion of myself, but now since Baby, I am starting to feel better. More at peace."

Shimi motioned Malone to sit down across from her in the wicker rocking chair.

"Your rape was October, if I remember correctly. A little over nine months ago," Malone said. "I have to ask ... is this baby ..."

Shimi hesitated for a moment and then quickly said, "Yes. Yes. The baby is ..."

"You never told me you were pregnant, Shimi. I'm so sorry. I feel I've let you down."

The two women sat together and talked for a long while. Sergeant Malone told Shimi about the death of Leon Birkshire. Shimi confessed she had heard of his death and that ironically his wife had been her midwife.

"That's PEI for you. Word gets around fast," Malone said.

Then Malone went on to tell Shimi of her other findings. Of all the other rapes, the trinkets kept by Leon, and how she had seen pictures of Shimi's antique button. Shimi started to weep uncontrollably. She put the baby down on the sofa beside her. In doing so Malone noticed the large red birthmark on the side of the baby's neck.

Malone pointed to the mark. "He had the same birthmark, didn't he? The mark you felt on his neck that night," Malone asked.

"Yes," Shimi responded curtly.

"Did your midwife, Birkshire's wife, comment on the matching birthmarks? Does she know her husband was your rapist?"

"At the birth she said these birthmarks can be quite common and often can fade."

"I see," Malone said. "It's a wonder she didn't mention her husband had the exact same one."

"She probably sees lots of birthmarks in her business." Shimi responded as calmly as possible and then continued. "Leon Birkshire seemed like such a nice guy. I never would have known he was evil like that. Should I tell Alice what I now know? But he's dead now, so now what happens?" Shimi tried not to stammer with her words.

"What do you want to happen, Shimi? I came here confused, yet I thought I knew what I needed to do. Now I'm not so sure. I see your precious little girl ... and now I wonder ..."

"She is almost enough to make the horror of that night disappear. It's like she is my most beautiful ... catastrophe." Shimi stroked the side of Baby's face.

"What's her name?" Malone asked.

"I haven't named her yet ... I know, I know that's weird, but there is something holding me back, and I can't really explain it," Shimi said. "Do you have kids?"

"Yes, I have two teens, thirteen and sixteen. They're a handful," Malone sighed.

"I know this is a strange question and very forward of me, but if I may ask ... are you glad you had kids?" Shimi asked.

"Well to be perfectly honest ... there are moments I can't breathe because my love for them is so powerful, and then there are times, I could scratch their eyes out. Sometimes, when they are bickering or things are crazy busy, I feel they have sucked every ounce of life and joy out of me. But then I come home late at night from work and I sneak into their bedrooms while they sleep, and I stare at their beautiful faces, and I could weep with the love I feel for those two brats." Malone stared off across the lawn and watched the birds at one of the feeders.

Then Malone continued, "Yes, believe me, being a mother isn't always a straight line of maternal fulfilment. It can be a shit show of mixed emotions and indecisions, love and even resentment."

Shimi nodded and also turned to the birds.

"Shimi, what do you know regarding the death of Leon Birkshire?" Malone asked.

Shimi looked shocked at the blunt turn of the conversation. "All I know is it's over. All the horror, all the pain he put women through," Shimi said as she put her finger out and let Baby clasp onto it.

"I think Leon Birkshire might have been murdered. Do you have any idea who might have done that?" Malone questioned.

Shimi said empathically, "Sounds to me like there could be lots of people who would like to hurt Leon Birkshire." Shimi looked hard at Sergeant Malone and kept her eyes from going to her lap. Inside she was terrified, and her mind was spinning, but she continued to look innocently at Malone.

"You didn't answer my question," Malone said.

"No! No, I guess I didn't." Shimi gave a quick glance at Malone and then picked up Baby.

"Hypothetically speaking, if Leon Birkshire was still alive and I had discovered this information, would you have been willing to come forward with your rape case?" Malone asked.

"I hope I would have. But I don't know, now that I have Baby. There would be lots of things to consider," Shimi said. "I guess I will never know now just what I would have been willing to do to bring Leon Birkshire to justice."

"Would you have wanted him dead?" Malone pressed the question.

Shimi finally gave in. "Yes! Yes, of course. I have daydreamed about killing my attacker. But I wouldn't have done it. Isn't that why most women are rotting away in prison? For killing their abusers? For putting an end to what the police couldn't stop."

The two women stared at each other for a long time, and Shimi's eyes never wavered. Malone nodded her head up and down at Shimi, and Shimi did the same. Their silent stare brought them to a mutual understanding.

"Okay, I'll be on my way," Sergeant Malone said. "Good luck to you and your daughter, Shimi. Despite how she was created, she is indeed a precious little one."

"Thanks. And for the sake of this precious little one, I hope this is over and done. We've been through enough," Shimi said quietly.

"Yes, you have," Malone said. "Yes, you definitely have." And as she walked past the sofa, she let the back of her hand caress the baby's cheek. Then she walked slowly to her car and left.

As she drove down the highway, she thought of her favourite novel, *To Kill a Mockingbird*. The scene where Sheriff Tate tells Atticus Finch that evil Mr. Ewell fell on his knife, even though both men knew that Boo Radley had stabbed Ewell to save Jem. Tate had said that prosecuting Boo Radley would be like killing a mockingbird. As a new cop, Malone had initially struggled with that scene, a police officer's duty was to tell the truth and uphold the law - but now she understood. She knew what she had to do.

Five days later, Detective Gallant would close the file on the death of Leon Birkshire, and label it, "Died of Natural Causes, Case Closed." Sergeant Malone would watch from across the office, as he took it to the evidence room for permanent filing. She would breathe a huge sigh of relief and hope that file would never be opened again.

Sergeant Malone called the forensics lab in Halifax where the results had been processed. She spoke with her buddy, Ken Burton.

Ken inquired, "What's going on with those reports I sent you last week. Looks like we have a serial rapist on our hands."

"Well, it's still under investigation and the guy is an American so they don't want us to say anything yet. You know how these things get tangled in political bureaucracy and it will all take more time than necessary," Malone said. "I'd appreciate it if you would just sit on this information, Ken. Keep it to yourself."

"American? Really? No worries, Melanie, but be careful. I trust you know what you're doing, and you have your reasons. It won't be the first cover up I've been a part of, and it probably won't be the last. All in a day's work, as the police say. Have a good weekend, my dear."

"Thanks. You too, Ken." Malone said, as she hung up the phone. She knew this conversation might not completely solve her problem forever, but at least it had given her some time.

She knew what she did to help Shimi Montray and her beautiful daughter was not helping Birkshire's other victims, who would always wonder if their rapist would ever be punished, or if he might strike again. She wished there was a way of alleviating their worry, but she didn't know how to do that.

As she drove home to her children that evening she pondered the case and knew it would sit on her shoulder poking at her, for some time. Was his death simply karma, after all? Or perhaps it was calculated retribution and Leon Birkshire did not die of natural causes? If that was the case, she knew, despite the poking of her conscience, she would be okay with this new modern-day Boo Radley taking matters into his own hands. She knew the truth was not purely black or white. That there is often a huge difference between the truth and its justice. And in this case, soon the difference would no longer bother her.

XXXI
(intensely)

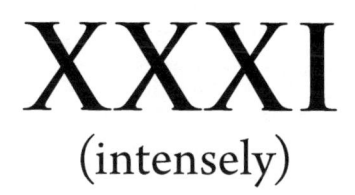

It was only a matter of minutes before Belladane and Eddie were in Shimi's kitchen. They had seen the police car at her house and couldn't wait to find out what was going on. With faces grave and curious, they both sat down at Shimi's mother's turquoise arborite table, a relic from the 1970's. Next to the fridge, Baby was sleeping in the clothes hamper with Darcy by her side.

Shimi poured everyone a glass of iced tea and then plunked herself down next to them with a loud sigh.

"Well? Don't keep us waiting," Belladane exclaimed, her voice shaking. "What's going on?"

"Well, first Sergeant Malone informed me that Leon Birkshire is dead. I told her I knew because of Alice being my midwife. She also informed me that he was the rapist and had raped at least three other women," Shimi said with a quiver in her voice.

"The bastard. I knew it!" Eddie cried, slamming his fist down on the table. Then he looked uncomfortable, surprised that he had blurted these words out loud.

"Oh my God! A serial rapist? He seemed so normal! That evil man!" Belladane rubbed her hands back and forth on the table. "Poor Alice," she added under her breath.

Shimi couldn't look her friends in their eyes, so she focused on stroking the petals of the daisies she had arranged in a small vase on the table. "She asked me if I already knew my rapist was Leon? She was suspicious. Of course, I said no."

"Good!" Eddie and Belladane said at the same time.

"But I think she suspects Leon was murdered. I thought the news report said he died of natural causes? So, she must have new information, but she didn't say what. And she asked if I knew of anyone who would want to kill him." Shimi looked up at her friends, her eyes wide with concern.

"And what did you say?" Belladane asked, her voice rising an octave.

"Of course, I said no. What do you think I said? Why would you even ask?" Shimi looked sternly at Belladane.

"Do you think she believed you?" Belladane moved her frantic hands under the table, where she dragged them back and forth along her red capri pants.

"I don't know. But she would know of course I would want to kill him, if I knew it was him. I'm not a good liar, but I didn't get the feeling she thought I was lying or that I was a murderer."

Belladane looked anxious. "All I know is when cops tell you or ask you something, they are normally fishing for something that they already know ... know what I mean?"

"What would she be fishing for?" Shimi asked, staring at her aunt.

"Let's not over think it. She probably just wanted to let you know about your case," Eddie interjected. He stood up and walked to look out the kitchen window. He pushed back his hair and sighed. He watched the tiny finches flit back and forth from the bird feeder.

"So, now what? Are they going to release all this information to the public?" Eddie asked, still staring at the birds.

"I don't think so. But she did see Baby. I didn't have to tell her. She knew," Shimi pushed her hair behind her ears. "She knew she is his."

"Oh dear, that's not good." Belladane shook her head and looked away. "That's not good."

"Why? What do you mean?" Shimi asked.

"Of course, she will report all this. It's to her advantage to close the case," Belladane said. "This is big news. Could be all across Canada by tomorrow!

"I don't think she is going to do anything. What would be the point? The man is dead," Shimi stared into her glass of water. "And ... I kind of begged her not to."

"Let's hope you're right. You, Baby and Alice have been through enough," Eddie said, sitting back down at the table. He gulped down his glass of iced tea, then smiled at Shimi and put his hand across hers. The coolness of his hand comforted her. "Everything's going to be alright," he said, looking hard into her eyes.

Shimi placed her other hand upon his and for the first time in a long time, she believed it would be.

She knew this was the moment, the moment she had been desperately trying to face since the night of Baby's birth. The moment that had crept into her every waking thought, shadowed all her daydreams and her frequent nightmares. She had the privacy and the undivided attention of Belladane and Eddie. "No time like the present," she thought.

Shimi walked across the kitchen and picked the baby out of the hamper. She placed the infant into Belladane's eager arms and then sat down beside her aunt. Belladane beamed at Baby and touched her finger to her tiny nose and to her hands. Her tight little fists were like tiny pink seashells and her slight whimper was a baby bird's cry. Baby sucked in her tiny lips and continued to sleep.

Shimi softly touched her aunt's paint-speckled arm. Shimi then sat up straight and cleared her throat. "I've made a decision about Baby."

"What? What do you mean? I didn't know there was even a decision anymore. I just assumed ..." Belladane looked at Shimi, her dark, brown eyes blinking anxiously.

"I've given my decision much thought. I've cried over it. I've prayed over it and I'm not even a religious person. I've looked for every sign under the stars, but I now know what I want to do." Shimi looked back and forth from Belladane to Eddie. "I was not meant to be Baby's mother."

"What? No! No! No!" Belladane cried quickly, hugging Baby tightly to her chest. "Shimi, you can't ..."

"Please! Don't!" Shimi blurted out sternly, holding her hand up to her aunt. "At the start of all of this, you said you would support me, no matter what decision I made. You wanted me to have an abortion. But I didn't. Now, you want me to keep Baby. But I can't." Shimi lowered her voice and let out a huge sigh. "I don't want to be a mother and I try to keep telling myself that doing this does not make me a horrible person. I love Baby, but I can't raise Leon Birkshire's child. And I simply want what's best for her."

"Shimi ... you're not a horrible person. I don't think that. But you would be a great mother. You already are a great mother. Don't be afraid. I will help you." Belladane began to cry. Huge tears raced down her face, dripping upon the baby's head. Baby awoke and instantly began to cry. Her tiny clenched fists shook back and forth next to her sweet face. Darcy jumped up, ran over to Belladane and laid his head on Belladane's leg. Eddie stood up and took Baby from Belladane's arms. He left the room and could be heard in the living room speaking softly to her, in his deep, soothing voice.

Shimi pleaded with her aunt. "Auntie, it's going to be alright. Please don't make this any harder for me than it already is. I'm sorry I went all Gordon Ramsay on you, but I need you to try to understand. It's not about fear; it's about doing what is right for me and Baby. I have made my decision. And it's the right one for me and for her. Please try to understand."

Belladane wiped the tears from her face, nodded her head and grabbed her niece's hands so tightly Shimi immediately felt smothered by her aunt's desperation and despair. But as Shimi began to speak some of the most sensitive words she would ever speak in her lifetime, her aunt's large hands wrapped around hers began to soften, and their hands became the comfort that their words could not find.

Shimi tried to explain to her aunt that someday she wanted Leon Birkshire to simply be a minor detail in her life, like a chipped fingernail or the slice of lemon in her tea ... something not noticeable or worthy of comment. She knew raising Baby would not make that possible. Was she selfish to feel this way? Probably. But did she feel she was wrong? No. It simply was what she needed to do.

"I am not a perfect human. And sometimes I wonder why I'm on this planet. Why was I born? What is my purpose for being here? I don't mean to sound all existential on you, but it's what I think. And having this baby has only reinforced these questions. So maybe, just maybe, this is why I am here. I was meant to meet Leon Birkshire. I was meant to conceive Baby, and I was meant to give her to someone who really wants a daughter."

They talked long into the night and Belladane listened carefully to Shimi's words, every painful one. Belladane finally promised she would support Shimi's decision to give Baby up for adoption. They hugged for a very long time. Shimi knew that within days she would lose her daughter, but she would not lose her aunt, and this gave her a tiny bit of comfort.

When the women walked into the living room, they found Eddie sound asleep on the sofa with Baby sleeping peacefully on his chest, his arms wrapped securely around her. Shimi's heart rose up to her throat. She never wanted to forget this image. She never wanted to break this beautiful bond, but she knew deep down, her decision was the right one.

Both women stood staring at this dear man and this sweet baby. They held onto each other and silently wept.

XXXII
(powerfully)

ALICE WAS BACK living full time in her own home, but she still made weekly trips to visit Belladane, Eddie, Shimi and of course, Baby. They had become the family she didn't have. Belladane had invited her to a family dinner the next night. She said it would be "a celebration of Baby and her mom." Alice was keen to support Shimi, knowing in the beginning she had had a difficult time bonding with her newborn. Belladane was rather closed-lipped about the party, but Alice was sure it was to celebrate Baby being officially named and welcomed into the family. To help Shimi continue with her long-distance serenity walks, Alice had bought her a backpack that would comfortably hold Baby. She knew Shimi would get lots of good use out of the gift. It was wrapped and ready for the event, sitting on the backseat of her car.

Alice had just finished baking an apple pie to take to the party, when a knock came to her side door. Alice opened it and found Shimi beaming at her with Baby asleep in her arms, and Darcy panting at her feet holding a plastic bowl in his mouth.

"Hey there, girlfriend," Shimi said. "Want some company?"

"Sure," Alice replied. Shimi handed Baby to Alice, and went to the kitchen with Darcy to fill up his bowl with cool water.

"This is a nice surprise," Alice laughed. "Let's sit in the gazebo. It's too hot in here. I've been baking a pie."

"Oh, you and your perfect pies. That's another culinary art I have never been able to master. Is there anything you can't do?" Shimi sighed, with her hands on her hips.

Alice mimicked Shimi, putting her own hands on her hips, and said, "Yes, one thing I can't do is get you to realize how wonderful you are."

Shimi rolled her eyes.

Darcy finished lapping at his cold water. Looking at him, Alice said, "Your Mamma's too hard on herself. Come on Darcy, to the gazebo."

Darcy was immediately at the door, leading the way.

In Alice's gazebo, Shimi plunked herself down onto the tattered sofa with a tired moan. Alice brought out iced tea and the two women chatted like they had known each other forever, instead of simply a few months. It had been over a month since Leon's death and she was recovering, slowly coming out from under the fog that was the reality of Leon's evil life. She was working on building a new happiness, despite the humiliation and horror that was attached to her husband. Now she could not think of one good memory of Leon without thinking about his evil deeds, as well. Everything she thought she knew was a lie. She realized she never knew the man to whom she had been married for over ten years. And this made her anxious and ashamed.

"You can't blame yourself, Alice. Leon was a chameleon. I never would have guessed the smart, interesting man who interviewed me was a rapist," Shimi said.

"I won't be able to live long enough to adequately apologize for my husband. What he did to you ..." Alice's eyes welled up with tears. "I'm so sorry. You know deep down inside I knew something was off about him. I knew he was up to something. I should have dug deeper. I just thought he had anger issues, or maybe I just really didn't want to know. I'm so sorry." Alice knew this was the umpteenth time she had apologized to Shimi. Her apologies felt like she was chanting the mantra of some obsessive cult, but she didn't know what else to say. She began to cry with her tears running down her cheeks and pooling in the cavity of her collarbone.

Shimi looked at her friend with sympathy and love. She knew there was no room big enough for Alice's shame and grief. "Wives often feel responsible for their husband's evil deeds, whether it is spouse abuse, or abuse of others. They shouldn't. You are not going to take ownership of Leon's life and choices," Shimi said, putting her arm around her friend's shoulders. "None of this, and I mean NONE of this, is your fault."

"I know that in theory, but it is so hard in practice." Alice tried to paste a fake smile upon her face.

"Well, you have to start living a new chapter. And thanks to Sergeant Malone no one knows about Leon, except us, so you have no reason to feel awkward or ashamed in public. Probably no one else will ever know. Which is good ... and bad, of course. But that's the choice we made, right?" Shimi stretched her legs out on the old sofa. For Alice's sake, she forced herself to look and sound confident and relaxed. She had thought on her drive here she might tell Alice about her decision about Baby, but now she was here, she was sure it wasn't the right time. Alice was struggling too much.

"Yes. I'm trying not to beat myself up every single minute of the day that I didn't know what he was up to. And I hope my future is not simply plagued with bad memories, or simply divided into the time before or the time after all this evil happened." Alice began to stroke the tiny bit of ginger hair on Baby's head. "Never mind me. You look really tired, Shimi. Are you doing alright?" Alice rocked Baby gently in her lap, but stayed focused on Shimi.

"Well, yes and no. If Baby isn't fussing or needing attention, then I'm thinking about stuff. So much chaos in my head. I call it the graveyard of my mind. So, I don't get a lot of sleep. I try to sleep when she sleeps, but it doesn't always work out that way. Sometimes I think someone else is controlling my thoughts. I have no control over them whatsoever. Sometimes I wake up crying and I lament ... I miss my old self. It's like there's a huge loss of my old, happy self. The woman I used to be is dead. I try to put on a happy face during the day for Belladane and Eddie, but at night when I'm alone ... well, at night the internal war rages. I'm fighting the urge to scrub my skin off in the shower. I am fighting the urge to sleep under my bed. It's getting much better, but often I still fall apart. I'm just a puppet, like Pinocchio." Shimi's face changed from serious and reflected a flicker of amusement, when she added, "A Virgin Mary Pinocchio."

"A what? What are you talking about?" Alice leaned forward.

"Oh, I'm just being silly. I got a Christmas card once, years ago, and it had the Virgin Mary on the front, holding her baby, but the funny thing was she had a big, long Pinocchio nose," Shimi laughed. "I thought it was hilarious. The whole virgin Mary thing. And then you know how the story goes. Mary's whole world was turned upside down, without her consent, just like mine. Now I can sort of empathize with her. She had a kid she hadn't planned on and she had no control over her situation. I'm just going through the motions of this motherhood thing, but everything seems like a lie. I feel like a big, fat Pinocchio liar."

"Oh Shimi. Maybe you have some postpartum depression going on."

"I don't think so. I actually think I am slowly coming through to the other side and finally have some clarity about things. I'm facing all my thoughts and even the lies with less fear and anger."

"The lies? What lies? What are you talking about?" Alice inquired.

"Oh, nothing! I just mean all the secrets we have to keep. The lies we tell ourselves about this last year." Shimi turned her anxious eyes from Alice and began to pet Darcy.

"Oh," Alice replied with a worried look on her face. Baby started to fuss, so Alice quickly lifted her up to rest on her shoulder and gently rubbed her back. Shimi breathed a sigh of relief, grateful for the distraction, the interruption.

Baby instantly calmed and went back to sleep. Shimi took a quiet moment and watched Baby comforted in Alice's arms. "You're such a good mother. How did you learn all this? I never know what to do with her. I'm afraid I'll never be a good mother. Not like you."

"Stop Shimi. Your baby will teach you how to be a good mom. And you're doing great. What you've been through this last year is enough to break anyone. And you have survived and come out the other side. Baby is alive and thriving, so you're definitely doing something right."

"Yes, Belladane and Eddie help a lot, but there's more to mothering than feeding and changing diapers. Maybe I don't have what's needed inside, know what I mean? That maternal instinct thing. Maybe I'm just a dog person." Again, Shimi instantly became uncomfortable with what she had revealed. She knew she loved Baby, but also knew there was something missing. But how to explain this to Alice, at this moment, was beyond her ability. Beyond her total understanding. Beyond her tears. So, she quickly added, "But enough about me. How are you doing?"

"I think you definitely have what it takes to be a good mamma. So, let's not hear that kind of talk anymore. But getting back to what you said about control … I know what you mean about things beyond your control. It's been really weird around here since Leo's death. The house is so quiet, empty. He wasn't home much before, but at least I knew he was coming home sometime. I mean, I know I wouldn't have lived with him anymore, knowing what I know now. We would have divorced. Maybe he would have gone to prison. I would have got my own place, so it would have been quiet anyway … but that would have been a plan. Know what I mean? My own control. My own decisions. Not just a circumstance that was thrown upon me."

"I know EXACTLY what you mean. It's tough living a life you didn't plan for. Kind of an emotional minefield. We have no clue what's coming next. Makes us feel rather … discombobulated."

"Good word. Discombobulated is one of those words that sounds like it means. Just all over the place." Alice gave a slight laugh.

I've been listening to a lot of Niykee Heaton music lately, especially the song, *21 Grams*. It resonates with me, for some reason," Shimi said, tucking her legs up under herself.

"21 grams? I hope you're not thinking of taking drugs?" Alice couldn't resist needling her.

Shimi was grateful for the small joke. "No, it's about the weight of your soul. That old disproven theory that your soul weighs 21 grams."

"Oh right. I remember hearing about that in university. The professor said the experiment was limited and flawed. Only one person out of six weighed at death, lost 21 grams; the others remained the same. But you know, I sat there, doodling in my notebook with my little Bic pen and thought, well maybe the experiment wasn't flawed. Maybe the others simply didn't have a soul." Then Alice added quietly, "Kind of like Leo."

"True … maybe most of us don't," Shimi added.

Alice looked at Shimi, raising her eyebrows in surprise. She then lay the sleeping infant down onto the lounge chair beside her and quickly adjusted a flowery curtain so Baby stayed in the shade.

Once again, Shimi instantly felt uncomfortable. "We're getting pretty deep here today, Alice. Don't make too much out of what I say. I'm running on no sleep, remember." Shimi sighed again and started twirling her ponytail.

Alice wouldn't be distracted. She earnestly asked, "Do you think we go on existing in a place, even when we're gone? Our energy, our soul, whatever you want to call it."

"I don't know. Good question. We've been trying to answer that one since the beginning of time. But if I were you, I would do my best to rid yourself of Leo's negative energy and his entire existence, and I will do the same. Get rid of his stuff. Sell this place. Start fresh in another house and maybe another neighbourhood. Just don't leave this province, okay?"

Alice looked tenderly at her friend's face.

Then Shimi continued. "Alice, you need to help all the future mothers you can. You need to paint pretty paintings and not be afraid to hang them all over your beautiful walls. You need to travel to beautiful places. And follow all your dreams. Let us make a vow - we are no longer going to live in the past. Let beautiful Baby be the only reminder of that asshole's life and what a wonderful reminder she is! All 21 plus grams of her."

"Yes, you're right, but you mean all 5000 grams of her,"

"How did you do that so fast?" Shimi laughed.

"I'm good at math, and I did just weigh her the other day, remember? That reminds me. I'll be right back."

Alice stood up and went into the house. She came out minutes later, sat down next to Shimi and said, "Open your hand."

Darcy raised his head from his nap, hoping for a treat.

Shimi put out her hand. Alice carefully placed something into it and then closed Shimi's fingers around the tiny item with her own fingers. "Let this be part of the closure you need."

Shimi opened the palm of her hand and gasped, "Oh my God! Where'd you ... where'd it ... how ...?" Darcy jumped up and came to Shimi's hand. He gave the item a sniff, decided it wasn't food and went back to his nap.

"The police dropped off Leo's stuff from the boat the other day. This was in his tackle box. I guess they didn't think it was important to investigate where this unique button came from."

"Thank God they didn't," Shimi said quietly, as she stared at the treasured heirloom in her right hand. She touched the bone button with the index finger on her left hand and rolled it around on her outstretched palm. "I can't believe I got it back. Thanks so much, Alice."

"I hope, Shimi, in some weird way, getting this button back and sewing all of them, perhaps, onto a new coat will give you some type of closure, maybe? I know that probably sounds trite, but I hope it's some kind of symbol, perhaps of better days to come, and your life can get back to some sense of normalcy. All six buttons of normalcy. Like it was before. But better! Know what I mean?"

"Thanks Alice. This means so much. It just makes me happy to hold it in my hand. Shimi hesitated for a second, then added, "And who knows, maybe someday Baby will wear them on her coat. And yes, I will sew it back on with real hope and in time maybe even a little forgiveness."

"Forgiveness? Well, let's not get carried away," Alice chirped, and they both laughed.

Then once again Alice's face turned serious. She looked over her shoulder to the neighbour's backyard and lowered her voice. "There were other items in the tackle box, you know. Items that weren't his. I wish I could also return them to their rightful owners. Sergeant Malone told me the horrible facts, but seeing the items in his tackle box made it even more real."

Alice's comments made Shimi feel ashamed that she was not pursuing the rape case and letting the world know what kind of man Leon Birkshire really was. But more than that, she knew the truth would have brought some well-deserved peace to his other victims. Her secret would forever prolong their agony. Safeguarding herself would agonize others. Her guilty silence mortified her. She also knew this decision was part of her emotional torment. This guilt would probably always be a stumbling block to her own healing.

"Yes," Shimi said. "Perhaps there are many women out there wondering who raped them and whether they will ever find justice. Is my privacy and my attempt to hold onto my pretend, perfect little world justification for other women's agony? Let's face it, I'm a shitty person for not helping them."

Shimi had felt shame in being a rape victim. She felt going public would have labelled her as weak and damaged. But now she realized that shame was small in comparison to the shame she felt now, instigating the cover up. Throughout her life she had excelled in everything she put her mind to, yet she felt helpless to solve this problem. And defeatism did not suit her well.

"Well, we all agreed to lie. We all agreed to keep the secret. So, then we are all shitty people. It's not just you, Shimi," Alice replied. "I wish there was some way Sergeant Malone could reveal to the other victims it was Leo, but not involve us. Maybe someday I will ask her … when I'm stronger … to go ahead and open the cases and prove Leo was a serial rapist to all those women. I will simply suck it up, and endure the consequences of the truth. It's not like the truth isn't already haunting me."

"I know right. Maybe when Baby is older and can understand things better, we can pursue the case. But even then, it will be tough on her. Could ruin her life."

"Things are so messy. There's no right or wrong way of doing this. I was always told the truth is always the right way of doing something. Now I don't know," Alice whispered.

"Like I said, sometimes I wake up in the middle of the night and I'm crying. Tears are streaming down my face and I don't know why. Yet I think I am on the right track, and I feel I am moving ahead with my life and my decisions, decisions that are both right and wrong … decisions that have seemed impossible to make." Shimi slipped the button into her skirt pocket and released another huge sigh.

Suddenly, Baby began to fuss, so Shimi took a baby bottle from her bag and handed it to Alice.

"Oh, you're bottle feeding her now?" Alice looked surprised.

"Yes, thought it was time I got her adjusted to a bottle as well." Shimi suddenly looked uncomfortable. She had considered telling Alice that she was giving Baby up during this visit, but since arriving she knew it wasn't the right time or place. Alice was really struggling with the conversation and her feelings. Shimi knew she should wait. She wanted the news about Baby to be a serene moment of understanding and love. Once again, she would wait.

Alice cradled Baby while she fed her, rocking her gently in her arms. Shimi watched the love and care in Alice's eyes when she looked at Baby.

"I know those spontaneous tears, Shimi. I have them too. But we are both resilient and are getting stronger every day." Alice bit her lip.

"I'm so happy Leon is gone, but I'm so sad that the truth about him gives you so much sadness, Alice. You deserve total happiness. But maybe we never hold complete happiness in our hands. Maybe it comes in sections, or percentiles, or whatever you want to say. We measure it against the happiness we had in another time or with another person, stuff like that. We always feel we need to quantify it. Maybe we shouldn't. Maybe we should simply accept the happiness in all its little clusters, in all the little ordinary moments of our life. You are ready for happiness, Alice. I can see it. I can see your strength. Your resilience. And your happiness will grow. Like now, I feel we're on the north side of happiness. It's a challenging happiness right now, but I know we're on the right path, and making the right choices. I'm living with all the guilt, shame, sadness and the happiness I own today."

"The north side of happiness! I like that. Our happiness does spin like a compass, doesn't it? Or a weather vane. I'm so glad I found you, Shimi ... that I saw that ad about art classes, that I had the courage to go despite Leo making fun of the idea, that Belladane was the teacher, and you were her friend, and you needed a midwife. All the stars had to align for us to meet, and here we are today." Alice finished feeding Baby and placed her on her shoulder. She rubbed her back gently.

"Yes, here we are. All those circumstances led to this moment and everything falls into place. Everything will be as it should be. For both of us. You'll see." Shimi's eyes glistened with tears. "Well, on that note, I best be going."

Shimi stood to leave and as she did, Alice jumped to her feet and followed Shimi to her truck, all the while rocking Baby in her arms. Shimi strapped Baby into her car seat, and Darcy jumped into the truck and sat down on the floor beneath the infant. Shimi lifted up his tail and placed it carefully beside his body, before gently closing the truck's door. "Oh, and we have decided not to have our party at Belladane's tomorrow. Instead, we're going to the beach for a low-tide evening picnic, so get your sunscreen on, and see you at my place at three thirty. Should be a nice day."

"Sounds great," Alice replied. "I'm intrigued about this party. 'A celebration of Baby and her mom.' Are we finally finding out the name of our sweet girl?"

"Yes, I think we should. All will be revealed tomorrow. Sleep well, my lovely." With that, Shimi jumped into the truck and slammed her door. She started the engine with a roar. Baby startled and began to scream, her tiny fists shaking in the air.

"Shit!" Shimi said with an exaggerated grimace and a shrug of her shoulders. "Bad Mamma!" she said playfully, with her face beaming through the open window.

Alice waved as Shimi backed out of the lane. As Shimi drove down the street, she stuck her arm out and waved. She then beeped her horn two short, perky goodbye beeps. Baby began to scream even louder and could be heard until they reached the end of the block. Alice raised her hand high and kept it in the air until they were out of sight.

Then, she slowly walked into her silent house.

XXXIII

(rightfully)

SHIMI INSISTED IT was time they all went on an adventure. It would be their first and last outing of their incredibly stressful summer. The tide would be extremely low this day, perfect for a picnic on the beach. Eddie was keen to go, whereas Belladane had to rile up some enthusiasm. On such a hot day Belladane would rather have sat at home, splayed in front of her huge whirling fan, drinking large glasses of Diet Pepsi with lots of ice. But always ready to support Shimi, she donned her ridiculously floppy, hot pink sunhat and sparkly flip-flops and they were off. Now sweating like a block of cheddar cheese left out in the sun, Belladane wondered why they had to walk "so gosh-dang-it far." She traipsed through the hot, loose sand behind Alice, who was carrying Baby in the backpack she had bought Shimi. Shimi had loved the present, but then said, "Why don't you carry her, and I'll carry the picnic stuff." Now parading along the beach, all anyone could see jutting out of the pack was a wide-brimmed, yellow bonnet protecting Baby from the blazing sun.

Shimi led the way at a quick pace, with Eddie close behind, balancing the picnic cooler on his shoulder. Shimi had the blanket slung over her arm and swung a red thermal jug of cold water from her side. Ahead of everyone sprinted Darcy, chasing seagulls and terrorizing the tiny sandpipers and crabs that scurried along the edge of the water.

Shimi had made all the preparations. She had declined any help from Belladane, wanting the day to be exactly the way she wanted.

In the cooler were devilled eggs, grilled vegetables and spicy Jerk tofu, sliced Honey Crisp apples with blue cheese dip, the best crusty buns slathered in garlic butter, and Eddie's favourite: freshly baked chocolate chip cookies. A baby bottle, a spare diaper, a water dish for Darcy, a big bottle of non-alcoholic sparkling wine, and four carefully-wrapped champagne flutes filled the rest of the cooler.

As Eddie followed behind Shimi, he admired her determination to find the perfect picnic place. Several times, he had suggested a lovely spot where the sand was soft, there was a bit of shade, and a large piece of driftwood would have made a comfy bench for Belladane and her sore knees, but Shimi kept saying, "Let's go just a little bit further."

Shimi spotted it from a long distance away, and as she drew closer she became more excited and more emotional. She knew exactly why. This would be the moment she had been waiting for all week. One she would always remember. The moment she would consciously let go of her past and take the necessary steps towards her future, making happiness a deliberate choice.

As Eddie came up to where Shimi stood with her hands on her hips, he dropped the red cooler to the sand. "Oh my God, Shimi. This is magnificent. So ... so amazing." He dropped to his knees and with his strong, tanned hands began to examine the bones of the bleached, whale skeleton half hidden by the sand dunes.

"I knew you'd love it," Shimi said, her sweaty face glowing with pride that she was able to find it again. She beamed like she had just discovered the Northwest Passage.

"Oh Shimi," Alice said, arriving with Baby. "This is incredible." She unsnapped the baby carrier from her back and quickly lay the sleeping baby down on a small blanket, tilting the large-brimmed hat over her tender, new face. She then began to examine the whale, as well. "So incredible," she kept saying softly as she circled the skeleton, touching it respectfully with her outstretched hand.

"I was beginning to wonder if this was where you were taking us," Belladane said, as she arrived, huffing and puffing, totally exhausted. "Boy, am I out of shape! Can we eat first, before you put us to work digging out this poor old girl? What a beauty she is. My, oh my!"

"We're not going to dig her out. I just wanted you to meet her. And yes, now we can eat." Shimi spread out a beach blanket and placed the delicious collection of food in the middle. "Dig in folks."

Everyone enjoyed the picnic, all the while gazing at the amazing whale skeleton. Afterwards Eddie dug, with Darcy's assistance of course, and they finally found the baby skeleton tucked safely inside the chest cavity of its mother, exactly where Shimi had left it. Shimi was thrilled. She wanted to hold it in her arms, and keep it forever, but she knew it was not necessary to own everything she loved.

With everyone gathered around her, Shimi took a small bag out of her pocket. She gently began to speak, choosing her words carefully, all the while focusing her attention on Alice who stood in front of her.

"I wanted to come here today because this is the spot where last winter I made my decision about Baby. For some weird reason this place, this poor mother whale and her little one, gave me clarity and in some strange kind of way, inner strength. And also, I thought this was a very fitting place to finally lay Leon Birkshire to rest, both symbolically and literally."

Hearing the unexpected name of Leon Birkshire, Belladane gave a soft, shocked gasp, "What?" Then, she clenched her jaw and forced herself to remain quiet.

Alice put her hand to her mouth, and looked at Shimi with curiosity and surprise.

Shimi continued. "This is where I want to say goodbye forever to Leon and all the pain he put us through. From this day forward, there will be no more Birkshire in my life, not in my nightmares, not in my fears. This is my plan, and this is my prayer."

Shimi took the small bag and opened it. She stepped away from her friends and began shaking the bag in the ocean breeze. Belladane, Eddie and Alice continued to look surprised and amazed at Shimi's pronouncement, but they stayed quiet, standing together and watching the ashes of Leon Birkshire float up into the air and dissipate over the skeleton and the protective dunes.

"Goodbye Leon, and thank you for Baby," Shimi said quietly, as she continued to shake the bag clean of all the ashes.

"Right! Good riddance to you Leon, but thank goodness for Baby," Belladane added, as she placed her arm around Alice's waist.

"Yes, goodbye Leo. May you be a better person in your next life," Alice added.

Baby began to stir on the sand, so Eddie reached down and picked her up. He stood silently with the baby in his arms. The three women stood looking at him, waiting for his contribution to their comments. Then like an ancient prophet he said, "As Søren Kierkegaard said, 'To understand life, we have to look backwards. To live life, we have to look forward.'"

Belladane, Alice and Shimi looked shocked for a second, and then they burst out laughing.

"Jeeze, Eddie, I thought you were going to say, 'F you, Birkshire.' Where'd you get that fancy quote?" Belladane's wisecrack made Eddie join in on the laughter.

"Glad you liked it. I googled it last night. Wanted to be prepared for today's celebration." Eddie gave an exaggerated little bow of his head.

Then he remained quiet and nodded at Shimi to continue with her speech. He knew he had no words for Leon Birkshire, no condemnation, no remorse, no fear. He was glad Birkshire was dead. He had watched good men die needlessly in Afghanistan. Men who were caught up in an ancient war between nations, a war that they would never understand. He would not mourn the likes of Leon Birkshire. He agreed with Shimi. Leon Birkshire would no longer be given any space in his head.

"Well thanks Eddie for that poignant philosophy. And yes, in the spirit of looking backward, I want to sincerely thank all of you, my dear family, for all the amazing ways you have helped me this past year. I wouldn't have survived without you. And I really mean that, literally," Shimi said, looking tenderly at each of her people, with tears welling up in her eyes.

They stood quietly for a few moments, staring at the mother whale and her baby. Then Shimi gave Eddie the slightest nod of her head, and Eddie stepped forward and gently placed Baby into her waiting arms.

"Yes, and in the spirit of looking forward, that's why we are here today. Right Baby?" Shimi gave Baby a huge hug, gently swinging her from side to side.

"Here! Here! And here's to all the happiness we will create from now on," Belladane said, raising her champagne flute to the sky.

"Yes, indeed," Alice replied. "We can all use a lot more happiness in our future."

Shimi placed her hand on Alice's arm and said, "Our happiness isn't in our future, Alice. It's right here, right now. We can make all the bad things that happened more right. Make all the bad things Leon did make some sense in our lives. And we can make ourselves happier. Like Eddie once said to me, 'Maybe it's simply a choice.'"

Alice smiled amidst her own tears and nodded in agreement. Tears began to flow down Shimi's cheeks, and she stood very still inside her happiness. She looked at Belladane and Eddie. They both smiled and nodded in support and affection. They knew what was coming next.

Through her sobbing tears, Shimi handed Baby to Alice. "She's your baby, Alice. She's always been your baby, your beautiful daughter ... Zavi. I think my body knew, even before my mind did. I was simply the circumstance of her birth."

"What? What are you talking about?" Alice's face showed total shock and disbelief.

Shimi continued. "I tried to be her mother, but deep down, even all throughout my pregnancy I knew she was someone else's baby.

And when I met you, I knew you were her true mother. She was meant to be with you. Always! From the very beginning."

Alice's tears were dropping onto Baby's head as she hugged her to her chest, "Oh Shimi! Shimi ... I ... I ..." Alice struggled to find her own words.

Belladane and Eddie stood arm in arm, tears also flowing down their faces. Then Eddie moved next to Shimi and put his arm around her shoulder. He knew how much this profound decision and heart-wrenching action was taking out of her. Something that was so painful, yet was such an emotional relief. Shimi leaned into his supportive embrace and grabbed his hand in hers. Placing her head upon his shoulder she knew that Eddie had become a big part of her happiness. Over the past tormented year, he had become her north star, her quiet sigh, her morning ocean of sparkling water. She was eager to begin every day for the rest of her life with him.

Eddie looked down at Shimi and felt an instant pang of love and happiness. He knew every step he had taken in his life, every decision, both wrong and right, had led him to this place, this moment, this woman. Together they would house their secrets, lock away their lies, and help each other keep one step ahead of their past. That was all they needed. That was enough.

Belladane beamed from ear to ear, memorizing this moment, realizing everyone suddenly looked perfect, how they were meant to be. She quickly snapped two photos with her cell phone: Shimi and Eddie supporting each other on the white sand, with the water glistening behind them; and Alice clutching Zavi to her chest and crying great, gasping tears of joy.

Oblivious to the emotionally charged moment that was happening between his humans, Darcy began to chase the seagulls, who were attempting to steal the remains of the picnic. They flapped in circles with loud, angry cries above Darcy and the four adults. As the dog jumped playfully into the salty air, several gulls furiously dove at his head. Another gull darted over Alice's head and dropped a huge dribble of poop across her shoulder.

"Oh, my God! These scary birds!" Alice screamed. She scrunched up her face, clasping Zavi to her chest with one hand, while covering her own head with the other.

Everyone, but Alice, laughed.

Belladane quickly pulled a tissue from her pocket, dramatically spit on it and began to clean the bird poop off Alice's tee shirt. "Now, now, they say bird shit is good luck, Alice. That's what they say," Belladane exclaimed in a fun, melodramatic English accent, playfully winking at Shimi.

Shimi looked up at the crying, mischievous gulls who continued to swoop just above their heads. She laughed at the crazy look on Alice's face, as Belladane continued to rub at the stain, and with tears of joy looked at baby Zavi in her mother's arms. She came close to Alice, gently took the infant's tiny, cubby hands, jiggled them up and down, until Zavi looked at her with her big, blue eyes.

Shimi leaned forward and kissed the infant lovingly on her forehead and whispered, "My darling Zavi, please teach your mom to love birds."

Epilogue

After the story is finished, all five of us sit silently for a moment. There is so much to absorb. I feel like a totally different person. Like everything I thought was true has been turned upside down. I do not know how to feel. I don't feel angry, or resentful about the secret they have held from me. I feel rather numb, but at least I know the truth.

I don't feel relieved to know the truth. How could I, being told these horrific facts? I wasn't a wanted baby. I was born because of a violent rape. Aunt Shimi is my birth mother, and my dad was a serial rapist.

During the story Mom had said if I wanted, I could talk to someone about my feelings. She meant a therapist, and maybe I will someday. But right now, I am in awe of what these four incredible people have gone through, so I could have this amazing, untainted life.

I somehow stand up and give my weeping mother a huge hug. And then I turn and hug my other mother, dear Aunt Shimi. We share the same auburn curly hair, same petite body and a love of animals and books. We have always had a special bond, and now I know why.

I take a long hard look at my aunt and uncle, who are finally sitting back, more relaxed in our big wooden lawn chairs, side by side. Aunt Shimi's eyes are puffy from crying. Uncle Eddie is holding her hand. I think they found the happiness they were so desperately searching for during that tragic year. Aunt Shimi and Uncle Eddie have been married for sixteen years now. Each winter they travel to exotic places, like Cambodia, Bali, and Australia. When asked, Aunt Shimi always says Thailand is her favourite. They live in a pretty little house in Halifax with their dogs, Lowkie and Murtagh. There's a little box on their bookcase, and in it are old Darcy's ashes. I can still remember that sweet dog. He was one in a million. Uncle Eddie is a retired insurance broker, and Aunt Shimi just sold her dog grooming business. Now they both are happily retired and still look into each other's eyes with love. It is pretty amazing, really, how fate brought them together.

I look at my Aunt BellaBell. She is sitting with her head back against her chair, her eyes closed, but I can see the tears moving down her cheeks as well. The replaying of the story was hard on her too. She suddenly looks older to me. Greyer. More serious. She's now 84 years old. She lives here in Charlottetown, about five blocks from us. She doesn't paint with her breasts anymore, but she did give me some of her crazy paintings for my sixteenth birthday. They hang in my room. I may take one to university with me when I head to Toronto next year. They are a fun conversation starter in a wacky kind of way. Her sweet wife, Gloria, couldn't make the party, as she is waiting for hip surgery, but maybe she decided to stay home because she knew the telling of the story needed to be intimate, the fewer people the better. Aunt Gloria and Aunt BellaBell met in her art class, and they have been together now as long as I can remember. They make a great pair, always laughing, cooking new recipes and massaging each other's swollen feet.

I look at my mom. What can I say about her? She is the best mom a girl could ever have asked for. She has worked tirelessly to be the best midwife this province has ever seen and a strong, resourceful, independent woman. She has never found her true love, but she says that's okay. She often says, some folks are lucky in love, then adds, she's been lucky in life. She taught me to be kind, patient, resilient, and forgiving. And most of all happy. Yes, and she even taught me to love birds.

And what, after all this, can I conclude about my father. The new burning question: Was his death a simple fishing accident? Or was he murdered?

Well, that is a question that will never be answered. Why? Because I will never ask. Even though I am young, I understand that a story is never told in full. There is always a little held back that only the teller holds in their hands, only the teller truly understands. Although the story moves from soul to soul, a secret needs to keep.

As I sit here staring at my family, Aunt BellaBell gets up and comes to me. She gives me the biggest hug and whispers into my ear, "Shakespeare once said, 'No legacy is so rich as honesty.' I hope you can take what we have told you, and fly my beautiful one. Fly. Don't let anything hold you back."

She holds me tight and I place my head upon her shoulder.

Then she quietly adds, "But some truths are rocks so deep in the earth no matter what force, they are never meant to come to the surface."

I'm not sure exactly what she meant by that. Maybe there is more that she will tell me later, or someone else might tell me after she's gone. I don't care. I learned their side of the story they wanted to tell, and I know their secrets and their truths are solely based on love.

And that's fine with me.

Additional Information

Before the 2017 HBO documentary, *I Am Evidence*, produced by Mariska Hargitay, star of **Law and Order: Special Victims Unit**, and advocate Kym Worthy, over 400,000 untested rape kits sat in facilities across America. Police departments deemed they did not have the funding to analyze the kits. Victims sought justice for decades with no results.

Due to the stigma attached to rape victims and the lack of prosecution, The Rape, Abuse and Incest National Network (RAINN) confirms that out of every 1,000 sexual assaults, 995 perpetrators will walk free. Also, only 230 out of every 1,000 sexual assaults are estimated to be reported to police departments.

Since the release of this poignant documentary more laws and bills have been passed in dozens of states in America to help solve this injustice to women. Some have mandated rape kits must be processed within 120 days of collection. Once kits were analyzed and databases created, hundreds of rapists were identified and 1 in 4 cases resulted in an indictment, and 1 in 4 of those cases constituted a serial rapist.

In Canada the stats are similar. According to 2019 Statistics Canada, over 4.7 million women – or 30% of all women aged 15 and older have been sexually assaulted outside of an intimate relationship. And alarmingly upwards to 50% of hospitals across

Canada do not have access to rape kits or the personnel to administer them accurately.

Statistics Canada estimates only 5% of all rapes are reported to police, although with the availability of analyzed rape kits and efficient law enforcement towards gender-based violence, reporting and indictments are slowly increasing.

About the Author

The North Side of Happiness is the author's second novel. In 2021, excerpts from her first novel, *A Murmur of Men*, won PEI's first prize for short fiction, and was shortlisted for book of the year.

    Before retirement, Sharon Lucy Robson was a teacher for the Toronto and York Region School Boards. Now she welcomes artists to her whimsical, recycled home, Satori Artist Retreat, Panmure Island, Prince Edward Island, Canada. She is a gardener, a world traveller, an environmentalist, and a lover of all animals, especially birds. Her three deceased dogs, Nikki, Atticus, and Ellie, were the inspiration for beautiful Darcy. (Her cats, Tony and Nudge, would be ticked off if they also weren't mentioned.) She is married to Michael Buffery, who is always eager to hear every draft of her writing. Her third novel is a work in progress, and as yet untitled.

With Appreciation

Thank you, Agnes Lee, for your tireless editing during your busy summer vacation. You truly are the Comma Queen. (Hope I now have most of them right.)

Thank you, Jen Lasci, for your attentive reading of my final manuscript and your astute advice on content and character.

And a big shout out to Meg Arnold, who gave advice on writing about PTSD. You are an inspiration.

The beautiful cover art was created by abstract artist, Sue Johnston, (@bridgewalks). Thanks so much, Sue. Long Live Art!

Manufactured by Amazon.ca
Bolton, ON